continued . . .

Praise for *Urban Oracles*

"Santos-Febres seems to write with hot oils, and the page glistens. . . . Mysterious and often disturbing, these stories are richly cloaked in lyricism and the pleasures of language."

—Harvard Review

"Santos-Febres shows a real skill for navigating the contours of urban loneliness—and better yet, she understands intuitively that if solitude can be miserable, it can also be intensely erotic. . . . There's plenty of mysticism and mystery in everyday life, and Santos-Febres knows how to read their subtler signs." *—The Village Voice*

"Throughout the stories is a careful probing of the materiality of the body—its pleasures and pains—bodies infused with the sweat of labor yet able as well to offer momentary escapes into pure sensuality." *—Review of Contemporary Literature*

"Her outspoken cameos of desire are lyrical and provocative."

—The New York Times Book Review

"This debut collection of stories of Puerto Rican author Santos-Febres arrives bearing beguiling hints of such past masters as Julio Cortázar, Clarise Lispector . . . revealed in flashes of prose that range from lyrical and baroque to inventive and erotically charged." *—Time Out*

"A seamless translation from the Spanish adds much to these innovative tales, which mix magical realism and gritty urban reality to memorable effect." *—Publishers Weekly*

"Fifteen erotic stories rife with furtive sexual encounters, voyeurism, and daringly sensual imagery . . . Much more than erotica, these blunt stories are crystalline glimpses of the psychology of obsession, by a writer whom we ought to know better."

—Kirkus Reviews

Any Wednesday I'm Yours

Mayra Santos-Febres

Translated from the Spanish by
James Graham

RIVERHEAD BOOKS
New York

THE BERKLEY PUBLISHING GROUP
Published by the Penguin Group
Penguin Group (USA) Inc.
375 Hudson Street, New York, New York 10014, USA
Penguin Group (Canada), 10 Alcorn Avenue, Toronto, Ontario M4V 3B2, Canada
(a division of Pearson Penguin Canada Inc.)
Penguin Books Ltd., 80 Strand, London WC2R 0RL, England
Penguin Group Ireland, 25 St. Stephen's Green, Dublin 2, Ireland
(a division of Penguin Books Ltd.)
Penguin Group (Australia), 250 Camberwell Road, Camberwell, Victoria 3124, Australia
(a division of Pearson Australia Group Pty. Ltd.)
Penguin Books India Pvt. Ltd., 11 Community Centre, Panchsheel Park, New Delhi—110 017,
India
Penguin Group (NZ), cnr Airborne and Rosedale Roads, Albany, Auckland 1310, New Zealand
(a division of Pearson New Zealand Ltd.)
Penguin Books (South Africa) (Pty.) Ltd., 24 Sturdee Avenue, Rosebank, Johannesburg 2196,
South Africa

Penguin Books Ltd., Registered Offices: 80 Strand, London WC2R 0RL, England

First published as *Cualquier Miércoles Soy Tuya* by Grijalbo Mondadori SA, December 2002
First Riverhead trade paperback edition: July 2005

Library of Congress Cataloging-in-Publication Data

Santos-Febres, Mayra, 1966–
  [Cualquier miércoles soy tuya. English]
  Any Wednesday I'm yours / Mayra Santos-Febres; translated by James Graham—
1st Riverhead trade paperback ed.
   p. cm.
  ISBN 1-59448-001-X
  I. Graham, James, 1955– II. Title.
  PQ7440.S26C8313 2005   2005042702

PRINTED IN THE UNITED STATES OF AMERICA

10 9 8 7 6 5 4 3 2 1

I dedicate this book to
Juan Santos Hernández, my father
Juan Carlos Santos, my brother
Juan López Bauzá, my friend

Whoever you are: when evening comes
Walk away from your room, away from everything you know:
Your house stands at the very edge of infinity:
Whoever you are.

With your eyes, so tired they can barely
Free themselves from the crowded doorway,
Slowly erect a black tree
And stand it against the sky: slender, alone.
And you have created the world, an enormous thing,
Like a word that ripens without being spoken.
And just when you think your mind has grasped it,
Your eyes will tenderly let it slip away . . .

Rainer Maria Rilke, "Entrance"

Wednesday A.M.

I parked the car, an old heap eaten away by sea salt I practically have to push around town. Riding the bus is out of the question. Nothing runs at night, and in the daytime nobody can bear the endless wait at the bus stop under a sun that never lets up and makes even the toughest ones break out in a sweat. Umbrellas are useless, those hats men wore in the '40s are out of style, and I am not the type of guy to wear a baseball cap all day, like some hip-hop fan or a jock from the gym, all pumped biceps and triceps, legs hardened by weights. Anyway, it was my first day working at the Motel Tulán. Make that my first night. In a few hours it would be Wednesday.

Walking to the motel's office I was distracted by the rain of light flickering, cold and metallic, in the puddles on the wet pavement.

It was a neon symphony that glowed insistently red, green, and yellow, ending in the shape of a small shiny pyramid, a river of curving tubes which enclosed the flow of electrodes bouncing off a surface of glass: Tulán, Motel Tulán. The words lit up one after the other announcing VACANCY, blinking on and off over the pyramid sign, which pointed straight up to the royal palms and the darkened sky over Route 52. Waiting for me by the motel doors was my friend Tadeo, whom I'd met while working on the copydesk at the newspaper and who'd gotten me this job later on.

They say cities are full of nameless crowds but in these islands adrift in the middle of the Caribbean, only a few loners cruise the cities at night, and they recognize each other. Once the sun goes down, the swarm of suits and workers running from office to office, from stores to delis to schools, retreats back to the suburban underworld in the shifting outskirts of the country, the swamps, and the beaches. The city is like a huge park in a small town, ready to welcome the night's marauders: security guards, cops on the vampire beat, whores, addicts, transvestites, taxi drivers, hotel and restaurant workers, dope dealers, and reporters.

That's where I met Tadeo, in the empty city. Owing to a strange coincidence—not so strange really if one takes into account the limited number of places open before the sun rises on a weekday—we were both going to eat at the same diner before heading back to our respective homes in hopes of sleeping through most of the day. At first, we just greeted each other from afar, with a nod. Then, late one night, before sunup, we shared two subs—tuna melt, steak and onion—and orange juice, sitting together by the jukebox. That's how our friendship began.

Tadeo broke the ice. Sandwich in hand, I was looking for a place to sit down, still wired from work and uneasy at the thought that the rest of the world was asleep. Tadeo was already chomping on his meal when he raised his hand and called me over.

"Hey, bro, sit over here so we don't end up eating all by our lonesomes. That way we won't look like husbands kicked out of their houses."

He chewed with his whole mouth, like he was trying to swallow an elephant. No manners whatsoever, I noticed, thinking what my mother, who worked so hard to teach her only child the rudiments of etiquette, would say if she saw me at the table with a slob like that. Tadeo's mother obviously didn't lose any sleep over such things. Maybe her biggest worry was just being able to feed him at all. And that's how Tadeo attacked his food, as if at any second his share might disappear from his plate. His big jaw moved from side to side, crowned by oversized, dark chocolate lips sprinkled with bread crumbs. Even then he didn't stop talking.

"A night worker is a born loner. Like a sleepwalker. You work nights, right?"

"At a newspaper."

"Just like in the movies, right? You're the guy who's always shouting, 'Stop the press, stop the press! We've got an exclusive!'"

"Not really, but I'm the guy who makes the last-minute corrections before the paper hits the street."

"Let me introduce myself. Tadeo Chamdeleau, at your service."

"Julián Castrodad. That's a fascinating name."

3

"Fascinating, no—Haitian. And your name, where in the world did it roll into this diner from?"

* * *

Tadeo was waiting for me at the motel's entrance, welcoming me with, "Hey bro, good to see you. I started thinking you'd come to your senses and signed up for unemployment instead." We went into the office together, where he offered a brief reconnaissance of my new working environment.

"That's your chair and this one's mine. We keep the room keys here. Back there is the kitchen and pantry with bottles of booze for the guests. Those are the cabañas of the illustrious Motel Tulán, laid out in numerical order, the first one over there and the last one right up against the hill. The cash register's over here, but we really only use it for keeping change. Most of the money is hidden under the counter, in that little metal box. So don't panic if you don't find much when you open the register. The real dough is down below. You can work at the Tulán for as long as you want. When was the last time you heard of a motel going belly up?"

As he spoke, Tadeo's eyes sparkled and he was smiling, always smiling. It made me think it wouldn't be all that bad working as a guard dog in such a strange place, a motel where people came to hide their dirty laundry.

As soon as Tadeo finished explaining things, the Tulán started to heat up. It was eleven at night by then, an auspicious hour for nighttime diversions. The first couple to arrive was an older man, sixty and then some, accompanied by an effeminate kid who looked like an angel fallen from heaven. He was the exact shade of cinnamon, with full, rosy lips and a little doll's nose that adorned a perfectly shaved head framed by discs of gold in each ear. His face was dominated by two oriental eyes, which stared at the dashboard with the arrogant aloofness of a Bantu prince. Mr. Sixty Plus took care of all the paperwork while the boy toy sat in the car waiting for his patron to return and open the door for him, perhaps even to take him in his arms up the stairs like a bride. When I was done giving the old man the keys to the cabaña and turned around to close the garage door, I heard the pretty boy mumble, "If Pedro Juan hears about this, he'll kick me out of the house. . . ."

More tenderly than a lover, Mr. Sixty Plus responded, "Don't worry, *mi amor*, I'll rescue you from Pedro Juan's house, or from the bottom of the sea if I have to." The boy toy smiled and, right there in the half-open garage, planted a kiss on his lover's lips as if he wanted to trap the soul escaping out of his mouth and into the other's body.

That first couple was my initiation. Tadeo let me handle them so I'd get an insider's taste of the motel experience. I've lived my entire life used to being the object of a thousand attentions, but now it was my turn to serve. Suddenly I was standing in the doorway of someone else's desire, as if half of me were there and half somewhere else. Walking back to the office it struck me that this job was double-edged. It immediately transformed me into an invisible being, less than a person, but at the same time, more: something like a reluctant ghost freed from the prison of its body. A door was opening into the secret regions, but my presence was too insubstantial to reveal itself. The secret hovered right there, between existing and not existing, surviving in a gray area. I was in limbo too, an unwilling witness.

"So, big fella, how did it go?" Tadeo asked me back at the office.

"Just a bit uncomfortably," I confessed, handing him the cash from the guests.

"Wait till you get stuck with a really difficult couple."

"Did you get a good look at the specimen you handed over?"

"That's our bread and butter, bro. What's more, I gave you a couple of regulars. That kid you saw getting out of the car is the devil himself. The other one is his third victim so far this year. I don't know how those older dudes let themselves get scammed so easily."

"Damn, Tadeo, the boy's beautiful."

"I didn't know you liked them apples."

"Not that one, not any of them. It's just a matter of rendering to Caesar what belongs to Caesar."

"And that just happens to be his name: César. Looks like an emperor prince but works like a high-class hooker. Don't worry, you'll get to know him. Pretty soon all of this will seem normal."

Half an hour later a gray sedan with tinted windows drove up. A woman stepped out of the car. She was stunning, but not because she was beautiful. There was something seductive in the graceless way she stepped out of her car, took the key chain (we gave her 23), and walked up the cold concrete of the motel steps in her high heels as if no one could see her in her quiet defeat, not because she wasn't there, but because she was already absent from herself. Before she shut the door, she asked for another bottle of hard liquor—it didn't matter what—to be brought to her room. She came alone, a strange thing at a motel; even I knew that much. But we assumed someone would meet her as the night progressed.

A few minutes went by before I headed back to the door to 23 with the bottle she'd asked for. I rang the bell. Muffled hints of a woman dragging her heels across the floor and colliding with various pieces of furniture came from inside. I remembered Tadeo's instructions that orders of any kind were to be delivered through the sliding panels of the room service compartment so that there were fewer interruptions for the guests, who might be caught in certain compromising positions. I found the secret compartment on the left side of the door and slipped the bottle in like magic, along with a bill for nine dollars. The woman, whose trajectory finally brought her to the door, peered out through the service window and stared at me. Her gaze slid down my shoulder to the hand holding the money tray, then up to the top of my belt, as if her eyes were determined to rub out my presence. My skinny forearms tensed up—an involuntary movement, a reaction that often gets the better of me and ends in trouble. I stared at my hands, and wished they were stronger, that my fingers fit the enclosure of the motel compartment better. That they weren't so delicate, so effeminate. Stepping back from the small panel, the woman opened her purse and took out a ten-dollar bill.

"Keep the change," she muttered, grabbing the bottle by the neck and pouring a double into the snifter, where what was left of the last round still swam on the bottom. "That woman wants to knock herself out," I thought, walking back to the office.

Tadeo spent the rest of the night teaching me the more subtle secrets of the motel arts. Between serving one guest and another, he described a worker's attire: how they—we—always needed to wear clean clothes, humble threads with no visible brands or logos, clothes "like the ones worn by a beat electrician who's come down in the world, a faithful employee."

"You see," Tadeo instructed me, "just about any old cat in my country knows this, but I've got to explain to you. Around here, people are too friendly and think they're dealing with tourists. As if showing all those teeth will make the guests dig deeper in their pockets. No, *hermano*, the trick is to disappear from your surroundings. Like you're not even there. Or better yet, like you're a gust of air that leads the car to the garage, that hands over the key, brings extra sheets. . . . You remember that cartoon character who takes his clothes off and nobody sees him? Well, that's who you gotta be when the buzzer at the entrance goes off. But despite appearances, you have to watch over everything. You Puerto Ricans have a hard time understanding this because you've forgotten you were once servants. That's progress, big boy. Makes people think that they've arrived just because they got a shiny necklace or a machine ringing in their pocket. But you won't get very far in this business thinking like that." I nodded, completely lost in Tadeo's dense web of logic.

The buzzer went off again. It was my teacher's turn. I decided to pull out my old journal, the one I always carry in my pants pocket, and was amused to find myself making notes again. I hadn't taken the journal out in a while, since nothing had grabbed my attention enough to make me feel the desire to write. I couldn't repress a smile.

At the foot of a distant stairwell, Tadeo was negotiating with a guest who didn't get out of his car. Sitting in the office, I opened to a blank page and wrote "peripheral vision." It was another trick of experienced motel workers, one that Tadeo had begun to explain to me before the buzzer at the gate interrupted him. Peripheral vision, according to my mentor, meant focusing your eyes on a shoulder or on the wall behind a guest, while still registering every detail out of the corner of your eye. If a car pulls in full of dents, if someone's hiding in the backseat or bringing bags and coolers filled with alcohol and snacks into the room. Or if their companion is conscious, just in case they're planning to dump a dead body so it's the motel staff who gets to deal with the police. All these details are essential if you want to avoid headaches. "Remember, big guy, the boss won't pay for the mess. You will. So believe me when I tell you peripheral vision is one of the most important weapons in a motel employee's arsenal. If you want to stay in the running, that is." I was trying to capture the essence of Tadeo's reflections in my notebook, without knowing that these notes would take me directly to what I had been looking for.

"Knock, knock, who's there?" said Tadeo upon returning, trying to spike my curiosity. "Bet you can't guess who I got up in fifteen."

"The governor."

"Close, very close."

"Don't tell me you've got a politician with a lover on the sly. With all the money they steal from the people, you'd think they'd have apartments reserved for that sort of thing."

"Even juicier. Labor attorney Efraín Soreno. And he didn't come alone. He's with four labor leaders from the Power Authority. I recognized them from the news."

"The ones from the strike?"

"The same."

"What are they doing here?"

"Scheming, my man. Nobody suspects they'd be here, meeting in a motel. . . ."

"You think it has anything to do with the work slowdown they announced?"

"Or something more hush-hush. No better place than a motel for shady schemes."

* * *

Tadeo's last phrase kept going around in my mind, preventing me from hearing the rest. I had no choice but to open my journal and write "shady schemes." I underlined the words a few times and let my gaze wander around the foggy hills and the steam rising off the blacktop on Route 52 and into the wet hills beyond. Along the edges of the overpass, the light posts jostled among spindly yagrumas and royal palms like skinny and weirdly luminescent trees.

"Big guy," Tadeo interrupted, surrendering to his curiosity, "what are you scribbling in that notebook?"

"Nothing, trying to inspire myself to write a book."

"A book? And I'm in it? Don't fuck with me. Let me tell you what I think: literature is for crazy people and chicks. Sure you aren't half man and half chick?"

That was his male game: whenever he found me writing after that he'd accuse me of being queer. His game and that of so many other animals of my species. But it was my way of proving myself, my form of bravery: Ulysses against the Sirens, Hercules against the lion, even though from up close the lion reveals his bald spot and his teeth are rotten, worn down century after century. It was all the same to me. I didn't want to do it any other way. Perhaps in the end I'd find what I'd been seeking for so many years, what had brought me to the newspaper and then got me fired, what had made me fight my whole family and had even turned me against myself. What was maybe even now slithering around inside the walls of the thirty-four cabañas of the Motel Tulán.

One-Eyed Pyramid

Chadwick says that to tell a story you need only three things: something to tell, the words to tell it, and, most importantly, the desire to tell it. I'm paraphrasing, of course. I never recall a writer's exact words. Must be envy acting upon memory.

Of Chadwick's three conditions, I have two under my belt. I know how to tell a story (I believe and trust I do; I've received enough practice on the job at the newspaper). I want to tell it (until utter delirium). But I can never find the thread of a story. Just cannot find it. Not one of them holds me by the balls with enough insistence.

And then, this job at the paper. Almost two and a half years and the routine's become a drag, a weight tied around my neck. And I thought working here would give me the perfect hands-on experience, that the paper would provide me with an inside look at the world around me, the

here and now, the one that seems like a phantom in retreat. But I'm
probably wrong. I only know that after seeing so many words crossed
out, so many tragic and senseless stories, after all that, my desire to
paint a portrait is turning into salt and water, and giving me a stiff,
mean temper I nurture with booze, cocaine, and watered-down coffee.
Anyway, I don't have time. I don't have time to think, to weigh what I
want to write and to figure out how it is that the newspaper spins and
weaves the succession of days, the hours, and the chain of current
events. The stress doesn't give me time to confirm my suspicions. Before
I can even reflect upon them, I already have seven more news stories
waiting for me on the monitor. And everyone has to eat. I have to eat. I
can't go looking for my story.

I was reading an entry from my diary. I don't want to call it a
diary, but that's what it was. Just like those melodramatic pink
notebooks—ferocious guardians of secret, yearning loves—that
sweet sixteens keep in their bureau drawers. My notebooks serve
the same purpose. I am in love, tragically in love. But the object of
my affection cannot be possessed. I describe my disgrace in these
silly little notebooks, and from time to time, when I want to feel
that all is not lost, I read them.

I was in the middle of a carefree afternoon before going back
to the motel. I had been working at the Tulán four nights already.
For the first time in my life something kept me away from a desk
and paperwork, and that something had to do with the skin
trade. It was a bit confusing, and I knew I needed to sketch out
some kind of road, wherever it led. I wanted to retrace the steps
that got me to the motel.

It was a quiet afternoon. Daphne, my live-in girlfriend for two years, was at work. I had the apartment all to myself and was surrounded by everything that breathes in silence: the bookshelf, the icebox, my desk, and the stove where I was making coffee. Outside the daily hustle made its presence felt, along with the presence of people who live off daylight.

I lit a cigarette and exhaled calmly, feeling my lungs expand and contract. I missed the constant commotion at the paper, but wasn't nostalgic for it. I smiled. I was free. I read the Chadwick entry in my diary again. The night I made those notes was the same one where my voyage began.

* * *

I took a break from the monitor. My eyes were dizzy from so many poorly written news stories, from endless sentences whose subject was lost in a crazy labyrinth of subordinate phrases. I couldn't stand it anymore, but was afraid they'd catch me zoning out, an activity to which I dedicated more and more time while on the premises of La Noticia. Of course, what my boss and his spies called "zoning out" was to me just writing my own stories, a jumble of incomplete sentences going nowhere. When I wasn't busy with that, I'd bitch about my lot in my notebooks. I, who wanted to write about so many things, had to live off correcting what others wrote so poorly.

Reception broke my train of thought with an announcement that there was a delivery for someone in editorial. That night some coworkers had invited me to Café Bohemio, where they had decided to go after our shift. I was sick and tired of heading out alone to parade my frustrations through the cafeterias of the night, or of going back to my apartment to listen to music until the morning sun lulled me into the fitful, sweaty slumber of those who sleep during the day. So that night I had added my name to the list of beneficiaries of a truly "stimulating" purchase, one of many made from editorial's telephones. As usual, we called our connection to the underworld, and everything was arranged. Someone would stop by the paper to deliver the order, at a discount since we were regular customers. And regular informers too, when we found out a raid was in the works.

When reception called, I offered to take care of the delivery guy myself, jumping at the chance to get away from the monitor where the next day's news drizzled out for the umpteenth time. The risk of completing a drug deal in the paper's parking lot gave me goose bumps, while the irony of the situation amused me. We journalists—who ought to be fierce guardians of the truth— ended up cowering like rats while we pursued the vices the rest of the world tried to conceal. I wasn't the only one: nearly all of editorial and some in administration were in on it, not to mention the printers. Alcoholics most of them, many partial to soft drugs, informants on the payroll of various politicians and traffickers. In the end, we were a corrupt pack with as fine a pedigree as any government agency.

I was almost out the door when a "Wait up, I'll go with you" stopped me in my tracks. It was Daniel, another guy with goggles for glasses, who worked in the next cubicle over. We were linked by a shared frustration: I was a halfhearted writer, and he worked as a copyeditor when what he really wanted to do was go out after a story. But there were no openings for an investigative reporter when Daniel applied, so he took the cubicle next to mine and, every once in a while, grabbed my ears to vent his frustrations. We made stuff up to battle tedium. Like this time, when we put on our brave faces so the rest of the guys could get high on coke before returning home to a lost morning. We went out to the paper's waiting room, commenting on office rumors and getting into character as action heroes undaunted by danger. Under our supposedly cool facades, our blood boiled with the faint thrill of adventure.

We were almost out the front door when I recognized Tadeo's face on the other side of the glass. He looked like someone else, so serious and brooding. Tadeo recognized me too. He immediately lowered his eyes, as if searching for something he hadn't really lost in the patterns of the waiting room's carpet. Once again my nerves got the upper hand. Even when I tried to play the lead in an episode of crime and action, circumstances outdid me.

"You take care of it, Daniel. I have to get back to the office. There are a few strays on my desk," was the excuse I came up with.

"C'mon, don't be nervous. You think it's the first time the guard at reception has seen one of these deals? He's the very first one snorting stuff up his nose."

"No way. You go. I'll wait for you inside. I'll explain later."

Daniel shrugged his shoulders and went out to the parking lot to finish the deal with Tadeo. When he returned, I was already back at my computer. I watched him as he approached the little parcel of paper and plastic that served as my desk.

"They laid this dime on me as a gift. Let's split for the bathroom right now and share it. And then you'll explain to me the little cloud you're hiding under."

"O.K.," I said, putting the tiny bag in my pocket and quickly making up a story that would not reveal Tadeo's identity, or even that I knew him at all. It seemed that my new friend, judging by the way he averted his gaze, was asking me for that favor. And I wasn't going to deny him.

Weeks later, they fired me from the newspaper. The competition announced it was going to put out a new daily specializing in violent crime. There were advertising banners in full color, island-wide coverage, and a foldout "Girl of the Day," exhibiting as much flesh as the page and social mores could take. Needless to say, our offices became a slaughterhouse. The president called all the division heads in to a meeting. They had to cut *La Noticia*'s budget. You can imagine what that means. The rope always pulls apart at the weakest strand, and I've always been too weak a guy for this strand of business.

Still, getting fired was a low blow and it took me completely by surprise, without savings, without cash in hand. I had already lived through so many journalistic crises that I never thought something like this would happen to me. I had been working at the newspaper for months when the island's current administration, upset over the frequent criticism leveled at the honorable governor, ceased advertising its campaigns exclusively with *La Noticia* (paid for out of the public purse, to be sure). Editorial went untouched. A few weeks later, the paper engaged in a no-holds-barred battle with the government, claiming its actions were

meant to bully the sacred right to freedom of the press. The owners spent thousands in lawyers. The copydesk was spared in the
shakedown. Right after that, a rumor made the rounds that the
government would launch an investigation into the connections
certain journalists enjoyed with members of the underworld. The
investigators never started their inquiry, but the budget cuts were
announced anyway. *La Noticia* wasn't selling well since the new
paper had hit the stands. That was the cut that did me in.

* * *

The first week of unemployment was dismal. Daphne gave me all
the support she could, but she began to despair because my body
clock was all screwed up. Sleeping during the day and going out
on the streets after the sun set: I would never find another job in
that condition. I hid from her in my favorite all-night diner. Every
once in a while, I'd run into Tadeo there and tell him what it was
like to not be employed. By then, he had already overcome his
embarrassment over the delivery at the paper, especially after
he explained to me it wasn't his regular job. He owed one of the
dealers in his neighborhood a favor and had agreed to do the
deal. He didn't want me to get the wrong idea.

One night, over two sandwiches, two coffees, and a pack of
cigarettes, Tadeo filled me in on his line of work: professional motel man. The pay wasn't bad, but with all his commitments, the
money evaporated from his pockets like thin air. So from time to
time he'd get a little extra work, something that paid well. "Listen, bro, you have to be flexible in this life. When all's said and

done, what's honesty to a poor man? He tries to be honest, but the truth, which gets fucked over, has more moves than a cat. It jumps right out of his hands, you see? Ain't that a bitch? . . ."

* * *

Several days went by after that conversation, I don't know how many. My situation didn't look any better and I was spending more time on the streets than in the apartment, which had turned into the mute trench of Daphne's frustration. I was telling Tadeo a bit about it when he interrupted me. "Bro, I don't know how willing you'd be, because I can tell from the way you speak you're not meant for this business, but there's a job at the motel." I listened to the offer and smiled. Me, work at a motel, a clandestine pimp? With a bachelor's degree, several stints as an exchange student in universities abroad, with so much education, so much refinement? Tadeo took pity on me while he chewed his bread with his mouth open. I saw myself reflected in his eyes: there I was, one more guy out of work, one more person without direction.

"I'll leave you alone to think about it," Tadeo said, taking the last mouthful and leaving. I ordered another beer, would've loved chasing it with a small line of coke, just so I could bear the burden of being alone. All my dreams and lines of flight came to a head on that table covered with bread crumbs and the sweat from empty beer cans. I felt like a palm tree battered by hurricane winds, couldn't stand being so vulnerable. I needed something to lean on, something that would shelter me from the elements. The next day I went to the motel to ask for the job.

* * *

Alone in my apartment, I finished reading my journal, went through my mail, swept the floor, and did the day's dirty dishes. Afterward I sat down to write a story about my meeting with Tadeo, a story growing episode by episode, night after night, with the tales he told me like a strange suburban Scheherazade, seeking to fill the shadow hours until day broke, crucified by power lines and the busy streets. In my pages, I traced the edges of the labyrinth his tongue unfolded. But this time, paper alone wasn't going to save me from the labyrinth that trapped me. Perhaps I would find my own way out through a story, a compass useful to all of us, to Tadeo, to me, to someone who might read it. All this vulnerability would've been worth it then.

I interrupted my work to connect to a web page listing literary contests. Then I made a schedule. I hadn't published anything in a while; a couple of stories that came out in now defunct literary magazines. One of them had earned me an honorary mention. Maybe I could earn another one, or win a monetary award this time, something to bring me closer to my distant goal. The motel was providing me with a different kind of time. The time I needed to get to the essence of the ordinary.

Daphne came back from work. I talked to her, even managed to make love to her as God intends, in the dark, tangling myself between her strong thighs and watching the incandescence from the streetlights bounce off her skin. She had been distant since I was fired. She made it clear to me several times how she was not at all amused to see me working at a motel. It wasn't that she disapproved of an honest job. "But Julián, please, a place like *that*? What have you lost on Route 52? Why don't you ask your uncle to give you a temporary job at his law firm? Why don't you bring your résumé to other newspapers? Why don't you go to city hall and ask for the job they offered you when you graduated from school?" I always answered the same way: those jobs were family favors, and I'd rather die of starvation than accept their charity.

"You're not going to die of starvation, but the future is slipping away."

"Daphne, the future is in my hands."

And in the middle of the fight, I would grab a pencil and a piece of paper to display my talent as a fringe artist. Her only answer was to snarl and retreat silently to the other corner of the apartment.

That night, after we coldly made love, I didn't want any more drama. So I pretended not to notice in order to avoid discussion of any kind. Daphne had let me make love to her, an improvement over the weeks of unemployment without physical contact. Besides, it felt good to have her in the flesh again. I didn't want to waste away the memory of my satisfied hunger; I wanted to take it with me to the motel to keep me company through the night, in between the moans and heavy breathing of my guests. My labyrinth . . . I gave her a good-bye kiss, showered, and left to do my shift at the motel.

* * *

Tadeo greeted me that Tuesday with a new game to kill the long hours of the night. It was his opinion that some of the cabañas had thinner walls than others. The game consisted of fine-tuning our hearing so we could identify which wall was the most transparent. Tadeo bet on cabaña 14. He was so sure of it that he rented it out to a spectacular couple who arrived early: a small man, almost a dwarf, accompanied by a giant woman, a fake blond with a light mustache, also blond.

"That one's a screamer, bro. I can bet on it. . . . We'll have a lot of fun tonight with the concert, just so long as her john gets a real go at her. You'll see. Fourteen's gonna clean up."

For the sheer pleasure of playing devil's advocate, I asked him, "How could that be, Tadeo, if this motel was built all at once?"

"No, *señor*, take a good look. After twenty you can see the difference in the other cabañas. I'm sure Don Esteban expanded after he made some serious dough."

"Where do you see the difference? I don't see anything."

"What could you see? You don't know anything about construction."

"I'll bet you twenty bucks cabaña twenty-eight wins," I shot back, to stir up debate. That's where we put the next couple that arrived at the motel minutes after I started my shift, a stunning, dark-skinned woman with her boyfriend, horny as hell, who was grabbing her ass as they went up the stairs and whispering in her ear, "Let me get my hands on you, *mamita*, I'm going to give it to you until you can't breathe at all. . . ."

We waited for things to heat up, for the first round to begin. In a matter of minutes they would both be naked and moaning out loud, freed by the illusion of secrecy. Meanwhile Tadeo and I listened and placed our bets.

At the stroke of midnight, while we talked about anything and everything, the buzzer rang. A car came up the entranceway. Tadeo leaned out the front door to see who it was.

"Gray sedan with tinted windows. *La Dama Solitaria* is back."

Water Chamber

"Back in my country people live with very little. Some land around the house, chickens, salted herring, bags of wheat flour and rice and that's it. I'm not saying life is happy, but you live on very little. That's why, when I left for Puerto Rico the first time, it was like a fog lifted from my eyes. I had already emigrated once, as a child, with the whole family. From one side of the Río Masacre to the other. But things don't change much either side of the border. I never thought being Haitian was different from being Dominican. Still, *la vieja* kept reminding me, 'Tadeo, son, you're Haitian and don't you ever forget it, especially when one of those big-city politicians starts blaming us when money gets tight. When that day comes, cross the river and don't look back.' I thought it was just one of her manias, so I let her give me the advice over and over. Because I didn't want to contradict her, understand? You don't want to get in your mother's face. It's a sin.

"I was in Salinas, in the south. They sent me to work at a construction site for a pharmaceutical company, digging ditches, mixing concrete. Made a pile of dough and didn't spend any of it. Took it all back to Baní, to rebuild *la vieja*'s house, which was practically falling on top of her. What a nice big house I built for her, bro, out of cement blocks, roof held up by strong wood beams, with a little porch so she could sit and enjoy the breeze. I dug a cistern for water and put up electrical lines. *La vieja* said to me, 'Tadeo, *m'ijo*, don't waste your money on that. I get along fine with my kerosene lamps. And for sure, the day electricity comes to this barrio is the day they announce the end of the world.' But check it out, man, the power lines finally made it there and the world did not end. What did end was the money. Half the house was still without power. No money for paint, and nothing to finish the small rooms for Ana Rosa, my sister, and her daughters. Her husband left them with my mother before crossing the sea in a *yola*, in search of a better life somewhere else.

"Then I, who had returned like the man in charge, found myself once again with nothing in my pockets. Hard as I tried I couldn't go back to the old life, working to put food on the table and nothing else, not being able to make good on the promise I made to *la vieja*, to provide for the family and make a decent life. So I came back here, legally. I signed up for seasonal work at a coffee plantation in the center of the island. They paid by the hour and not by weight. You had to kill yourself digging your claws into the ground to keep yourself from falling down the steep slopes where the coffee trees were, but I ended up earning good dough. Only that time I did spend a little, because I had time to go out to see more than the barracks where they kept us workers. I took off for the capital. My eyes lit up when I arrived.

"I was done with the plantation. My plan was to find a native *Boricua* who would marry me so I could stay here legally. Fortunately, or unfortunately, I knew a man from my country who told me how to go about it. First, I had to get a hold of twelve hundred dollars. *Boricuas* charge a high price to marry Haitians, even if they think they're Dominican. Then I had to find more money to pay for the marriage license, health examinations, official seals. If that wasn't enough, you have to pay the intermediary who finds the *Boricua* for you. And I had to get somewhere to sleep.

"Life is expensive here. There's no farmland. You have to pay for everything. But you can make some money and the sharp ones know how to save. I worked wherever I could, making deliveries, cleaning houses, gardening, landscaping. Right when I almost had that small pile of dough for the intermediary, Immigration got their hands on me. Over something stupid. Every day after work I went to the corner bar to watch television, just to kill time. One day, a stupid drunk decides to start a fight. And since even the biggest screwball on this island has a gun, the drunk was no exception. He started shooting. I was scared: I dove onto the floor from where two policemen grabbed me and tied my hands behind my back with plastic handcuffs. When they asked for my papers, I didn't know what to tell them. A big mouth like me, can you believe it? I didn't think to say, 'Don't have 'em on me, officer. But hang on a second, I'll be right back!' and then go flying through the barrio like a soul fleeing the devil. No, I kept quiet. The next day I awoke in the belly of an airplane, minus the six hundred dollars I'd saved. Immigration took all of it. Even though I'm a grown man, brother, that makes me want to cry. With that money I could have finished *la vieja*'s little house.

"But the lure of this island had seeped into my veins like bad dope. For better or worse I had to return. Couldn't find a job because I'd been arrested. So I hopped on a *yola* to cross the channel. Won't tell you that story because I don't want to hear it myself. We got caught on the first attempt. But I made it the second time. The rest is history. I settled in Paralelo 37 the best I could.

"That's a real den of thieves, bro. Nobody knows why they call it Paralelo 37. Even from afar the name sounds like something on fire. Doña Cándida, my neighbor, says that Paralelo got its name from the young soldiers who came back crazy or drug addicted from the Korean War where there was a place with the same name. But I have a hunch they call it that because it's like living in a war zone.

"I lived in Paralelo 37 for some weeks, without knowing what to do. The scare from the crossing in the *yola* stuck with me. I couldn't shake it off. Doña Cándida looked after me like a stray dog, took me to her church. They say opportunity slips away fast, so right away I offered to clean the place for a few pesos. One day I stayed for the service. I don't know if it was the exhaustion or the stress I was living under, or bad memories from surviving those long nights on the high seas, but halfway through mass I started shouting that I was a sinner, a real sinner, and that a divine angel told me to give myself to the Lord. I heard myself shouting in tongues. Inside I was saying to myself, 'Tadeo, what's this nonsense?' But I couldn't explain it, no *señor*.

"I went to the Pentecostal church for a few months. Then I got over it. It was a brother from the church who got me this job at Motel Tulán. Since they gave me the night shift, I stopped going to worship. Thank heavens. Those people wailing really got on my nerves. I began working at the motel just as Don Esteban, the owner, was retiring, but I got a chance to talk to him several times. Smart guy. He came up with the idea of building a guesthouse on his plantain farm, which at the time was so strapped the bank was threatening to confiscate. Little by little, his motel was transformed into what you see now. He didn't do it on purpose. Like he also didn't choose the neon pyramid outside, glowing yellow all night like a sign for an Adventist temple. Something to do with Esteban being raised a Mason, but I have a hunch the pyramid reminded him of a dollar sign. It's like with everything else, bro: When you call on money, money comes. His son, who's very active in church now, liked the logo. He thought it brought luck to the family, so he didn't touch it when old Don Esteban, tired of all those squeaking bedsprings, retired from the business and left it to him as his inheritance.

"So that's my life, *caballero*. That's how I stumbled on this motel and now I don't know when I'm getting out. Don't get me wrong. I'm not uncomfortable. It's just *la vieja*'s house still has kerosene in one part and electricity in the other. And before she dies on me, I want to make good on my promise. I don't want her to leave this world thinking that her son wasn't a man of his word."

Dark Flower of Flesh

"Hurry up, bro, and take care of that nice piece of work. I'll stay here and hold down the fort."

There she was inside the sedan, her mane of hair flying in all directions. "Good evening," she said casually. Once again her breath smelled of cigarettes and alcohol. And once again I gave her cabaña 23. As I opened the door I felt the Solitary Lady looking me over from head to toe, sizing me up. "This woman is a real trip," I thought. Her gaze made me uncomfortable, but I had to admit it aroused me, too.

Hardly a quarter of an hour went by before she called the office for room service. Tadeo looked at me. Without saying a word we understood each other. I walked up the stairs slowly and tapped on the door, just enough to announce my presence. When the Solitary Lady opened it, she was wrapped in a black slip, holding the knob for the thermostat in one hand.

"It came loose when I tried to adjust the temperature. It's freezing in here."

"We always keep the air conditioners on high. These rooms get pretty hot sometimes," I said, flattering her and trying to sound confident, even brazen. The sight of her slip and the look she gave me earlier made me forget my place in the motel for a moment. She was unfazed. She gestured for me to come into the room and with her thick, arched eyebrows ordered me to solve the problem. Disappointed, I obeyed.

"The other night I almost froze in this bed, between these dirty sheets."

"I'll bring you fresh ones right away."

"That's right, handsome, bring them."

I ran back to the office, my tail between my legs. An uneasy feeling charged through my body like a neon current. Did that woman think that I was her slave boy, that she could toy with my desires like that, that she could show herself to me in a slip, check me out from head to toe, and treat me like a child or a eunuch? I barely even noticed when the phone rang. It was her again. She asked for a bottle of wine and an order of French fries. And for me to bring a thick comforter along with the sheets. Otherwise the cold wouldn't let her sleep. I hung up.

"Nice work, man. Seems like you hit it off with *La Solitaria*. Let's see if you manage to get her telephone number."

"Come on, Tadeo. What that woman wants is a little servant to satisfy her every need."

"So make it your job to take care of her, *verdad*? The customer's always right."

Tadeo heated up the fries in the microwave. When they were ready, he opened the bottle, put the fries in a box, and sent me on my way back up the stairs to cabaña 23. In the garage outside her room, the woman's lead-colored sedan sucked up the light from the single bulb dangling from a naked cord. I announced my return with a light rap on the door, opened the wooden service compartment, and slipped the fries, the cheap bottle of wine, and the bill inside. I never expected to feel her hand on mine.

Her cold fingers felt like a small reptile brushing slowly against my skin. I couldn't help flinching and stumbled backwards toward the edge of the staircase, almost dropping the bottle of wine. She immediately opened the door. Outlined against the empty light of the room, she stuck her face and half her body out, perhaps to make sure the motel employee hadn't fallen down the stairs and broken his neck against the sedan's hood. As I tried to regain my balance, I looked up at her. Her eyes were deep and dark, bloodshot. You really couldn't lose yourself fully in their darkness, even if you wanted to. There were pale streaks across her pupils, pale veins that hinted at jagged edges underneath, not unlike the rocks a diver high up on a cliff senses under the surface of the murky water below. Stumbling on the stairwell, I had already crashed on the rocks at the bottom of her eyes.

Her gaze froze me until a sarcastic smile spread across her large carmine lips. In her best femme fatale voice, she asked me:

"Everything alright?"

33

My mouth and head moved without knowing what to say. She started in again:

"I didn't mean to scare you," she said and closed the door halfway, and then opened it again, so she could pay me for the wine and fries.

I took the money without saying a word, trying to apply one of Tadeo's lessons to this abnormal situation: "A motel employee must always look serious. But not too serious, like something bad's happening, but rather serious enough to erase every trace of emotion. This face should look like a piece of wood. That way he makes sure he stays in control of the situation." But there was no going back to the safety of an austere and blank presence. Our skin and our eyes had built a bridge that was difficult to destroy. A personal rapport had been established. And it had been on *La Solitaria*'s terms. To top it all off, I didn't have a clue how to make this beautiful creature in her transparent slip yield to me, as she stood on the threshold of a motel door, outlined in light, looking me over with amusement.

"Keep the change," she answered, reacting to my silence. And then, she confused me even more by brushing her cold fingers against mine. Those fingers, so like a manicured corpse's, stirred something inside of me. I couldn't be sure if it was desire. Impossible to say.

She arched her eyebrows. I started to back away, pissed off about losing control of the situation. On the fourth step down, I heard the door creak once again and her grainy, dark voice.

"Hey, handsome, knock on the door next time. I don't like

34

sticking my hands in that little box. It's straight out of a haunted house. Plus, I'm much too old now for that much privacy."

Back in the office, I tried shaking off the bad feeling that had come over me. The landscape around the motel soothed me, the hills stretching out like green, stormy seas, the light posts amid dense foliage, dark power lines tracing a pentagram against the sky. Night dew began fogging the windshields of the cars parked outside. The red, green, and yellow neon from the luminous pyramid reflected on their hoods. The night crept slowly, as if balancing on some strange, slick surface. Almost by chance, my eyes rested on cabaña 23's garage door. The memory of her cold touch passed through my hands again. Hoping to shake it off, I looked at my watch. It was Wednesday now.

When I looked back outside, I thought I saw something peculiar. Right on the belly of the sloped entrance, two luxury cars were parked side by side. Something passed from one window to another, an envelope perhaps, a package small enough to get lost in the quick sleight of hand that was undoubtedly intended to hide it from view. Afterward one of the cars drove up to the office. The other waited its turn, as if the driver were carefully timing his entrance to the Tulán.

Tadeo went out to the car. He placed his elbows on the car's door and started talking to the passenger, who never made a move to step out or even to lower the window all the way down. Once again a quick movement hid a transaction of some sort. Then Tadeo stepped back and watched the car speed up the hill to the motel.

The other car drove up. From where he stood, Tadeo signaled me to take care of it. I grabbed a key and led the driver to room 18, where three men with cell phones and stacks of paper got out of the car. One of them was labor attorney Efraín Soreno.

"Tadeo, it's Soreno again in cabaña eighteen. This is getting hot."

"Tell me about it. The one you saw me talking to is Chino Pereira, the big boss in Paralelo 37. He wants two deluxe cabañas for next week, catering and absolute discretion included." I looked at Tadeo with a blank expression, expecting more information. Tadeo's response was to put a hundred-dollar bill in my hand. "I'll explain it all later, big guy. I can trust you for now, *verdad*?"

I leaned against the Tulán's front door. I was intrigued, chewing on this Paralelo 37. It was the second time Tadeo had mentioned the place, first when he had told me about his life, and now in reference to the guest who made reservations. There was something weird in the air, trapped within the syllables of that name. Paralelo 37. I took out my notebook and wrote it down with a reminder, "Call Daniel at the paper." Maybe he could give me the lowdown.

Back at the office, Tadeo shook his head like someone laughing at a secret joke. "Don't worry, big guy, nobody has ever gone to jail for what we're about to do." I frowned but he ignored it, meeting my eyes with a sly smile. Tadeo was luring me on with the oldest trick in the eternal contest between men. He wanted to gauge my fear, weigh my courage, see if it was for real. And I, finding strength in the sheer force of his provocation, wasn't going to cave. I wasn't going to let him think I was afraid, or hesitant. Another smile spread across his face, an approving smile. And then, just to toy with me, he added:

"Anyway, come with me to the register, we need to change your hundred-dollar bill. You owe me twenty bucks. Remember our bet? Well, you can't hear jack shit from cabaña twenty-eight, but there's an opera going full blast in fourteen. . . ."

Breakfast for Daphne

The city spread out through blinking red lights, narrow streets lined with discount jewelers, money transfer outfits, tailor's shops, and markets hawking their fresh tomatoes on loudspeakers. A harsh and ragged city, awash in colors—sky blue, fuchsia, mango yellow—whose skies were crisscrossed by power lines, where pigeons perched after their constant search for bread crumbs on the hot tarmac. Right in the middle of the city, in front of the square converted into a temporary parking lot, tucked between the discount stores and government agencies, stood La Jerezana, my favorite bakery.

La Jerezana is one of the last bastions of another time, a time in which each building tried to imitate even older Spanish towns, with their central squares, three- and four-story buildings with

ironwork arabesques, locally produced roofing tiles, and bal-
conies and rooftops decorated with mosaics facing the sea. With
its clay oven and smoked hams hanging from the ceiling, La
Jerezana stood its lonely ground, hemmed in by progress a little
more each day. A block away, on the top floor of an aging building whose entrance imitated a house in Andalusia, was the apartment I shared with Daphne.

It was five thirty in the morning and La Jerezana already
smelled like bread. Fresh bread, white bread as hot as the inside
of Daphne's thighs, bread with that aroma of toasted grain, that
smell of vegetable matter that generates more life even as it dries.
I took a number and sat down at the counter, where I could see
outside. Daphne's car was parked across the street.

There were many days when my body simmered over a low
fire as I went down at daybreak to get some bread for my woman.
Later I started going less and less, and finally I only went for solitary sustenance. The worst thing about it was that I don't know
how it happened, what I, or both of us, had done to make the
small blaze that kept us warm go out little by little. It was probably because Daphne was tired of waiting hopelessly for me to
find my place in the world, be it at the paper or inside my own
pages. But sometimes it felt like it was something worse.

"Thirty-eight." I got up to order.

"A loaf of French bread, a quarter pound of *jamón serrano*, a
quarter of *queso Manchego,* and another of Gouda. How much is
the prosciutto?" The man behind the counter was covered with
flour.

"Same as always, or have you forgotten? You deserted us."

I remembered I had close to a hundred dollars in my pocket.

"O.K., man, so put in a quarter of prosciutto and a dollar's worth of eggs."

"Right away. The customer's always right."

Those last words pierced the center of my chest like a poison arrow and sent a shudder through my hands. I couldn't help smiling, and worrying too. The memory of the Solitary Lady burrowed inside my head. My skin crawled and something stirred between my legs. The man finished weighing the order and wrapped the eggs in brown paper.

I met Daphne at a bar after leaving the newspaper one day. I told her I was a writer. It wasn't a lie since at that stage of our encounter, I'd already published some stories. True, they were in defunct magazines—a local one, *Prodigios*, and another one from the Universidad del Oriente de Barranquilla, in Colombia. Don't even ask me how I got the addresses of those magazines, let alone why they decided to publish my work, because it's still a big mystery to me. Another story had recently been posted on a webzine edited by a friend whose poems I had helped translate into English as part of her application to a writers' colony up in the Adirondack Mountains in New York. Plus, there was that honorable mention I got in a small-time contest sponsored by a Spanish savings bank. Those were the only things that allowed me to consider myself a writer, that and the dozens of first chapters, heavily revised, of my great novel, the one that was sure to strip away my anonymity. Those things and my desire to impress Daphne.

In the beginning, Daphne and I spent all day sleeping on each other's chest, making love in the afternoon. I read her my stories, my notes, and she commented on them as best she could with her pharmaceutical background. "You know Leo Buscaglia is my favorite author, but what you wrote about a man searching for his destiny is so beautiful," she'd tell me, her eyes filled with an admiration I knew to be undeserved, but in which I wanted to believe. She told all her friends, "My boyfriend's a writer." After a while, though, when there were no new publications, she stopped saying it. "Maybe you should write more upbeat stuff, give a positive message, like Paolo Coelho." Later she'd complain about my downtrodden stories: "Your problem is that you're always writing about life on the edge. But everyone wants to escape the dreariness of everyday life." Out of frustration, I argued that the paper was drowning me in words. "So why don't you focus just on being a reporter? At least your future's more certain there." I began to resent her and started to leave a mess of papers all over the house, but in a show of defiance I didn't read them to her. She got the message and stopped paying attention to them, to me.

When I was fired from the paper, her demeanor became even more disheartened. I'd failed her, the man she thought she'd found, next to whom her own inner light would be revealed. I was no longer that man. She said so with her body and a choreography of distances that slowly dominated her touch, the smell of her skin, her light brown face which frowned at me. It got worse when I told her about the job at the motel. I don't know if it was out of pity or what remained of her love for me, but she tried to be comforting, to tell me not to worry, because "the motel's just a temporary thing. That's all you can expect from it. Soon you'll find something that's up to your standards." Her words came out twisted. At least that's how I felt as they hit my chest. I defended myself as best I could, explained to Daphne that maybe at the Tulán, I'd find what I thought I'd seen between the stories killed at the paper, ink-stained yet lifeless, the story that was always being replaced by a new one and newer one. "It doesn't matter where I work, that doesn't change who I am. I'm a writer," I told her with a muted rage that forced me to swallow the ends of my words. "You and your dreams . . . ," she answered, the worst possible thing she could've said. I responded with a long silence.

I walked into the house to find Daphne still asleep. Everything about her—her small eyes, her black mane, her big hips and little doll's hands with immaculate fingernails—had a clean air, and a chemical smell. And I arrived filthy, foul smelling, dismissed and aimless, forced to act like a servant and a witness to what everyone wanted to conceal beneath the cover of a motel room. Daphne was no longer welcoming me. Even if the right thing to do in a case like this would've been to pack my things and move out, the last thing I wanted was to be the villain, to make Daphne suffer by being left behind. Truth is, I didn't have the strength or the courage to go ahead with it. Perhaps that's why I still insisted on the impossible, on erasing the evidence of my defeat from Daphne's face and body, and proving to the world, by starting over, that I was still capable of making a woman's eyes sparkle. My woman's eyes. Daphne's.

I went in for a quick shower, took off my pants and underwear. A smell not unlike ripe papayas rose from my pubic hairs. It was the smell of a willing woman, or of having slept with one. Not knowing what to do or where it came from, I decided to declare war on that smell. I stood under the hot water, lathering up and letting the water rush to my aid. Suddenly an avalanche of images assailed me, tons of warm semen spilling out and staining a motel carpeting. I tried to shake it off, but my flesh was already hard. I couldn't face Daphne like that. I was too vulnerable, especially if she was going to look at me like she'd been looking at me lately, as if I were a child who dreams of flying by flapping his skinny arms. So I took matters into my own hands, touching myself in silence, biting my lips, thinking of the Solitary Lady.

When I went back into the room, wrapped in a towel, carrying coffee and omelets, Daphne was just starting to wake up. I surprised her with the steaming breakfast from La Jerezana. My body was steaming too, from another kind of feast, and full of its own little fire. Daphne sipped her coffee.

"What's all this?" She took a bite of *pan con queso Manchego* while I answered:

"A welcome-home gift."

"But I was home all night."

"Yes, my love, but I welcome you to the day, with the soul back inside its body."

"Whose body?" she asked. I was on the spot.

"Yours."

"How about you take it out of me again?"

"Take what out?"

"The soul from my body."

"Let's see if I can."

"Of course you can, all you have to do is give me a kiss."

"Where?"

"Here."

Daphne opened her legs to my mouth, which was once more full of tiny caresses. The inside of Daphne's thighs tasted like wild oats. Her smell blended with the aroma of bread and coffee and the bitter fruit growing in my hard-on, fruit I still couldn't name, citric and fresh, the kind that offers its juice as soon as it's opened. We fondled each other like two strangers, each lost in a hunger stronger than the meeting of our bodies. Inside Daphne, I recovered from the shock of finding myself with the odor of another woman, one I hadn't even touched. It wouldn't happen again. It couldn't happen again because there wasn't the slightest reason for it. And this ritual of making love to Daphne, no matter how melancholic it felt, was what my body was there for.

Daphne rose from bed and dressed without bathing, taking the two odors that clung to her down to the pharmacy with her. I would wait for her, wandering around in the apartment until late in the afternoon. Maybe I'd write a little and then we'd have supper together. We would enjoy the fresh loaf of bread before it became hard and stale. Then I would leave for the motel.

Alone in the apartment, I fell into a deep sleep and woke up at noon, wanting to write. I went over the notes of my conversations with Tadeo, which covered page after page inside my notebook. I came across the name Paralelo 37 and picked up the phone to call Daniel at the paper. Surely he could shed more light on the subject.

The phone rang three times before my old colleague answered. "Daniel Figaredo, copydesk." After the requisite greetings, I lied and told Daniel I was working as a government investigator.

"Housing and Community Development," I said. "I'm looking for information on a barrio known as Paralelo 37. All we've got here are a few maps. Do you think *La Noticia* has a file on the place?"

"Of course we do, it's one of the hottest spots in the country. Do you have e-mail? Because if you want, I'll send it to you right now."

The Sambuca Factor

For many years the area didn't have a name. It had sprung out of thin air fifty years ago, behind the soda-bottling plant. Houses there still had dirt floors, even if they never lacked a television. Those who knew the place thought of it as an abscess growing off from another district to the north known as Parcelas Falú, which was bordered by swamps and mangrove thickets and whose canals would fill up with water from the ocean when the moon was full. To the south, Paralelo 37 was hemmed in by plots of land taken from a vast citrus farm, plots given to the black and mulatto Falús who were slaves so long ago that by the early part of the century they no longer remembered the meaning of the word *boss*. As it always happens on this island, the darkest blacks sought out respectable women, which is to say as white as possible, and began to marry off. The weddings resulted in land disputes among wives, cousins, and sons, who in turn also handed out ever-smaller parcels on which their relatives built little houses of wood and zinc. Paralelo eventually spilled over onto land the white Falús kept fenced in to sell to foreign investors when they fell on hard times, which were considerably hard just before World War II. That's when the bottling company arrived and announced its dominion over the lands along the coast.

It came too late. A bramble of small hovels—scourged by moths, parasites, and termites—had grown roots in that quagmire and multiplied like wild reeds. The executives from the bottling company called in the authorities, asking them to "relocate" the families to the public housing projects the new government was building alongside high-scale urban developments. Perhaps the workers would pick up manners from the country's emerging middle class. Always acting in the name of progress, the authorities went in peacefully to persuade the families to move to new facilities. They were called "public residences," but the people of Paralelo christened them "projects." Many were suspicious of the quality of these new homes, even though the government promised that each unit would have fresh water and electrical and gas lines, with open spaces between the four-story buildings for young and old, basketball courts, baseball parks, civic centers for grand occasions, and roads with easy access to schools and hospitals. With so many promises being made, many moved into the projects: cement boxes, each named after a national hero. The government celebrated their decision with perfectly calibrated bribes: employment opportunities, free children's shoes for the school year, a welfare check that couldn't be delivered to houses in Paralelo because they weren't on any mail route.

But Paralelo 37 was a hydra with a thousand heads. As soon as the old settlers packed up and moved, other families would come in and occupy the little half-collapsed shanties that were left behind like the peeled skin of a fruit. They raised them up again with cardboard tinder and never gave the steamrollers enough time to reclaim the place, which was a hard enough task in itself, given the serpentine nature of the swamp.

There's always a solution to the disaster of poverty. The white Falús sold Paralelo to the government. The bottling company had to settle for a seven-acre parcel of rescued land, around which they built a cement wall. On the other side of the wall remained the labyrinth of muddy roads and alleyways cordoned off by barbed wire fences and pieces of wood. On that side, the clucking and crowing of hens and fighting cocks could be heard mixing with the screams of pot-bellied children all the colors of the rainbow, who were raised in that quagmire by the grace of an unknown god. Some grew up to find work at the bottling plant as security guards, workers, or company janitors. Others took a different road in life, working for Víctor "Sambuca" Cámara, the old boss of Paralelo 37.

Sambuca was a dark, thin mulatto who used brilliantine and hair spray to tame the kinky locks that crowned his royal palm of a head. His eyes were the color of caramel, just like his father's. Doroteo Cámara had been a black stonemason who eventually fell on hard times on account of his drinking. Years before, Sambuca's family had lived in the countryside, but when wealthy islanders began to build stone houses near the urban centers, Doroteo Cámara's steady hands emigrated in search of fortune and the chance to show off his art.

Besides embellishing their homes, the rich folks had to be entertained as well. That's how in those districts, along with stone-masonry and woodworking, another profession arose among black people, one that had been lost by their forefathers. Blacks became musicians. Professional musicians. Bar after bar opened all over the city. And Doroteo Cámara gave himself to those bars.

The music came about slowly, originating in the fiestas of the Cross, the strolling carolers at Christmastime, whenever a child's wake was held in the sugarcane fields or the coffee plantations, and when orchestras in town played Spanish operettas or marched on Sundays in the main plaza. The drums of old, which during slavery times had given the signal for blacks to escape or for disgruntled laborers to burn down the cane fields, now played underground rhythms vibrating off surfaces very different from the traditional goatskins stretched over the mouth of a drum. The ancient rhythm could now be heard on pulsating guitars played by light-skinned fingers, from musical metals that took in the wind and from the flat pieces of animal teeth arranged in the wide black and white smile of a horizontal harp. Doroteo remembered that as a child his parents told him that down south, the mulatto son of a washerwoman and a bricklayer had become a composer of popular *danzas*. The island's first composer. So it was clearer than water: To get out of the slums, you had to know how to entertain the rich.

The cleverest blacks found a way around their traditional positions in the workforce. They moved to the city, far away from the hated fields that broke their backs. Once there, they got around working all over again by refusing to climb up the scaffoldings or to carry sacks of lime and long wooden rafters. They were smart and saw it was just another version of the old ways. When the Americans arrived on the island, those blacks, mulattos, and light-skinned blacks were ready for what came next. They put their hands to work with the new instruments the Yankee soldiers had placed at their disposal in the different wars and bars. Between the society soirées, the military galas, the partisans of the Spanish Republic and this show or that at the casino, they managed to eke out enough for a living, a good living, maybe even enough to improve their lot.

Doroteo Cámara moved from the country to the city ten years after the Americans arrived. He came in search of his fate. There he met Georgina Falú, who worked as a maid in the house of one of his most demanding clients, a frail old widow (also named Georgina Falú) whose old house, inherited from her cane baron father, was always in need of repair. The *señora* would call Doroteo because he was a serious, hard worker who still hadn't developed the bad manners of city blacks, who treated proper ladies as if they were their godmothers back in the slums. Doroteo would take the jobs on account of the pay, which wasn't much but was steady, and to see black Georgina smile. Two months later he had fallen in love with her. Three months after that he made love to her in one of the servant's rooms, on the *señora*'s freshly washed sheets. Nine months later their first son was born. And since Doroteo was a decent man, he took Georgina with him. They settled in a lot his mother-in-law gave them in an undeveloped spot near the big city. Doroteo woke up every morning at dawn to take a bus downtown, where he continued to find work building houses. Gina became a laundress. Their little home prospered. They had their own vegetable patch and the kids were going to school. But still a strange uneasiness embittered the mason's life, something he couldn't put his finger on.

Doroteo saw the black musicians, the same ones he ran into at the bars in the slums, buying houses near a tall building known as the University, whose tower was adorned with small statues. And he saw them riding in cars dressed like whites. While he was working like a beast of burden, they were moving forward. He was trying to save all his money so he could buy a little bit of land closer to town and take his family out of Parcelas Falú. But every dollar slipped through his fingers like water.

In any case, things were turning ugly in Parcelas. Doroteo would look out from his porch at wave after wave of country people crashing over the area, overcrowding the narrow, muddied alleyways and swamps the neighbors used to raise pigs. Many came without any real know-how and worked on the docks or ran errands for a few pennies in the middle-class neighborhoods. Yet masons, carpenters, locksmiths, and woodworkers kept arriving in great numbers, making it all the more difficult to find work. Standing back to back, they filled the small plots of land still up for grabs in the area, raising shacks from odd pieces of wood and tin cans, sleeping on the sacks of rice the Americans gave out to alleviate the hunger of those years, and enlisting in the military when it was broadcast that another world war was looming. Those who returned alive from the war either made it in society or hid in a dark corner of their shacks, overwhelmed by strange scabs and mysterious ulcers, letting themselves die off.

Doroteo didn't want that for his children. So he worked harder. And then harder, and still more. Little by little, he began to spend more time out of the house and in those bars where four or five musicians played *charangas*, the Cuban *son*, and songs that seemed to relieve the terrible burden breaking his back. The music was a respite, the music and a little *aguardiente*, the illegal kind.

Georgina was becoming estranged from him, as estranged as he was becoming from his own trembling hands. Doroteo noticed that, month after month, he landed fewer jobs. So he dug into the tin can that held his savings and got a bottle to suck on so he could drown the sorrows he felt inside. Georgina wasn't helping; from time to time her skin, the shade of walnut, would swell and give birth to yet another mouth to feed.

Sambuca was the last to be born and he came into the world in a rage. As a newborn he wailed like a wild beast in the mountains, and even when he was tethered to his mother's languid breast he didn't calm down. She had to wean him sooner than the others because he would leave her breasts raw, suckling even the blood with a thirst that had no measure or explanation. Doroteo had already died when Sambuca went to grade school. All he remembered was his father's reddened, yellow eyes, swollen gut, and a trembling hand. The other one, stiff, rested against the right thigh, which was paralyzed too. They called him Sambuca because that's what his father called him, since he was no longer capable of saying his son's real name. His mother still insisted on calling him Víctor Samuel, but he found it hard to respond to that name. When all was said and done, it was his father who took care of him when Gina worked from dawn till dusk. Sometimes when Sambuca's little fingers managed to open his bottle and bring it closer, his father ruffled his hair and looked at him tenderly.

After Doroteo's death, Sambuca's older sisters closed ranks around their mother. They learned how to knit and clean houses, how to make dresses for the proper young ladies, the daughters of teachers, engineers, and lawyers. Later, pretending to be older, they managed to find jobs at the municipal hospital. In that way they were able to pay for the education of four of their five little siblings. One became a secretary, another an accountant, and the other two, Spanish teachers. Together they all bought a house in the subdivision that had been built near Parcelas Falú. They did what their father could not: they got the family out of Parcelas.

Esteban, Sambuca's second oldest brother, had gone half mad after one too many wars. Talking to him was like trying to hold on to a slippery fish: his eyes wandered, he kept a close watch on the doors to the house, and at night he'd wake up screaming and sweating even when it wasn't hot. He began to come home with bloodshot eyes, reeking of alcohol like his father. Georgina would let loose, yelling at the top of her voice, wielding the Bible given to her by the missionaries from the new Pentecostal church, to which she had converted. Beside herself, she shouted at him: "Son of Satan! The demon of drink will finish you off just like your father!" But if Esteban didn't drink, he couldn't deal with his soul. Soon liquor wasn't enough and he had to look for something stronger. He moved out and drifted around Parcelas by himself. He fixed up the old shack as best he could and lived there like a dog. Only a couple of years older than Sambuca, he'd take his little brother with him to all the bars in Paralelo. What's more, Sambuca was becoming an ace on the clarinet. It was only a matter of sticking the instrument in the boy's mouth during the music class at school. It seemed as if he was born blowing through that labyrinth of metal. But he lacked discipline, or so his teachers and the local bandleader said. His brother didn't lecture him. He loved to listen to the boy play *charangas.* He even stopped trembling when he listened to his little brother make music. They were always together, Sambuca playing the clarinet for Esteban. That his older brother was stranger than ever and more incomprehensible didn't weaken the love Sambuca felt for him. It made him follow him closer still. It was in making the rounds with Esteban that Sambuca discovered that there existed a business rife with danger (to satisfy his rage) and fast money (to fill his pockets), one that took him no time to master.

* * *

The people of Paralelo 37 adore him. Every year on the day after Christmas, Sambuca throws a huge party, with expensive gifts for the kids of the area and white-gloved waiters serving ice-cold Champagne to residents and friends alike. They roast dozens of pigs on an open fire and cook up thousands of pounds of rice and pigeon peas, as well as pastries with cherries in marinade. The best bands provide the music and everybody sleeps well that night, basking in a luxury that for a few hours replaces the daily hassle of living in poverty. What's more, everybody in Paralelo knows Sambuca is responsible for getting the city government to pave some of the roads, bring in electrical and telephone lines, and get mail delivered to the sector, which finally allowed most families to receive their much-anticipated welfare checks at home. Sambuca godfathered hundreds of kids in Paralelo, buying them book bags and textbooks and advising them to stay in school so they wouldn't end up like him. Those he couldn't persuade to live within the law, he would place in small, risk-free positions in the chain of distribution. But if he found out they were using what he supplied them with, he removed them from his organization. More than a few times Sambuca had turned into a rabid beast who didn't hesitate to draw the blood of those who opposed him. His loathing for addicts was as great as his generosity to the people of Paralelo. It is said that he had ordered more than a few of his own surrogates killed.

His undisputable favorite was Chino Pereira. They called him Chino because his eyes were slightly slanted, even though his skin was the color of burnt wood. Some believe he is Sambuca Cámara's own son, or maybe his nephew, the lost vestige of the junkie brother he cared for until his death. Chino doesn't know. He never met his own father. But he did meet the legendary Sambuca, from whom he inherited the empire that is Paralelo 37.

Point Blank

Another week of work went by at the motel, and I got used to seeing how other people lived out their fantasies and frustrations, until I realized mine were not so terrible. Daphne was right. My fall into the motel was something transient, an experiment perhaps. A happy accident that yielded bountiful advantages. I had spent all week reading about Paralelo 37 and suddenly my mind was burning with words, words that flew out of my fingers. The result was a long story in which Paralelo came alive, at least for me. Sambuca, Tadeo, and Chino would live there and everything that happened to them would be a reflection of the power of the place, of that force that draws the floating periphery toward the center, a center that feeds on the pain of poverty, on the tragedy of proving oneself a man, on the melancholy of having to destroy those you love so you can control them. That was Paralelo to me. That was where my story would be born.

I would have to change the names of my characters, of course. I wasn't going to be so foolish as to get on the bad side of the island's most powerful players, not men of legitimate wealth but rather those bosses born in the sticks, architects of the surest and most ruthless routes to wealth. Daphne's aloofness didn't move me anymore, just as the memory of the Solitary Lady failed to move me, although I dusted it off every so often when I played with myself on those afternoons Daphne ignored my caresses, doled out more for my own relief than to make any real contact. I have to confess that I was beginning to like my life again and that I had decided to work at the motel only until I finished my story. The e-mail from Daniel had restored my newspaper contacts; my old colleague quickly informed me that there was a new boss (the previous one had to be sent to detox in Miami), and that, financially, things were stabilizing. He would keep an eye out. Most likely it was a matter of months—two or three at the most—and I would get my old job back at *La Noticia*. Everything would be back to normal.

What's more, the motel kept offering me new reasons to dip into the ink. It seemed as if the Tulán's passions ran parallel to mine. On that Tuesday night, a beautiful lesbian couple kicked off my shift. One was young and short, but very strong. She looked like an athlete. The other was much older. She had the lost eyes of someone who knows she's defeated by a passion far stronger than will, like an old virgin, fallen prey. Her profile shone with the same brilliance the images of saints have in the ancient testaments, the ecstasy experienced by those who give themselves up to the pleasures of their martyrdom. She wouldn't get out of the car until the other one had picked up the keys and then she stepped out alone, and without asking for anyone's help, opened the garage door. I imagine her sacrificing a bit of herself with each rise in the stairs leading to the door, like someone pausing at each point along an intimate Stations of the Cross, in all its slow and sensual death.

A young guy with long hair, drunk, arrived with his girl-friend. They looked like college kids, one of those young couples still living with their parents who have to find a place to quell the hunger that attacks them in the middle of a crowd, someplace far from the beach or the library's parking lot, someplace where they can leave the car and tear into each other. So they look for a motel.

Tadeo took care of an older man who arrived in his car with a very young girl, almost a child. The girl, absolutely free of guilt, looked at herself in the rearview mirror while slowly chewing bubblegum. She had the face of someone who had seen too much too soon. Fixing her runny lipstick and looking at herself in the rearview, there was something withered about her. Something far away and free from the lure of fresh excitement for anything new. Upright in his car, the old man, probably a husband who'd slipped out of the house on the sly, looked like a wretched cow: bovine through and through, always obedient to someone else's dictates.

Soreno the attorney and his associates were hiding out in cabaña 18 again. They called to order coffee and cigarettes.

"I'll go," Tadeo volunteered. "I'm anxious to see what's up with those guys from the union, see what I can take in with my peripheral vision. Listen, brother, truth is whatever's going on in there is a real mystery. It's not normal to come back to the same motel so often. You keep an eye on the register. I'll tell you what I learn when I get back."

I stayed in the office, minding the paperwork. More or less thoughtlessly, my eyes lit on the sign outside cabaña 23. Shadowy, probing eyes, the touch of a reptile in heat. That was my way of refreshing the memory that warmed my flesh from time to time. I couldn't have cared less about playing the union spy. I would've liked to play other things instead.

Tadeo was back in the office, his hands signaling that he had valuable information. The bell for new arrivals rang: a lead-gray, four-door sedan. *La Dama Solitaria*. I walked up to the car confidently. Opening the garage door, I steeled myself, determined not to let this woman take me by surprise again. I'd already spent a week holding myself back, and I had been waiting for her all night, had developed a strategy to keep to this side of the line, to continue possessing her in my mind, a sound, safe haven that allowed me to take her from afar. This time, any game with the Solitary Lady was going to be played according to my preconditions. To prove it, I changed the rules of the game and the number on the key. I'd give her cabaña 20, one of the rooms that Tadeo said had thin walls. I could have her right where I wanted her, at a distance yet exposed.

Giving me a faint smile of acknowledgment, the woman stepped out of the car.

"What happened to twenty-three?"

"Occupied. But this room is just as cozy."

I handed her the key and her fingers brushed mine as she took it. Once again her cold hands made my skin crawl, but this time was slightly different: I expected it. She didn't say anything else. She left and went up the stairs, weaving on her brown stilettos. I gauged the swing of her gait and knew I was safe. She would go into the room only to hide and do what she did behind closed doors. Perhaps she'd call in her usual order of liquor, or fast food, which I would deliver unseen, filling the empty parts of my memory with new observations of her body and new questions as to why she was here. She had to be hiding from something like all the other guests who took cover in the suburban night, hiding out in the motel until sunrise.

Back at HQ, Tadeo told me that the first thing the attorney and his associates had done when they arrived was to recharge their cell phones.

"Seems like they're waiting for a call, and from what I could read in their faces, this will be their last night at the Tulán. They're closing the deal tonight."

"What kind of deal?"

"These guys are doing business, bro. They didn't bring any paperwork, like the other night, and they haven't made themselves comfortable, smoking and drinking to kill time. These guys are on their way and they're in a hurry. I think they're just waiting on something and as soon as it's taken care of, they'll split."

61

An hour and a half went by before we saw any more action. Only a few of our regular guests arrived: a young insomniac who brought his books to study for finals; a couple, both married, looking for a way to steal a little passion in the night. Tadeo and I kept a lookout for room 18. And out of the corner of my eye I was checking *La Dama Solitaria*'s door.

A red car, European make, came up the hill. When Tadeo approached, gesturing toward an empty garage, the driver waved him over. Then from the office, I saw Tadeo let him idle while he opened the garage door of cabaña 18. He came back to the office at a trot.

"This you won't believe, bro. The guy who went into eighteen works for Chino Pereira."

"Are you sure, Tadeo?"

"Of course I'm sure. I never forget a face, even when I try. Names I'm not so good with so I couldn't tell you what they call this particular character, but he works for Chino Pereira. I've seen them together in Paralelo, splashing mud on the tires of their car as they ride around the swamp impressing the locals. Everyone in the neighborhood knows he's rising through the ranks."

"So what's his connection to Soreno?"

"That's what I'd like to know. And I bet you it's got nothing to do with the work slowdown at the Power Authority. This smells like something else."

"It doesn't smell, Tadeo. It stinks."

"That, bro, is the smell of money."

We bandied about theories to explain the transactions taking place that very moment in cabaña 18: investments in illegal arms sales or in drug trafficking, with the miscreants diverting union dues for private use. Or maybe it was the other way around, maybe the traffickers were using Soreno and his cohorts to launder money through secret accounts opened on behalf of the union. Every trafficker needs allies with one foot in the legitimate world. Money needed to be put to good use in a front to buy houses and land, invest in businesses, all to strengthen the profits gained from others' weaknesses and vices, from those lost in the morass of tedium, who search for some substance to make their life a little more bearable. And on that night, Tadeo and I had discovered what many suspect but rarely get to confirm. The Motel Tulán allowed us a close look at the internal mechanisms of the wheel that keeps the city moving. Lawyers, traffickers, undocumented workers, adulterers, and women on the run, they all converged under the night sky over Route 52. The city itself concealed them in its most secluded spots, as if denying the existence of encounters and transactions which she herself provoked and which she counted on to multiply her splendor. Each and every one of those invited to the city's carnage carries with them not only the weight of their guilt but also the burden of believing themselves to be acting on the fringes of the city when in reality they are the blood that keeps it alive. Tadeo and I were the sole witnesses to those frenzied banquets that take place on the margins of a city that needs them to feel alive.

Half an hour later the deal was done. Walking slowly and

steadily down the steps, the man got in his car as if nothing had happened, and drove away from the Tulán. The phone rang. Tadeo jumped up to get it, thinking it would be from cabaña 18. Maybe now they would order some drinks and give us the chance to go into those rooms where power, in its criminal and destructive form, had been lounging around for hours. Even we who watched from outside and knew the dangers involved still itched with a morbid curiosity. We wanted in, we wanted to smell the aroma of intrigue, the same way our eyes fix on the corpse as we drive by an accident. Tadeo and I (yes, me too, why deny it) wanted to go into that room and steal at least a little of the spectacle, a discarded shoe, a small pool of blood, some remainder of the crime scene before our own consciences protected us from the sights and forced us to think about good and evil, about how lucky we were to be seeing it all from the safety of the law. But deep down we envied the powerful, those who dared to break the law and take advantage of it. The phone rang three times. Tadeo picked up. The call wasn't the coveted invitation to the scene, it was for me. *La Dama Solitaria.* Tadeo gave me the message that she wanted a bottle of wine.

"She expressly asked that you bring it over."

"Man, look at the time. I'm almost out of here. And anyway, I don't want to miss—" I grumbled, but Tadeo calmly interrupted me.

"The customer is always right."

I took the bottle. Walking to the guest rooms I noticed 18's garage doors opening. Some of the guys from the union were getting in the car, ready to go. Soreno was in the driver's seat. I continued using my peripheral vision, learned without giving myself away that four of them were leaving, the same number that had gone in earlier. Thank God they hadn't left any presents wrapped up in 18's sheets. I didn't have time for a closer look. I had to make the delivery. I opened the garage doors and went in to drop off the bottle. The Solitary Lady was waiting for me by the door to room 20. I wasn't counting on what I saw.

Wearing just a small black slip, she showed off all her smooth skin, pampered by every luxury. She was long and tall and I could see her ribs under the flesh. Her nipples were like closed, bulging eyes, through the transparent fabric; they were small and hard, as if she had had them enhanced or at least lifted. Her endless legs and wide hips revealed a small ass that came to a point in a tiny pillow of soft flesh between her legs. That small pillow seemed to be the only tender spot in her body; that and the large velvety lips between her inviting thighs. A flower of flesh. Her arms were crossed, a glass in each hand.

"My shift's almost over," I said as a prelude to leaving without a drink.

"That's what I thought. Now we'll have time to talk. Come in."

Her voice was so casual and decisive, I didn't have time to hesitate.

Two glasses of wine and her hand was already on my thigh.

"What are you doing in a place like this?"

"I take care of guests while I work."

"On what?"

"On a story."

"You're a writer?"

"I try to be one. And you?"

"What about me?"

"What are you doing in a place like this?"

"If I tell you, it's going to end up in your writing."

"I know how to keep a secret. That's why they gave me this job."

"That's good."

"Good, what's good?"

"That you know how to keep a secret. . . ."

Her hand slithered up my thigh like a snake. I looked into her eyes, dark as a night full of precipices. The tip of her tongue slipped past her lips, calling mine.

"If you feel like it, do it."

"Do what?"

"Kiss me."

"I could lose my job."

"You're off the clock now. Are you afraid to taint the hotel's good name?"

"Let's just say there's a conflict of interest."

"So you're interested?"

"Very much."

Her hand was resting between my thighs, where a fierce rush of blood was making my skin smolder. She smiled again, this time a bigger and more inviting smile. She came closer. The large bags under her eyes, their dozens of tiny wrinkles fanning outward, made me want to kiss her, and at the same time to push her away. I wanted the wrinkles to repulse me, to give me enough room to hold back, so I could take control of the situation at last. I put my hand on her shoulder to keep myself from giving in to the urge to run my tongue over the wrinkles under her eyes. She guided my hand down to her raised nipples, still wrapped in the dark, cool slip of black silk. Then I couldn't hold back any longer, and I fell on her with my lips.

Her wet mouth tasted like fruit about to decay, vaguely like the flavor an overripe papaya has when it's ready to be pressed into sweet marmalade. I let myself enjoy the taste of that woman's mouth for who knows how long. Suddenly I was on top of her, lifting her slip while she slithered under me, holding the slip in place so she wouldn't be completely naked. I pushed up on my arms and kicked my pants halfway down. In a flash she thrust her hips against mine. I stared at the carpet, trying to get a handle on what I was doing. She read my mind and slid down to my waist, grabbing hold of me in her mouth. I let myself go while she caressed me, never taking her eyes off me. Her slip was halfway off, exposing her nipples, and what had been a broad smile exploded into a burst of laughter. I watched her laugh and felt deflated; she was going to make me come too soon. I held back. She got on top of me and I let her ride. I rested my hands on her waist so I could feel her heaviness, her curves, and her rocking back and forth, losing myself in the rhythm of her hips. And so I could pull out before I came. Moments later she was blowing me again, while I shivered on the Tulán's carpet, my mind empty, except for

that stupid phrase roaming around inside my head: "The customer is always right."

I crashed for a few seconds and then snapped out of it and
started rummaging around for my clothes, which were strewn
around the room. *La Dama Solitaria* watched me with an amused
look on her face while I fought with the legs of my pants. I ran
away as fast as I could. I don't remember how I did it, only that I
was out of there as soon as possible, taking advantage of what
was left of the darkness to sneak away from the motel room. I ran
up the hill to where I'd parked my old piece of junk, trying to
think of something to say to Tadeo, of how I could apologize for
the hour and fifteen minutes I had lost inside that woman's body,
leaving him to man the register and face the people from the day
shift on his own. But Tadeo was already gone.

I drove toward home with the radio at full blast. I didn't want to
think. People listening to the radio were calling the news show to
vote for their favorite radio personality. I flicked the dial. On this
station they were commenting on the impasse in negotiations between the workers' union and the Power Authority. No agreement had been reached and the union was threatening to put the
strike to a vote. I hit the station again. Music, I wanted to hear
music, anything. It was the only way I could escape the questions
teeming inside my head: Why couldn't I stop the seduction? Why
did I let that woman drag me wherever she wanted? Her tone had
invited me to surrender to the events of night turned into day,
and this Wednesday had given me a gift no man can refuse. I
smiled. It was true. No man in his right mind would decline the
invitation I had been given. An experienced woman whom life

had led to a motel room alone had chosen to seduce me. I, the chosen one. The lucky winner. Standing out from all the others, just this once.

A *gauguancó* was playing on the radio, and I surprised myself when my fingers fell in with the beat. Maybe the feeling of the tips of my fingers against the wheel awoke the memory of touch. I remembered M.'s body, her saliva, juicy and spent, her hips pressed against my skin. M., that's what I decided to call her from now on. M. for *miércoles,* Wednesday. There are some beings better left unnamed. Names have the power to summon. The secret name of Yahweh, the warnings from a witch's coven, invoking Satan, the Kabala. I had summoned that woman not with a name, but with flesh, and smells. And now she'd gotten under my skin.

But I had touched her body as well, her taut thighs, which knew all about caresses, the wrinkled bags under her eyes. Those fingers—*my* fingers—had traveled over her like a cartographer, fearful yet hungry for the discovery of her landscape. Those nervous fingers, full of anxiety and wild plans for taking action that doubt and daily life interrupt. Yet my fingers were, they had dared to be, the lucky winners of a prize. A dubious prize, but a prize nonetheless. Because even more than knowing that I was the object of desire—I definitely didn't make the first move, although I didn't exactly put up a fight either—I had slept with M., formerly *La Dama Solitaria*. She would now be riding less alone in her car on the way home, smiling with satisfaction. Feeling mischievous, she'd open the gate, go up the stairs, throw herself on the bed perhaps, and rest her worn-out body.

Later she could attend to the day and its obligations. I was doing the same, driving my piece of junk en route to my woman, who wouldn't suspect a thing. I was outside law, order, and morality, stronger than all the rules that keep men tame and subject to society and its insignificant little prizes—nothing more than consolation prizes—that only serve to conceal the slaughter of the spirit. Civility, civilians in thrall to organized fear. For the other half, there was manhood—mine—a savage thing that sinks its teeth in and tears things apart, which imposed itself that Wednesday in the hours before dawn simply by exercising its desires.

I wanted to feel satisfied with my accomplishment. Pleased. Proud even, but there was something that wouldn't let me entirely enjoy my victory. It wasn't guilt, which I was amazed I didn't feel. I even knew without a doubt that my peace of mind wasn't a defense mechanism; I just didn't feel guilty, plain and simple. I was running out of love. Even worse, I sensed Daphne was. So instead of guilt, I felt that volatile impulse, like a longing for relief or a raging body demanding to fly, to be free in this new station of life, celebrating that which Daphne would never value as much as I did. That weighed more inside my chest than all the love that I felt. What had taken place would probably never happen again. It wouldn't happen again because there was no reason for it to. And, finally, if it happened, so what? It would never get past the walls of the motel.

Just the same, I couldn't shake off the uneasiness that kept me from fully enjoying my morning and my return home after a bounty of unexpected flesh. I, the great fucker, the unfaithful, the unbeatable. And yet, there was a thorn under my skin that wouldn't let me see precisely what sort of manhood had manifested itself that Wednesday morning in the motel, and whether it had belonged to M. or to me.

Stacking Up the Goods

He arrived late Thursday evening. Tadeo filled me in beforehand with the details about our mysterious guest: Chino Pereira himself. I had already taken the time to learn through Daniel about Paralelo 37, but the electronic data my mole sent me said a lot more about Víctor Samuel Cámara, alias Sambuca, than about his most renowned protégé. There was something on a case in juvenile court and a confidential document, obtained illegally by the newspaper, in which Social Services stated his name and age at the time—José Pedro Pereira, born in San Juan, fourteen years old—with a psychological profile that revealed more about the social workers than the minor. Nothing but the same sad, generic tale blaming society and the lack of family values for the violent and criminal tendencies shown by the young delinquent. What was impressive were the results of a mental aptitude test included in the report: a high IQ. The rest was straight from the book: teenage mother, unknown father. Raised by the grandmother first and then in various foster homes. And later on, in the street.

I have to admit the information on Chino Pereira—or the lack of it—intrigued me. But after Wednesday, and the fleeting encounter with M.'s body, everything else became secondary. Daphne, my work, the story, the motel. I had completely erased from memory being there the day—sorry, the night—Tadeo met Chino. Not only should I have remembered it, I should have been expecting it. I could feed it into my story, finish it, and then consider my time at the Motel Tulán done. I could even go back to my old life. Although I have to admit that by then I didn't want to leave the motel as much as I had wanted to a few days before. One of its doors was now calling me in a different direction, and not necessarily toward the exit.

Tadeo didn't know how much I knew. And I was not about to tell him that I had requested information on Paralelo 37 and the traffickers he had named as he killed time telling me about his life. I didn't want him to feel like a snitch. Nor was I interested in letting him know I was violating his trust by sticking my nose into the places he revealed to me as a secret. I put on the innocent face of a man ignorant of the underworld and its inner workings, and got ready to listen. My friend had a hard time finding the right words. "Let me see how I can explain this, my man," he started, and he looked up and down, trying to get a hook on the easiest way to explain whatever he was getting us into. He found it at last and started telling his story.

"I was about to move away from the neighborhood. I had gotten this little apartment in the back of a house in a subdivision, right here, near the motel. And that's when I met Chino Pereira."

Tadeo paused, looking at me out of the corner of his eye to gauge how I took the news. My sole reply was to pull up the closest chair, light a cigarette, and sit down to listen. I expected Tadeo's story to be a long one.

"Chino is the right-hand man of Víctor Samuel Cámara, alias Sambuca, the drug trafficker who's been around the longest in Paralelo 37. Must have been about eight months ago when Chino Pereira came up to me. You see, pal, the lady who rented me the place wanted three hundred dollars, water and light included. I had a month's rent, but no deposit. I was telling Charlie at the bodega back in the barrio about it, to see if maybe he could give me some work to make ends meet. Then Chino walked in. To tell you the truth, the man is impressive. I remember he had patent leather shoes on that were so shiny you had to use sunglasses to look at them. Super expensive watch, beeper, cell phone . . . Chino strutted into the bodega, as if he had lived all his life surrounded by abundance. But it was known in Paralelo 37 that it was something new, something he'd come into since serving a nine-month sentence at the state penitentiary and doing important business for Sambuca inside. After that, wherever Sambuca had business Chino was never far behind.

"The man ordered a six-pack of cold beer and looked at me all serious. But, I wasn't concerned. Everyone in Paralelo 37 knows Chino Pereira doesn't smile, not even for his guardian angel. I bid my good-byes and went outside, didn't want to interrupt some business deal. But it turned out to be nothing. Chino is a nice guy, although you might not think so from that funeral home face he's wearing all the time. Seems he heard the tail end of my conversation with Charlie, because when he came out he offered to lend me the three hundred dollars for the deposit. 'I know what it is to live up to your neck in water,' he told me.

"Just imagine, cousin, the situation I found myself in. On the one hand, I needed to get out of Paralelo. Cops were going in more and more and any day I was going to find my hands cuffed behind my back on an Immigration plane to Santo Domingo again. On the other hand, it was Chino Pereira who was offering to help me. If I refused, I could get in trouble. And if I accepted, the same. I knew he would somehow charge me for the favor. You pay for everything around here.

"So I weighed my options and accepted his offer. Thanks to Chino, within a week I was in a new home, making good money and sending some every once in a while to *la vieja*, Ana Rosa, and the nieces. The girls needed school supplies, uniforms, and I needed to try and save to buy construction materials to finish the little house. Ana Rosa had plans to come here and leave the girls for their grandmother to raise while she saved to buy a little land of her own. I had to help her with her trip too, because she isn't going to come over in a fishing boat as long as I'm alive.

"What I was afraid of eventually happened. Before long Chino began making me pay back the loan I owed him. At first I was a deliveryman. Do you remember that, my friend? That's how we saw each other at the newspaper where you used to work. Now he's charging me another way. Two deluxe cabañas and my silence. He pays for three nights even though he only uses the cabañas one. And he spends all this money on liquor, sodas, chicken, and fries. He did it once before, and he swears this will be the last time. Both times he's thrown in something to keep my mouth shut. Five hundred dollars, brother, easy money. The first time I saw that bunch of bills in my hand I almost started talking in tongues, like the time I went to the Pentecostal services.

"Can I count on you or not? All we have to do is keep our mouths shut. I take full responsibility. And I promise you that if you get into it, a little something something will find its way to you."

To tell the truth, the little Tadeo told about Chino Pereira was disappointing. Looking at my partner sitting there with an eager expression on his face made it clear to me he wasn't up to any probing interview that would reveal details of the trafficker's personal history, who his mother and father were, and why, if he was so intelligent, he had gotten involved in the world of drug dealing. O.K., that last question answered itself. What other opportunities and challenges could this island offer a poor kid with brains? Anyway, questions like that were of no use in this case. Chino Pereira was a gangster, a powerful one. The less we knew about him the safer we would be. Working for him for a few nights would fill our pockets. For Tadeo, that was the information that counted and he'd already shared it with me. The only thing left for me to do was to be seduced by the love of money and answer in the affirmative.

I never imagined Tadeo would be so desperate. Maybe it was

something else. Maybe he thought I was stupid enough in the street-smart sense to think there was one iota of truth in his guarantees of safety. Tadeo assured me there was no harm in our little exploits. I knew there was, that if the police ever discovered our connection to Chino Pereira, as employees of the motel our heads would be the first to roll, straight downhill from the motel to prison. We could even get the motel seized from its rightful owners. But that night, those types of considerations weighed less on me than the dewdrops on the hoods of the cars parked outside. They mattered as much as they had when I started to feed off my connections to the underworld inside the paper, driven by the frustration and anger, I now realize, I had developed toward my job. They mattered as much as my two years with Daphne when M. dramatically offered me all of herself in that motel room. Perhaps for the first time in my life, the past, the future, mattered less than the present. I was freed from them. So that night, due to the strange designs or solidity of life itself, I didn't hesitate to accept the dangers Tadeo invited me to share with him. In absolute denial of my previous life, I let him think of me as the Naïf, and what's more, the Daring. I had a duty to him and to the new turn my life was taking. In any case, there was little I could do. I had already spent the hundred dollars from last week, and I didn't see how I could pay him back. To top it all off, Chino's car could be heard rumbling toward the Tulán's office.

Four guys stepped out of the gray Mercedes and carried two blue coolers with white tops up the stairs. They must have weighed more than a convention of stiffs, judging from how the men broke their backs trying to climb up the stairs with them.

The driver took off in the Mercedes, which was quickly replaced by an olive green Cutlass Supreme, out of which stepped four other guys carrying sharp leather briefcases and another cooler. They too walked up to the deluxe cabañas Tadeo had reserved for the occasion, and that car also took off down the hill. Twenty minutes after that, in the original Mercedes, accompanied by a brute who looked like he had just retired from the riot squad, Chino Pereira made his appearance.

Tadeo was nervous. He didn't show it on the outside, except for the extra glint in his eyes and the way he wrung his hands as he stood by the office door checking on the new guests' comings and goings. He wasn't smiling much that night, which was something for Tadeo Chamdeleau.

He had picked out 10 and 11—the fanciest "deluxe cabañas" the Motel Tulán has to offer its lovelorn clientele. They were equipped with brand-new AC, clean carpets, Jacuzzis with cleverly positioned underwater jets, wide-screen TVs, and stereo systems. When Chino arrived, Tadeo insisted we both go with him, all the way up the stairs, in order to make sure he approved of the accommodations—or maybe he just wanted me along to give him courage. "It's a bit much, Tadeo, for what we came here to do," the dealer said with an expressionless face. But Tadeo swore to me later on that for a brief instant he thought he saw the faint, hazy trace of a smile cross Chino's face.

"The adjoining rooms will remain unoccupied until you're done," Tadeo assured Chino and his companions. "So now, if there's nothing else—"

"Three bottles of rum and a gallon of coke. And glasses, lots of glasses, this is going to take a while," Chino said. "We got plenty of ice."

"Listen, bro, aren't there any more ashtrays around? I can only see one," a young kid, frail and freckled, asked. He had a scraggly little mustache over his mouth and was wearing an extra wide shirt which could be wrapped around him twenty times, with fabric to spare.

"Bring some more ashtrays for Bimbi, before I get mad at him for leaving his smelly butts all over the place."

"You gotta quit smoking, *hermanito*. You'll get cancer," said one of the guys, a rotund mulatto who didn't fit inside his own body.

"Life kills, bro. You gotta enjoy it while it lasts."

"Well, then, smoke it all up, bitch."

"C'mere and smoke this, *papá*," Bimbi answered and grabbed his crotch. "You know I got your favorite tobacco right here."

"Enough already, Bimbi and Pezuña," Chino ordered in his full steady voice. It was enough to silence them. "Help Michael put the table under that lamp."

Tadeo and I left the room to go to the pantry for the rum and coke. He placed everything on a tray that was too heavy just for him. I helped him carry some glasses, an empty cooler, and the soda back to the room. The riot squad giant opened the door and it was as if he'd opened a dimension I'd never seen before.

Under the lamp three portable scales were sitting on the long table. Scales like the ones they use at health food stores to weigh food. The air was thick with distinct aromas. It smelled like cigarettes and motel humidity, like the bittersweet fragrance of newly cut grass, which goes in your nose and lodges itself in the back of your mouth. The smell of marijuana floated out of clear plastic bags smeared with petroleum jelly, a smell that spread every time someone opened the plastic. Slices of pineapple and bitter oranges sat on top of the grass "to give it a fruity taste." It was the winning recipe that made Chino Pereira's stuff so popular. There were four guys on two chairs and the bed, all of them busy untangling the buds, weighing the weed, and patiently filling small plastic Baggies. At the end of the assembly line, Bimbi slapped on Chino's identifying seal, a small dot the color of the sea.

"So you see, little man, they criticize me because I smoke," Bimbi was complaining when Tadeo and I brought in the bottles and glasses. "But this taste of glue will stay in my mouth for weeks. If I kiss a pussycat later on, she'll bitch about it. Who likes to have their mouth taste like an envelope?"

"Bimbi, you are a dumb son of a bitch. Those little stamps come ready to use. You don't have to lick 'em."

"Oh, is that so?"

"No wonder you got kicked out of seventh grade, brother."

"Pezuña, you fucker. You told me I had to lick them."

In another corner of the room, two dudes were digging through the coolers filled with ice and beer, looking for "the lid." There was a false bottom under the ice that concealed its true contents. The boys pried it open with pocket knives and pulled out several bags of rice. From among the grains they rescued a number of powdery white rocks. Then, from out of their leather bags came boxes of baking soda, the kind they sell in the supermarkets to bake cakes with. They were going to cut the rocks with it.

Sitting in a stuffed chair embroidered with the motel's logo while he channel-surfed with the remote, Chino oversaw the operation. With his impeccable haircut, his skin the color of dark cinnamon, and his large serene eyes, he watched over the room's proceedings with apparent indifference. He couldn't be older than me, and yet he looked like he'd just returned from a trip around the world. His demeanor spoke loud and clear: "I have seen it all and I have tried it all, and what I haven't tried I've made other people try and tell me about it. There's no trick or con I don't know." When he saw me walk in he frowned for a second, and looked around waiting for someone to tell him what this slovenly guy with glasses and stringy hair was doing getting a look at things he shouldn't see. Tadeo wanted to avoid any confusion, so he tried to clear things up.

"No hassle, Chino. This is the friend I talked to you about. One hundred percent solid."

Chino looked me over closely without moving. It didn't look like he believed a word Tadeo said. I had to follow up my friend's introduction if I wanted to cut the air of suspicion building up in the room. I stretched out my hand to pick up one of the little bags piling up on the table. I saw the blue spot and smiled.

"For a while there I was a regular client," I added in my best waiter's voice.

"A regular what?" I heard someone behind me ask.

"It's just that I used to work at *La Noticia*, the newspaper, and sometimes, when the night dragged on . . ." I kept talking with the bag between my fingers.

"Tadeo, didn't I send you to *La Noticia* once to make a delivery?"

"That's right. That's where I know him from."

"So why don't you work as a journalist anymore?"

"Budget cuts. I never was a journalist. I worked at the copy-desk, as a proofreader."

"The copydesk. I have a friend there."

"Matías Lomerado. My boss."

"Every once in a while I run into him. Who knows, maybe one of these days I'll talk to him, and you'll get your job back."

"Forced to resign. Addiction sucked him in."

"Well, then, he's a jerk," Chino said, nearly drowning out my last few words. "Addiction doesn't suck anybody in. It's the mind that chases after dope. Whoever controls their mind has control over drugs. It's as simple as that, my man."

I knew Chino Pereira was finished with me when he went back to flipping the channels with the remote. I was stunned. It seemed I had passed the test. But as I went over our conversation inside my head again and again, I couldn't figure out how. I began to get nervous and signaled to Tadeo that I wanted to leave. He got the message and we tiptoed out to return to the office. Downstairs I really had to have a smoke, so I lit a cigarette and filled my lungs. Tadeo came over to join me in the corner where I was trying to calm down a little.

"I hope I don't have to go back up there the rest of the night. Those people really put me on edge," he said.

"So why do you get involved with them then, Tadeo?"

"I don't have a choice, bro. What about you, why did you follow me into this mess?"

"Didn't you tell me it was all taken care of, that you had talked to Chino about it?"

"Thing is he didn't expect it would be someone like you."

"And what's so strange about me?" I snapped at Tadeo, giving him an angry look. I had a knot in my throat, which I tried to undo with nicotine. But the knot stuck there like a tumor, making it hard to talk. Right then I would have loved not being myself.

Tadeo gave me a serious look but then he relaxed. A good-hearted smile spread across his face. He took his time taking a cigarette out of the pack, lit it, and contemplated the night while smoke streamed out through his nose.

"Brother," he said at last, his voice as friendly and thick as syrup. "Have you looked at yourself in the mirror lately? Did you get a good look at Chino, at the people up there; have you checked me out closely? Give me a good haircut and put a Rolex on my wrist, or take an unshaved Chino without his brand-name threads, and what do you have? Two creatures of the same breed. One good, the other bad. One lucky, the other not. Who knows which is which? But it's obvious you're different, even from afar. Sometimes even I wonder why you decided to work at this motel."

I was silent, wondering the same thing. At that moment, my theory of entering a different life from the one I knew no longer impressed me. The odd condition of being half present in the doorway to someone else's life only underscored the transparency of those who live by taking notes; an uncomfortable state of affairs, unbearable if there's no way out. But a way out to *where*? And M., where was M.? When would she return to the motel?

When all was said and done, what was I doing at the Tulán,

working among people and in a place so obviously alien to me? Where did I belong? Not at the newspaper, which I always knew wouldn't last long. I never wanted to be the defender of truth, nor an investigative sleuth searching for the clues to the schemes of artists and politicians. I've always been in love with lies, the revealing power they hold when disguised as truth. The newspaper never allowed me to tap that power. Its writing—automatic, clean, without feeling or real inquiry—existed for the sake of information. Information was God, or better, a perverse changeling who could easily be replaced by another. Because there is always another scandal, another catastrophe to denounce so that you give the impression your every written word buttresses the bastion of truth. And yet that truth is something no one believes in or practices but which everyone professes to uphold, if only to maintain the illusion that some truth still exists. The truth of society, public truth, the people's truth. Everyone betrays it on a daily basis, on the street and in offices and newspapers.

No, the newspaper was never my home. But it seems my home was not in the street either. A guy like me on the street, my soft hands unstained by blood but discolored by too much ink and paper, only provokes suspicion. I am neither stupid nor cold, brave nor bold, nor a coward. Taking risks is not my thing. Violence is not my thing. I betray halfheartedly, and don't gain anything by it. I only know how to lie, relying on pieces of the things I see, feel, and ultimately invent. So where does a liar, a writer, belong?

I felt someone walking up behind me, coming close to where Tadeo and I were taking refuge in the night to avoid looking at each other, our faces full of unanswerable questions. It was Bimbi, Chino's chainsmoking little helper, out for fresh air. He greeted us by raising his chin and then joined us for a smoke.

"Damn, I just had to get outta there for a sec. Chino is good people, but he's too serious. He won't let me shoot back when the guys are ragging on me, or fuck with Pezuña. Pezuña's got it in for me, because I'm new to the game. If he weren't so fat, I'd jump on him and beat him until he lost twenty pounds. But what good would it do? You could break your back hitting him right in the chest with a bat and that fucker wouldn't feel a thing. What with all that fat he's as stuffed as a mattress. . . ."

We pretended to listen, but were lost in a silence that finally went down like aspirin, relieving the tension of what was going on inside, soothing my throat and Tadeo's heavy chest. Bimbi didn't even notice. For him, nothing existed but his frustration. Gangly and nervous, he was spitting mouthfuls of smoke out into the night. He couldn't just let go.

"Hey, man," he said, this time looking at me, "what's a girl like you doing in a place like this?"

Another finger pressing on that sore. I took a deep breath, calmed myself down, and answered. "I swear on my blessed mother, I have no clue."

"Don't worry, man. I don't know what I'm doing here either. But that's life, just like a new bitch. You go wherever she tells you to."

Alpha Male

Chino Pereira's crew was still at the motel the next day. They hadn't finished the job. It was a big shipment. Plans were set in motion. Bimbi, high as a kite, had spilled the beans the night before. Chino was opening new branches, expanding Sambuca's territory to Los Lirios, the housing project next door, which until then had been a no-man's-land, a war booty for two gangs fighting over distribution after their leader was sent to jail. The defeated dealer had left behind a successor with huge weaknesses, the principal ones being luxury cars and bags of coke. From prison, Chino had brokered the deal that brought Sambuca more fame and fortune. He would manage the site on behalf of a new consortium of fallen and retired kingpins. This made Chino

Pereira not just the most powerful protégé of Paralelo 37: His power would spill over the entire urban coast all the way to the mangroves by the shores of the project's lagoon.

That was why he took major precautions and hunkered down in our motel. He still had to uphold an agreement with the cops inside Los Lirios, which had been taken over six years ago by city and state police. One day back then, the sky over the project woke up crisscrossed by riot squad helicopters with sharpshooters poking out of the sides. Military trucks blocked all access to the area while dozens of soldiers in combat fatigues and helmets, with M-16s and machine guns, took up positions. They went into the buildings and, searching floor by floor, got rid of the scum, by which they meant the people who received social security and housing from the government, the people who had never learned the good manners of the country's middle class. The underworld, with its jaws open wide to the fragile legality of the projects, took a well-organized slap in the face, and a publicized one at that. It was all over the newspapers and television. Even so, the entire operation netted just one drug lord: Miguel Hurtado, also known as Cano Capota, who was the guy Chino met at Oso Blanco state pen. But Los Lirios, like Paralelo 37 before it, turned out to be a hydra with a thousand heads. Cano Capota's head rolled, but it was replaced by an even more hideous figurehead.

While Los Lirios was being privatized, the city decided to intensify the occupation, placing police at the entrances and building a guard station, to better control access to the project for residents and visitors alike. Video surveillance was installed on all four rooftops: shiny objects that seemed to put life on hold and gave the housing project the feel of an open-air prison.

Thankfully many of the policemen were from the area, meaning they had been raised in the barrios of Paralelo 37 and Los Lirios. Cops and traffickers often grew up together, sharing bottle-cap batting sessions, girlfriends, and godmothers. Later, time placed them on opposite sides of an elastic law that never outweighed common blood and familiar faces. The cop at the guard booth, Pezuña's first cousin and Chino's childhood friend, agreed to talk business with the project's new administrators. With another ten cops backing him up, they came to an agreement on the percentage they were to receive twice a month to look the other way. They made but one condition, that the material couldn't be stored or packaged in Los Lirios. They couldn't guarantee anything if there was an unannounced raid looking for large stashes of dope.

There was no other way. Chino had to find a safe place to process the material needed to supply the new distribution network. He couldn't open his house to a mob of amateurs working for Cano Capota, most of them street kids and high school dropouts. Not one was more than twenty-five years old. To top it off, one faction of Capota's gang had staged a revolt against his successor, who was found one morning riddled with bullets on a country road far from the city. And they were still looking for trouble. Chino had to maintain a low profile until he consolidated power. He couldn't operate from Paralelo unless he wanted to be found out by the renegades, their heads full of coke and their fingers poking into metal and gunpowder.

Bimbi was from Los Lirios and he knew the whole story. He crossed over to Chino Pereira's side because the trafficker was interested in hiring local guys, rather than bringing in new faces. He could move up in the ranks. And furthermore, there was also the small detail of protection. Sambuca's thirst for blood was well known. His arsenal was the stuff of barrio legend. Chino Pereira had all those guns at his disposal, plus a huge network of people who owed him: people to whom Sambuca, as well as Chino, had given money to make bail or business, to cover the expenses of a sudden sickness, to buy Mother's Day presents, to pay for sweet sixteen celebrations or recordings of rap groups. Those people were Chino's borrowed eyes, who watched his back and supplied spaces like the Tulán Motel whenever large-scale raids loomed along the coast.

Tadeo and I would have to stay through the next shift. It wasn't hard convincing the morning guy to switch. Seems he owed Tadeo some favors. On this island, it's the currency with the widest circulation: favors owed, accumulated. Plenty of businesses get off the ground owing to that kind of capital. The motel was no exception.

* * *

I escaped back to the house for a while just as the sun's rays were peeking over the horizon. Lulled to sleep, I had a short dream in which I introduced myself to my double. What I mean is, in my dream, I was watching myself being Julián, sitting in my living room with the TV on, leafing through the day's paper. Try as I might, I couldn't read the words printed on the paper in front of the other me. The dream letters were unrecognizable. I could see the paragraphs, the sentences, and the words but couldn't read them. They were written in a secret code I had no access to. The Julián I watched read the news and wrote something down in his notebook. Then the door to the bathroom opened and M. walked out, wrapped in a towel. Her back was wet and shiny in the light coming in through the window. It was daytime.

M. sat down next to the other Julián and he sat there captivated, looking at her, forgetting what minutes earlier he had taken so much trouble to read. A woman's purse lay on the table, under a pile of newspapers. M. took out lipstick and a powder case. She let the towel slip, showing the top of a nipple. Julián couldn't stop staring at her while she lovingly applied the makeup. It looked like she was getting ready to go out.

Suddenly she grabbed Julián's notebook. She began to write with her lipstick while posing seductively. She wasn't looking at the page, and yet she wrote with astonishing grace while staring at Julián, as if she were holding a telepathic conversation with him. They both laughed. The message had been received. But I, meaning the Julián who watched himself laughing from afar, never knew what the message said. Julián kissed M. slowly and began caressing her naked nipple. In absolute control of her body, M. continued writing with her free hand, without looking at what she was doing. Then she let go of the lipstick and it slowly dropped from her hand in slow motion.

I woke up startled. There wasn't time to decipher the dream because I had to hurry back to the motel. The car started with a kick and I headed out to Route 52 at full speed, with my hair still wet from a quick shower, still swallowing the last mouthful of my breakfast.

Tadeo was waiting for me. I had to watch the office while he went to the bakery to pick up the sandwiches ordered by the deluxe cabaña.

"I'm beat. I had to go to sleep in the utility room. Chino is going to end up owing me big time, after spending the night locked up in there."

I read my notes and waited. In the meantime, a red Mercedes came up the hill to the entrance. It was the same car that had brought Chino's partner to the motel to meet with the union brass. Tadeo had been right. It was the drug dealer's partner, again.

More coolers went from the Mercedes to the first-class cabañas before the driver sped off in the direction of the city. That's when Tadeo arrived back and unloaded the breakfast. We both headed to Chino Pereira's temporary base of operations.

"The munchies have arrived, gentlemen. Time to stuff your faces," Bimbi announced when he saw us walk in. My only response was to smile and begin calling out the orders: two ham and cheese with egg, three mortadella, one grilled cheese, and toast with mayo.

"Toast with mayo?" asked Chino's bodyguard.

"That must be for Bimbi, he's so finicky," answered one of the guys. "Even after getting high he doesn't want to eat. Between that and the cigs he's going to disappear. Look how skinny he is."

"Man, I just don't like butter. Makes me break out."

"And mayo doesn't?"

"Mayo is good for your skin. It lubricates."

"And who gave you that little beauty tip, your personal cosmetics consultant?"

"Nah, your sister, when I was screwing her from behind."

"Oh, really? Mayo, huh? I'll pass the tip down to your mother, when I see her tonight."

"Don't diss my mother."

"Chino, I gotta leave early, I have to stop at the supermarket for a jar of Hellmann's."

"That's enough," answered a voice from the back of the room.

It was Chino Pereira, sitting in his usual chair, rolling a blunt with weed. His hands, with their long, gangly fingers, looked like a concert pianist's. Nails like a vulture's, which followed the curve of the fingers, tore at the aromatic weed and then stuffed it inside a tobacco leaf whose edges were moistened with saliva. Watching Chino concentrate on his task, I began to wonder how the saliva of such a powerful man tasted; a man of impressive composure and calm, whose agility allowed the war of words to surround him, without drawing him in except to set the acceptable limits that gave way to the silence he always wore like armor.

Chino lifted his gaze from the nightstand where he was rolling the cigar and looked at me. I looked into his eyes, a little taken aback by their intensity, and tried to hide the thoughts running around inside my head. What was I doing wondering about Chino Pereira's saliva? What kind of fascination could that man provoke simply by showing himself immersed in the spectacle of living?

"No breakfast for me?" he asked.

"Here's an extra coffee, Chino," answered one of the guys as he held out a steaming cup. "It's already got sugar."

"This will do," he replied, as he brought his lighter to the tip of the blunt. The thick, heavy smell of marijuana filled the corner. The grass smelled good, fresh. It had been a while since I smoked and my mouth watered. Before I knew what was happening, Chino passed me the blunt. "He read my face," I thought, but said:

"Just a little hit. I gotta get back to the office."

"Tadeo, could I borrow your assistant for a while?"

"As long as you return him in one piece," Tadeo said as he went out the door.

Chino got comfortable on the chair and leaned back, letting the smoke tickle his throat as it went down. He calmly emptied his lungs and took the cap off his coffee, drinking it in little sips. I smoked, nervously at first, but the weed soon began to make itself felt. Tingles of electricity cruised up and down my body. I wore a dopey smile and my eyes, my unlucky eyes, came to rest on Chino Pereira's face once again.

I have never been the type of guy threatened by another man's beauty. I guess that makes me liberated. It's hard to admit another man moves, thrills, or turns you on, especially when you live like I do among a pack of machos preoccupied with hiding the mysterious charge that makes you admire someone else's power. The terrible fear of being taken for a woman, meaning, for a vulnerable being, delicate yet open to the other's hardness, provokes all manner of jokes and violence aimed at breaking the man close to you down until you turn him into a piece of clay where you can embed your besieged virility. Looking at Chino sipping coffee with his fleshy lips, his wide face with its strong yet strangely feminine jaw, I couldn't shake the feeling that I was in the presence of a beautiful man. The cinnamon cast of his skin and his pitch black, slightly slanted eyes, his hair and impeccable hands, the width of his shoulders, the narrowness of his waist, and his broad, muscular thighs visible through the fine thread of his cotton pants. He smelled of grass with a slight hint of musk. A thin gold chain nestled in the straight hairs on his chest. I began fearing my thoughts and my eyes. I was a liberated man, and I acknowledged male beauty from a distance and with respect. But this man was too close. Offering me the blunt with his outstretched hand, he had invited me to an unusual kind of proximity.

I decided to act as if I didn't notice. I concentrated on smoking the blunt, and tried to divert my attention, to act distant and in control, closed off from his gaze. I sucked in the smoke from the joint, letting it down easy into my chest and accepting the sensuality of the sensations goading me to close my eyes and just let go. But the very same pleasurable act set off an alarm inside. I opened my eyes. On the other side of the smoke slowly escaping my lungs, something in the way Pereira was looking at me told me danger was close at hand. Maybe it was the light in his eyes, as he watched me enjoy his product, relishing my passive satisfaction. Maybe it was the way I remembered the blunt stretched out between his fingers, offering in a wordless language the possibility of a pact between lips and air, and various other suctions. Even faced with my bewilderment, Chino kept watching me insistently, as if penetrating me with his eyes. And then with his voice.

"You remind me of this guy I was in jail with. They called him Cerebro, the Brain. We were cellmates."

"Do you keep in touch with him?"

"Nobody wants to rehash memories from jail."

Another long silence. Chino passed the joint back and I took a drag, but without the serenity of a few moments before. The conversation had piqued my curiosity. Plus, the window Chino was opening into his past offered me the chance to escape his gaze.

I went ahead cautiously. I couldn't tell if his comment, followed by a silence that swallowed his last words, was only a decoy to pull me even closer. But it was a risk I had to take. That I wanted to take, to be precise, because the man was a stone whose mystery I wanted to decode. And to be honest, I didn't even know why.

"Cerebro . . . he must've been smart."

"A genius, man. Nobody knew more about books than him."

"And why was he in jail?"

"First-degree murder. Two life sentences. He had more than enough time to read."

"And you?"

"No, man. I was just there for a short spell. Anyway, books are not my thing."

"And I remind you of Cerebro."

"He was kinda blond, but unlike you—no offense, man—he was always clean-cut. Even so, you two are a bit alike. You're the type who thinks too much, *verdad*?"

"What?" I answered, caught off guard at how he'd read my character.

"You people have to be protected from yourself. Get crazy over any little thing. The mind is a trap. You have to respect it."

We were both silent for a second, while I brooded over what Chino was saying to me. His advice seemed to come from an old man, or better, an old child who has lived through a lot. Confused, I reconsidered the strange look he'd given me at the beginning of our encounter, the one that seemed like an open door to seduction. I must have misinterpreted it. Surely he had been taking my measure, a necessary step before he could make up his mind about me. Those eyes had seen how much I went over things, how often my mind became a labyrinth. How I got lost trying to find the right road, and then went around in circles in my head, laying innumerable traps for myself. He had realized all of it in a few seconds.

Or maybe not. Maybe the understanding I perceived, and the fact that it seemed so obvious, was a product of getting high and the odd complicity that develops between two men who open their hearts to each other in a bar, or in a gang of smokers at the park, sharing their most intimate secrets and finding the perfect excuse to show each other the wounds that are killing them. But they would always be safeguarded by the specter of "controlled substances," meaning the numbing effect they could blame for revealing their vulnerabilities. Yes, of course, marijuana was responsible for the strange electricity and bizarre connection. But the moment was still turning to my advantage. Pereira was opening up, and he could count on me to listen and to remember. All of a sudden I had stumbled on the gift of getting inside his mental machinery. And I wanted to get inside.

"Cerebro helped me get used to life in prison. 'Chino, the dead won't let me sleep,' he used to complain. 'I keep them company with books so they'll leave me alone. And if nothing else, I tell them about other dead ones I haven't killed.'" Chino stared at me and smiled. My face was almost as hot as a piece of coal.

Out of habit I looked at the clock. Almost an hour had gone by, time that the marijuana stretched even further. I couldn't explain why Chino's stare had burned my face and made me blush, but I was uncomfortable. What's more, my mouth was dry, and I couldn't abandon Tadeo in the office alone for such a long stretch. We could arouse suspicion, and we needed to keep our necks in the clear.

"You have to go?" Chino asked, picking up on the detail.

"It's been an hour."

"Time flies. . . ."

"Pleasure talking to you. For real."

"Likewise," Chino answered, stretching me his hand, a large hand with delicate fingers.

I was almost out of the room when I heard Chino call my name again and then, very quickly, he was standing next to me at the door. He grabbed my shoulder and started talking to me in a low voice, his face close to mine.

"What are your days off?"

"Sunday and Monday."

"Have you ever gone to a *Batá* ceremony?"

"I've heard a lot of talk, but I've never been. I'm sure it must be a real trip."

"So I'll take you. We can talk about it later," Chino said. I went out to the stairs, leaving behind Bimbi's jokes, the sweet smell of marijuana, and all the empty coffee cups. Chino's fading smile was the last thing I saw as the door slammed shut. The sun baked the motel parking lot without mercy. Tadeo was looking up, watching a plane cross the sky. I walked over to him.

"Shit, big boy, I was starting to worry. I was afraid Chino had taken you hostage."

"We lit up and time just flew. Sorry."

"Don't worry about it, but I'm glad you're back. I got serious news."

"So spit it out."

"It's nothing, but while you were there chatting up the dealer, a messenger came by. Chino wants to talk to me later. He's got a juicy offer for me to take a shipment to Miami."

"But why you? Doesn't he have more than enough people who know how to slip the goods through?"

"This way they lose the scent. You know, since I'm not part of that world. And get ready for this, brother, I make thirty thousand dollars, plus expenses, on the job. You hear that, big guy? Thirty grand, plus expenses for my time in Miami."

"It's hardly a vacation."

"That's why I didn't want to take it on before I went over it with you."

"Don't even look at me. I'm not going to Miami as a mule."

"No, brother, I just want you to help me think it through. Thirty thousand dollars is a lot of money. With that much, I could build a huge mansion in Baní, get naturalized, and bring my mother over here to live. Give her some comfort in life before she dies on me."

"Do you even understand the risks you're taking?"

"I do, bro, but shit. Nothing ventured, nothing gained. It can't be worse than crossing the Mona Canal in a fishing boat in the middle of the night. There are no sharks in the sky."

"But there are police dogs in the airports."

"I know that. But I've got brains."

"You're going to need them, Tadeo, you're really going to need them."

Games in Bed

"So, how many lovers have you had before me?"

M. laughs.

"Come on, tell me, you don't have to be honest."

"No?"

"Sometimes a lie sounds more seductive than the truth. Tell me, how many lovers . . ."

"None. You're the first."

"I knew it!"

"How did you guess?"

"I'm very perceptive. That's why I'm an artist."

"Really?"

"Yeah, we artists are extremely sensitive guys. We ache all over."

"Like women."

"Do you ache all over?"

"Sometimes."

"That's why you're here."

M. doesn't say a word.

"You don't have to be honest about why you're here."

"I couldn't even if I wanted to."

"Is it that terrible?"

"Even I don't understand what's happening to me."

"Maybe I can help."

"Help me? So you want to rescue me too."

"Why not?"

"Because the last thing I need is to be rescued. What's happening to me is because I looked so hard for someone to rescue me."

"Tell me what's going on."

"I categorically refuse, my dear. I'm not going to ruin a night like this by sharing my sorrows."

"So then?"

"So then what?"

"What do we do?"

"I don't know. Let's enjoy each other and rest."

"From your life?"

M.'s smile was full of sadness.

"You could say that."

"M."

"Hmm."

"Tell me about your husband."

"What?" M. raises up on one elbow.

"Am I taller than him, stronger, more attentive? You don't have to be honest."

"Are you going to keep spinning that broken record?"

"Tell me, do I spend more time with you in bed? Do I understand you better?"

M. leans over and reaches for the pack of cigarettes on the night table. She takes one out and lights it.

"No. You don't understand me at all. Neither does he. That's how the two of you are alike."

"Let me tell you, you are very much mistaken. He doesn't want to understand you and I do. That's how we're different."

"Alright, you're different. In other ways too."

"What other ways?"

"He's not here with me."

"Why don't you leave him? Why don't you tell him to get lost if he hurts you so much?"

"Why don't you leave your woman?"

"Me? Who told you . . ."

"It's obvious. If you didn't have a woman we'd be in your apartment. You wouldn't run the risk of losing your job for one fuck. And if you were happy with her, you wouldn't be here with me. So you're not that different from my husband. And who knows if your woman is not so different from me."

"I wouldn't mind . . ."

"What?"

"If Daphne found a lover, somebody with whom she could explore the things she can't with me."

"And who told you going to bed with a stranger is a game of

exploration? Perhaps it is for men, or for girls who've just lost their virginity, but not for women. Of course you'd like it if your woman found a lover. That way you keep your indiscretions to yourself and feel less guilty at the same time. It would also be easier to forget the question I just asked you."

"Which one?"

"Why don't you leave your woman?"

"We'd better change the subject."

"We'd better."

"If you want me to, I'll leave."

"I don't want you to leave."

"You want to sleep?"

"I'm not sleepy."

"You don't want to sleep and you don't want to talk."

"I want to talk, just not about myself."

"You see? You see how wrong psychologists are when they say men have intimacy problems? Here I am, trying to convince a woman she can place her trust in me."

"And wasting your time miserably, when you could be doing other things with such a delicious mouth."

"Then there's nothing I can do."

"No."

"..."

"..."

"Nothing to assure you that I can keep a secret, that whatever you tell me will remain under lock and key."

"Nothing..."

"M., you can tell I don't lift weights, that there's no cell phone attached to my belt. And believe me, I don't go around showing off my car or my conquests. If it weren't for this part-time job at the motel, Daphne would be all but supporting me. I clean, cook, and iron for her and the rest of my free time I try to write. You can tell that I'm not your run-of-the-mill macho, that I'm different. Come on, M., why don't you trust me?"

"Because it's not what I'm looking for. I don't want to be in a motel at dawn on a Wednesday, tangled up in the legs of some-one who wants to *understand* me. What I want is a man who'll tear me apart and jump all over every inch of me until I'm empty, dead, until there's nothing left of me."

Silence.

"Listen."

"Yeah."

"Why don't you rough me up?"

M. gives me a seductive look.

"Me?"

"Yeah, you."

"It's not the role for me."

"Of course it is."

"I'm not that type of guy."

"You're a guy. Come on, tie me up like this, with the sheets."

"Is that what you think men are really like? You think we're all animals?"

"Let's not talk about it."

She kisses my cock.

"But M.—"

"Come here, try. You don't have to be honest."

"I don't?"

"I think I like it more when you lie."

It was Wednesday morning. I got up from beside M.'s body as if spending the night with her had turned me into a creature that lived on the bottom of a swamp. Dazed and confused, my mind went over our bedside conversation fragment by fragment. I couldn't even tell how much of that conversation had been real and how much a dream. Even so, there was no doubt the sensitive man routine wouldn't work with this woman. The problem was that the other role, that of the soulless, distant fornicator, didn't really suit me, no matter how much I wanted it to. Not with her. Maybe that was why every encounter contributed to further complicating a never-ending labyrinth of partial perceptions. That Wednesday morning I couldn't help asking myself why I was finding it so difficult to feel satisfied with what I already had of M., her raging body hiding out from the night and what it could offer. Why did I want to find out more about her? Why couldn't I stop asking myself what M. was doing in that motel, what she was doing with me? Why had she chosen me to keep her company?

Maybe what attracted me so much was that M. was a wanderer like me. That is to say, she hadn't found a safe haven where she could take shelter from the shadows that suck in the daylight. As far as I was concerned, it was time to admit it. I didn't have a home, I had lost it a long time ago. I had tried to find one in the paper, in the relationship with Daphne, and in the distant promise of writing, but without success. Now I found myself stealing a roof from this motel to take refuge from the storm outside, hoping to gain some respite. Perhaps that's why M. had become a small celebration for me, why I waited for her body every Wednesday, so I could use it as a compass, or at least, a short retreat of peace and quiet. No such chance. The last thing M.'s body gave me was peace. After satisfying our hunger, that strange, almost mandatory hunger which didn't originate in either her or me, life stayed where it was, dancing on the surface of our skin like something cold, something we could not absorb. Sleeping with M. was like waking up after a long binge. My head splintered, my knees were weak, and my eyes screwed up in the sunlight. I lost my sense of direction, the one thing I really needed at that point.

Two Arrows

If I were a winner? I would die of boredom. "Success" is not my forte. I nourish myself on what is left of me, and there isn't much. But there remains a certain secret silence.
— Clarice Lispector, *A Breath of Life*

When I was little, my father told me fairy tales about a certain princess who lived in a castle teeming with fountains, with peacocks and fawns prancing around in the gardens inside its walls. All the animals in the castle and the ones in the forest loved the princess because she cared for them, giving them food, petting them, and talking to them sweetly. After tending to the animals' needs, it was her habit to sit in front of her bureau every day, brushing her long, honey-colored hair.

One afternoon, a prince on a hunt rode into the grounds of the castle while following the trail of God knows what animal. It was most likely a deer, or some other creature known to abound in the land of fairy tales, but that one seldom finds on the roads of life. The important thing is that the hunter aimed badly and the arrow landed inside the princess's bedroom. The princess, stirred from her boredom, stood up and peered out the window, perhaps catching a glimpse of the princely cape as the hunter disappeared into the woods. Her heart was inexplicably shaken. Without understanding why, she held on to that arrow as if it were a talisman.

It was a magic arrow, my father said, a gift from the prince's tutor, who always spoke to him wisely about destiny's direction. He had to recover the arrow at all cost, for at the end of his search he would find his future, like a coveted prize. My father's eyes grew misty whenever he reached this part of the tale. It was the sad part. At only eight or nine years of age, I knew it intuitively, not by the words he was saying but by the feeling hidden behind his voice. Maybe that's why I kept asking him to tell me the fairy tale of the princess. I liked seeing him saddened, a little lost and clinging to me, as if I were his arrow.

Although the prince, my father went on, wanted to ignore his tutor's words, he couldn't forget the arrow. He dreamed of it at night and forgot the dream each morning, but he woke up with the strange feeling he had lost something small and significant, like when you see someone you know and are about to say hello and suddenly you forget their name. Yet each night, the prince's head was filled once again with the dream of the arrow.

One night while he was sleeping, the prince dreamed he saw the princess. He woke up that day overwhelmed by the desire to go hunting. Once again the deer reappeared and once again the prince aimed, missed, and the arrow entered through a window he was sure he recognized. But this time, instead of going after the fleeing deer, he went to the castle doors in search of the arrow. The princess came down the stairs of the castle to personally hand him two, the one he just missed and the very one he had lost so long before. Miraculously, a fawn appeared at his feet. Right then and there the prince remembered all his dreams. He married the princess and they lived happily ever after.

This was the tale my father told me while my mother worked. She was the real head of the family. Order was everything to her. At night she would tell me, "It's late, you have to get up early tomorrow," and she'd take me by the hand and lead me to my room. She changed my clothes, put me in bed, tucked me in, and she was done. If I asked her, "Mami, tell me a story," she would reply, "Ask your father." Then he would come in to give me the fantasy I needed to sleep through the night. Still there were times I managed to convince my mother to put aside her papers and her work to spend a little time with me. She didn't tell me stories. But she spoke to me.

It wasn't that she didn't take care of us. She oversaw the way I dressed, how I ate, what I studied. She explained to me a thousand times, "That's not how little girls sit," "That dress is too short to wear to church," or "It's unbecoming of a woman to smoke. Look at Abuela Maru, your grandmother, her teeth are yellow and her mouth reeks of tobacco. The only one who puts up with her is your grandfather Ramiro." At night, when we talked, she asked me what I wanted to be when I grew up: an astronaut, an engineer, or an attorney like her. But whatever it was, the one thing you couldn't do was lose your femininity while beating men at their own game. That was essential, because then you wouldn't find a husband and you wouldn't have kids. "If you're too strong, they will punish you for it," she would say with a sigh. And she went on talking to me about things that in those days made me very happy, because I thought they were very adult.

But in between sighs, conversations, and orders, I began to suspect *the existence of another story, a story my mother didn't tell me. Not a fairy tale: a story made out of pieces of silence.*

Once upon a time there was (or so my mother thought, underneath the words she spoke to me) a very wealthy and beautiful young woman, almost a princess, who lived in a Spanish-style house. Her father was a surgeon, and her mother was a woman who smoked and played canasta. The Almost Princess had a nanny called Mami Alicia and it was she who cared for her, who taught her to prepare soul food and talk to the dead. The young woman wanted to leave the house, and every day after school she sat before the bureau in her room to daydream about seeing the world. She wanted to swim in misty oceans, wander about in gigantic cities with thousands of neon lights, hear sirens cut through the night and spill wine on her party dress, ski down snowy slopes and visit great universities. Her father gave her everything she wanted, as long as her wishes fit in through the main gate of the house. "You must stay inside. This island is full of thugs," he said. "It's dangerous outside for a girl like you. I promise you that next summer I will send you to Europe or the United States with your mother." She looked to her mother for support. Her mother smoked and smiled, unable to look at her, or her father.

The Almost Princess waited and waited. One day she persuaded her father to let her study far away. While the driver took her to the airport, she saw beaches where she had never swum, trees whose names were unknown to her, people that got close to her daddy's sky blue Packard to offer her bananas or newspapers or to wipe the windshield with a dirty rag. "Thugs," she said with the arrogance of someone on the go. And she looked away, imagining instead what would be waiting for her on the other side of the ocean.

When she landed where she was being sent to study, she saw shores where she had never swum, trees whose names she recognized from books, and people hoping to sell her newspapers or fresh fruits or who just used a dirty rag to wipe the windshield of the Lincoln Continental, which belonged to a friend of the family who picked her up at the airport. In a state of shock, she hid in the girls' dormitory, only coming out to study and to have tea with girls of her class, all of them almost princesses yearning to leave the glass prison where they were locked up, where the walls were so translucent and eternal that they extended over islands and continents, over land and sea. But the Almost Princess found a way out. One spring evening she kissed a boy from class, and then another and another. They made her believe she could go outside the walls that trapped her and that, if she held on to their strong arms, the thugs outside couldn't defile her. But, for some strange reason, the boys' mouths always tasted like the cigarette breath from her mother's dark tobacco. She kissed and kissed, until she found one with fresh breath, with sweet and considerate lips, one who seemed unlikely to turn her into the dry smoke coming from her mother's mouth. He was the one she married and returned with to the island.

I never knew how my mother's story ended. When I became a teenager, I lost interest in the words she concealed behind her orders and her silences. Her advice seemed even more boring. I didn't obey any of it, and what's more, I broke her rules just to go against her, like my daughters do nowadays, as daughters always do. I don't know what happened, but right in front of me my mother disappeared for many years. She was there but I could not see her. And then all of a sudden, she materialized before my eyes, when I found out about Efraín and his secretary and I wanted to set fire to my home, to my whole life. To keep myself from doing that I ended up at Abuela Maru's apartment with the two girls in tow. And then my mother arrived. After getting filled in on what was happening, and listening to my grandmother's coughing and her shitty advice, my mother spoke to me like she always did, surrounded by silences:

"Don't get divorced, if you can avoid it."

"Why?" I asked defiantly.

She shrugged. For the first time in my life I saw her take a cigarette from my grandmother's pack and light up. Sucking in the smoke, she looked at me calmly and said:

"I was not unfaithful to your father, not with other men. With work, yes. . . . But together we gave you a nice home and a future with more opportunities, more freedom than the ones we had. And only as a married woman and a mother was I at last able to go out into the world. Can you believe it, eh? The missus goes to work. But she is still the 'missus.' I don't know if things have changed much and it's already another world, but in my world, a woman on her own is worth nothing. Feminists have to stop talking nonsense. There may be this or that law to protect us, this or that door may be opened, but in the real world, a woman is still worth what a woman has always been worth."

My mother and grandmother sat right in front of me smoking. They were so different, and yet they were so much the same. Abuela Maru, always so ladylike, allowed the pretense to percolate under all the colors, gloss, and hairspray. She barely managed to fulfill her duties as a wife and mother. Obviously it was just a role to her, and she did only what was strictly necessary to fill the quota of respectability people expected, and then didn't maintain the farce a second longer. Afterward, like someone who has just finished a daunting task, she sat down to smoke her black cigarettes, play canasta with friends, and find some sort of release from her life. My mother for her part was proper, iron-willed, accomplished, and determined. Quiet and organized, she went to work, tended her family, and made sure her daughter saw more than just the department store's makeup counter, that she went out to ride her bike, had boyfriends, took an interest in her education. But the daughter turned out to be frivolous. She was crazy about men, and worked hard to look beautiful. The only thing she wanted was to avoid being like her mother.

We were three women who walked different paths in life and yet all three of us were washed up on the same shore. Destiny is such a mother-fucker. God must be a real son of a bitch.

Puddle

That last encounter I described with M. took place a week and a half after Chino Pereira and his gang left the motel. They went as they came, leaving no trace save the wad of bills they pressed into Tadeo's hands and mine. I invited Tadeo to celebrate our windfall with me, and we decided to go shopping. I didn't want to stop by my house or run into Daphne, so I waited, idling in my car while Tadeo showered.

"I'll go with you, bro, if you take me to a place where I can send some money to Baní. I'd give anything to see the surprised look on *la vieja*'s face when she gets this bunch of bills." Tadeo blew the cigarette smoke out the car's window. I relaxed behind the wheel. The highway smelled of freshly cut lawns and sea salt.

We took Las Américas Expressway. The tarmac sweat out the day's fumes as if it were exhaling its last sighs. One of those blessed, surprise cloudbursts had fallen. It brought the heat down, but then all kinds of vapors rose out of the earth, turning an already hot and stifling day into a stew. The best thing to do was to escape into the air-conditioning of the mall, an artificial environment where even the light is plastic, and everything is impeccably arranged beneath an acclimatized breeze that offers a break from perspiration. Plaza Las Américas was the place.

And there it was, huffing and puffing like an enormous elephant in the middle of the expressway. The capacity parking lot could be seen from the exit ramp onto Roosevelt Avenue, packed hood against hood, the sunset bouncing off car after car. A mob of people were going in and out with bags or with their hands empty, trying to amuse themselves with the city's favorite pastime: shopping. Which is how the masses cast away—for at least a few hours—the empty, bewildering feeling they live with the rest of their lives.

After ten minutes of going round and round, we found a place to park in the multilevel and went up to the *terraza* to get something to eat. "Plastic food," Tadeo called it. Under the Mall's roof and sheltered by palm trees (also plastic), we sat down to go to work on the steaming piles on our trays, foods that fulfilled nothing of the promise of their exotic names (Szechuan chicken, calzone, gyros, *pollo a la barbacoa*). Funny how the *terraza* could take any cuisine, be it Greek, Mexican, Puerto Rican, or Chinese, and make it all taste the same.

We went to the office supply store. With the money in my pockets I stocked up on paper and bought a computer software program, two ink cartridges, notebooks, and a fancy fountain pen. I even had money left over to toy with the idea of buying a copy machine for the house. But no, it was too expensive. Maybe if Chino Pereira needed me for another gig. I composed a list of everything I'd want to set up my own personal home office—the latest WordPerfect, bookshelves, a laptop perhaps—all of it sponsored by Chino Pereira.

Just the idea of being able to count on that money alarmed me. The bills I had earned made my palms sweat, as if it could give me away as an accomplice to crime. Moral scruples weren't bothering me just then. It was the fear of being caught. I only wanted my hands to be stained with ink, to be fit for ink, or at least to bear the promise that they would at some point find a way to stain themselves in the dark stream that was calling them. I didn't want to go through the motions of writing lost in an ivory tower, but I also didn't want to be this close to the absolute rawness of action and its shadows. What I'm saying is, I wanted to live in order to write my stories, knowing them in the flesh, but not at the price of living an unmanageable life. For me it was crystal clear. Blood and ink (might) run parallel, but they don't mix.

That wad of bills reminded me of the price paid by those who only dealt with life, which is to say, with survival and the absolute power money confers. It had to go as soon as possible. Spend it, spend it, burn it up. Feeling nervous, I decided to buy a fax machine. I would use the rest to pay off my debts, buy a few

Graham Greene novels I'd had my eye on for quite a while, and keep a couple of dollars in my pocket. Walking back to the parking lot carrying my electronic equipment I felt a little foolish. A fax? Why would I want a fax? "Idiot," I said to myself. Tadeo gave me a strange look, as if he wanted to be sure the insult wasn't directed at him.

"Don't worry, Tadeo, I didn't mean you. It's just that I realized I should've saved myself a little for later."

"What did you expect? To open a retirement fund with what you make off Chino Pereira? Don't sweat it, bro, there's plenty more where that came from."

"That's what worries me. Better to crawl out of the river as soon as the water rises. I don't want to be carried off to the deep end and be unable to get out."

Tadeo just looked straight at me and nodded his head in agreement.

"Don't think I don't catch your drift."

"What's that, Tadeo?"

"I know what you're talking about. My little trip to Miami."

"You got that right," I lied. "You've got to think about that very carefully."

"Sure, brother, but I can't think about it too much."

"Tadeo, it's a big risk."

"The payoff's bigger. What's more, you know that a horde of people have worked as mules without ever getting caught. Schoolboys, old ladies in wheelchairs, stewardesses, businessmen, nondescript tourists. They catch fewer every time."

"But they could catch you. And you have a lot to lose."

"What, Julián, what do I have to lose that is so valuable? My mansion in the Virgin Islands, my golf course?"

"Your freedom."

"You call this freedom?"

We walked together for a while in silence, out to the car, and then we opened its doors and threw the mess of odds and ends we had bought inside. We felt like new and different people. It was as if those little pieces of paper could erase the agony of our past needs, the pity and disillusion of all of our women, the mothers and girlfriends whom we had failed by not being generous providers, the backs upon which to construct a home, and a shelter against instability and uncertainty. But the joy disappeared as quickly as the money we'd blown. It seemed like a lot at first, but it ended up dissolving into a couple of books, two reams of paper, and some wires tied to a plastic case with shiny buttons. Money always blows away, like a drug. And then the body begs for more. More dollars, more things still to buy, more gifts, more proof that you can indeed be a lucky winner, a well-adjusted participant in a growing society.

After shopping, I went with Tadeo to send money to his mother, who was waiting for him in the distant town of Baní with her half-built house and a lonely heart. Tadeo was so proud he could have sent himself by wire transfer. "Just want to make sure that what Ana Rosa tells me is true, that my mother is alright, that she's already recovered from her stroke last Christmas. Then I'll stick around here and I won't go back until I finish raising the dough."

* * *

That conversation I tried to have with M. took place over a week after that. At almost seven in the morning, I departed with a kiss on the cheek, went down the stairs, and walked out to my car. The morning sun struck the asphalt as it does only in the Caribbean. Light that burns the eyes. Light that forces you to squint through your eyelashes. Light that in any other place would signal a nuclear holocaust, an environmental anomaly. I glanced at my watch, blocking the sun with one hand, and then used that same net of fingers to fish for the keys in my pocket. It was barely seven in the morning and nothing could hide from the sun, not my body after an all-nighter, nor those cement walls stained by the humidity. In the morning, the Motel Tulán looked more like a mausoleum, like a place that instead of brimming with pleasure only sheltered lost souls. I had never left so late from an encounter with M. in cabaña 23. How many had there been? Three. I had been wrapped up in that bed a total of three Wednesdays. But they weighed on my heart as if they were a thousand.

Tadeo had already finished his shift. He was nowhere to be seen. A good-natured older man with rosy cheeks approached my car and signaled that I shouldn't get in. I became alarmed. What did this old dude want with me?

"You're the new kid working for us?" A question that cried out for a quick affirmative.

"Yes, sir." I was face-to-face with *Señor* Tulán.

And so that morning, Don Esteban Tulán, the legendary founder of the motel, stood in front of me. He pulled an impeccable handkerchief, white as a dove, from inside his pocket and calmly daubed it on his neck, drying the exertion from his walk across the small stretch to where I was. He jiggled his shirt, a white *guayabera*, in that way country men do when they want to get rid of the sweat soaking their sleeves to avoid soiling their fancy clothes. My grandfather did the same thing. Not my father. He didn't wear *guayaberas*. Every once in a while, I revive them.

"Hope it rains by noon, so it cools off," he said in passing.

I smiled back at him, catching the scent of Old Spice that escaped from his handkerchief and permeated the air in the parking lot. The sun beat down upon him without mercy too. His eyes were slits as he watched me; the light was making it difficult for him to detect whether I showed any signs of being a trustworthy, reliable employee. But I was already well trained by Tadeo. I put on the motel ghost face, a warm yet closed visage that can't be read. I crossed my fingers and hoped the trick also worked in broad daylight.

"You have a minute?" Don Esteban asked without waiting for an answer. "Come with me to the office before this sun melts both our brains away."

I followed him without a word, a little nervous. I couldn't foresee the consequences of our meeting.

* * *

"Tadeo tells me that sometimes you stay after your shift to finish some work. A writing project, something about history. He didn't really say what it was," old Tulán went on, making a disapproving face as he walked toward the office. Good old Tadeo. For sure he played dumb, taking advantage of the boss's detachment to squeeze in a lie that would conceal my adventures with the guest in cabaña 23.

I gave in to my nerves and my paranoia. And the owner of the Tulán looked at me as if he expected an explanation.

"The room is paid for."

"Yes, Tadeo mentioned that."

"I hope it's not an inconvenience."

"It doesn't bother me just so long as your project doesn't interfere with your job."

"No, sir, not at all. That's precisely why I rent the room, to take advantage of my alertness to write before I become too tired. If I wait until I get home, I'm useless."

"I know, son, when you have to stay up all night it's better to keep going. One ends up living upside down, sleeping during the day and working at night, but what can you do? That's why I decided to leave the business to my son. I still make my rounds every once in a while, just to keep an eye on things. 'Supervising,' they call it now. I just like to know the employees, and be sure that they are decent, hard-working people who want to get ahead. Forgive me for asking, but what is it you are studying?"

"Studying?"

"The project you're doing, it isn't for class?"

"No, it's independent research."

Señor Tulán propped himself up behind one of the office chairs. He looked me up and down disapprovingly. I am sure he'd never in his life heard of anyone researching anything that didn't have a concrete, practical goal. Better not even to mention that the alleged investigation Tadeo invented for me would help me write a novel. It would only add to his misgivings. Because in the end, to Don Tulán, or for that matter to any motel owner on the face of the earth, what kind of person was a writer? Decent, hard-working people interested in improving their lot? Definitely not. Eccentrics, half crazy bums, that's what people think writers are, unless they are dead or embalmed in life, which is the same thing. I felt like I was in the presence of the school principal and I had to justify some mischief. The mischief of M., the mischief of my writing project. The truth had to be disguised.

"You see, Don Esteban, before I started working here I was a journalist. When I left the paper I was working on a piece about the history of the island's inner-city neighborhoods. I think it's a good project. Maybe if I finish it and turn it into a series of articles, I could improve my portfolio and my chances of finding a job in journalism again."

"And what neighborhoods are you researching?"

"I'm working on one they call Paralelo 37."

"The Thirty-seventh Paralelo? As in Korea?"

"That's the one."

"I fought in the Korean War. It was hell, young man. You have no idea how easy you have it, or what I had to go through to build myself up. You've interviewed the people in the barrio?"

"Interviews are the basis of my investigation."

"That sounds right. This country should remember its past. Everyone here lives as if the world were invented early this morning. And older folks, well, we're worthless. Nobody wants to listen to, or preserve, all the knowledge stored in our brains. I'm not

125

a man of much schooling, but I know a few things. We'll sit down to chat one of these days when I have the time. I may not be able to tell you much about Paralelo 37, but I can tell you about the Korean War."

"That's very kind of you, Don Esteban."

I took a deep sigh of relief. The old man just wanted some attention and was apparently beginning to trust me. He wouldn't fire me this time. I kept on answering his questions and pretending to listen to his conversation, using the time to unwind from the unexpected interrogation. I looked at the clock with an expression meant to make Don Tulán believe I had things to do, but that out of courtesy and respect I didn't want to interrupt him.

"Well, son, I won't take any more of your time," he finally said in reaction to the expression on my face. We parted with a firm handshake and a smile. But when I was halfway out the door, Don Tulán hit me with another question: "What about your papers?"

"Excuse me?"

"Your research papers."

It took me a second to make up something.

"I must've left them in the room. I'll go get them, if that will be all for today."

"Don't bother. I'll tell the maid to save everything she finds there and leave them in the office for when you get back tonight. They'll be safe here."

"Thanks," I said a little concerned by the turn of events. What if the maid told old Don Tulán she hadn't found anything? My web of lies would vanish in thin air. Maybe I had better go up to the room to retrieve the alleged papers. But I couldn't insist, since he would see M.'s car parked inside the garage when I opened the door. I had to hope that the old man would forget to relay the message to the maid, that some delay would prevent them from running into each other, or that nobody would care about the existence of some scribbled papers related to alleged research on Paralelo 37.

I said good-bye to Don Tulán and went home to sleep. Daphne had already left for work. I would see her in the afternoon, when she returned. It was better that way. That day I had a million dreams; I don't remember what they were but I woke up more tired than when I had gone to bed. I took Daphne out to dinner. We talked about anything and nothing. Two days went by, uneventfully. It looked like the old man and the maid had not crossed paths. Punching in to work the next day, I chanced upon the maid from the day shift, who was covering the afternoons as a favor for a coworker.

"Did you see the papers?"

"What papers?" I was a little distracted and had already forgotten about them.

"The ones you left in twenty-three. Someone had thrown them in the trash. I rescued them for you. They're under the counter, up against the cash box."

"O.K. Thanks very much." I returned to the office to look for what were supposedly my notes. While I poked around under the counter, I laughed at how events had somehow changed my tall tale into the truth. As if my mouth were capable of uttering the Holy Word, the one that said, "Let there be light," and there was light. Against the dark metal box hiding the night's cash was a disheveled notebook with a bunch of papers wedged between the covers. The handwriting wasn't mine. "Love is the first thing that rots," I read and then I didn't want to go on. My heart missed a beat: I knew the papers were M.'s.

Maybe she had left them there to test me. Maybe it was just another way of luring me in to play with a mysterious woman. Maybe this notebook was the reason she came every week to the motel. Another aspiring writer? I looked over the papers carefully. They didn't look like the thoughtful pages of someone trying to write a book. They seemed more like verbal remains, like an exorcism aimed at expelling a ghost from within. What would these papers say, what window could they possibly open to at last get to know something about this woman?

I didn't give in. I put the notebook away in my car and resumed my routine at the motel. I wanted to see her in person as I read, wanted her to watch me running my fingers over the edges of the pages where she had scrawled her confessions. I wanted her to watch me reading them and for my reading of her notebook to become a kind of surrender on her part, giving me power and some sort of control. I was going to wait until the following Wednesday to confront her. All the while I resisted reading the notebook, I didn't feel like answering the entrance buzzer, didn't feel like smiling for anyone, or handing room keys to anyone, or gazing at the moon and talking to Tadeo until the next slow-moving guest arrived at the Motel Tulán. My whole being wanted something else: to hide in the storeroom and stay back there until I finished reading every last word in that notebook. But I resisted.

One day went by, then another. The notebook sat where I had tossed it on the backseat of my car. I waited patiently, without reading it. Then it was Wednesday again. But this time, M. didn't come back to the motel.

Abuela Maru's Mulatto

There they were, my mother and my grandmother, Abuela Maru, trying to convince me not to get a divorce, but neither they nor their advice was enough to change my mind. Me, divorced. Now I say I don't care; I almost believe it myself. But not at that time. Before, no matter how much I tried, I couldn't come to terms with my misfortune. "I don't care" became my pet phrase, a verbal crutch that failed to provide any consolation. It was a bad habit, like when people add "Right?" after each sentence to make sure the other person is listening, or so they can at least imagine someone is paying attention to every word coming out of their mouth. Only I started saying "I don't care" at the end of every phrase when I was talking to myself.

Later I got overwhelmed with so many empty crutches. I had all kinds of them. I was saying them to get away from Efraín. For ten months I was saying them. Ten months of torture. That's as long as I lasted the first time I was separated from him. Now it's more serious. Now I truly do not care. But then this happens, and look at me now, going up another blind alley.

During the entire ten months, I would wake up and go to bed with a thousand words entangled in my mind, as if they had all decided to turn against me. I couldn't stop thinking. The damn words went to my throat, and ended up seeping into my conversation after dinner during coffee, at the gym, or when I was stuck in traffic in my new air-conditioned car. I finally had to start repeating them to myself so that they would dissolve into thin air. I couldn't shut up. I'd spend all day muttering a speech to myself, an endless fight with Efraín. I waited for the stream of words to finally stop, because it wouldn't let me sleep or cry or be anything else but an endless litany.

The girls began to worry. Sometimes they looked at me frightened, trying to understand my mumbling, my mouth's perpetual motion, and then they would ask me: "Mami, what's wrong? What are you talking about? Tell me." Rosaura started to cry one day in the schoolyard and wouldn't get in the car when I went to pick her up, because she couldn't stand seeing her mother talking to herself like a loca. Perhaps to compensate, Talía stopped speaking and we had to take her to the child psychologist. One day it occurred to me that maybe I could quiet my mouth if I wrote those damn words a thousand times on a piece of paper, as if it were punishment from school. The nuns at the Catholic school I went to made us write our offense one hundred times so that we learned the error of our ways. I decided to impose the same punishment on myself. But penance turned into something else altogether. Other words succeeded and began to fill pages and notepads. I was writing for months at a time. That was the only way to recover my inner silence. Everything I scribbled I threw away. They were my stinking sores, my vomit. And here I am again, with the same bad habit.

Of course it mattered to me the first time I found out. It wasn't until after the second time that I made up my mind. But the solution was equally awful. Divorce. People think getting a divorce is like changing your underwear. Since there's no physical body to bury, people treat the widow as if they had just run into her in the supermarket parking lot after grocery shopping. You behave the same, when in reality you're torn up inside from so much crying, from signing so many documents that leave behind a record of something irrevocably destroyed. When I arrived at Mom's house crying and later at Abuela Maru's apartment with the girls all packed and me ready to become a widow, Abuela told me a story.

She was nineteen years old and he twenty-seven. He was a musician, one of those educated mulattos, and it's anybody's guess how he became a clarinet virtuoso. My grandmother had been raised like a proper little lady, but she told me how they were never able to flush out the appetite for adventure she felt under her skin. Perhaps it was a trait inherited from one of her aunts, a bohemian at the turn of the century who later became lovers with different landowners in the Manatí Valley. From her lovers the aunt inherited farms she readily made available to the new governors when they settled on the island. She made a pile of money selling the farms to the Americans. (None of her lovers ever found out about the others; it was quite a feat to keep such a huge secret in a small town.) She moved to the capital, where she opened a chic restaurant, a laundry, became a caterer, and ran other services for the young soldiers from Wisconsin who were surprised to find themselves stationed at the

Ballajá Military Hospital. She married her younger sisters to gentlemen from the new aristocracy and with help from money and connections erased her unruly past. Her sisters learned every bit of the choreography necessary to look like reputable ladies. She didn't think that lesson was important. Abuela Maru used to say that until her aunt was very old she saw her receive lovers in her big house in Old San Juan.

One night, Abuela Maru was chaperoned to a Philharmonic concert given at Casa de España for the immigrants who came like flies on shit (my grandmother's words precisely) fleeing the Spanish Civil War. Her mulatto arrived late to the concert, making a triumphant entrance with the conductor eyeing him severely and directing harsh words at him, words that were lost in the orchestra's shaky attempts at tuning their different instruments. Paying no mind to the director's scolding, Abuela's mulatto laughed mockingly. He had the swagger of a pimp and the elegance of a landowner. His skin was the color of toasted almonds. Whoever saw him in haste would think he was a Gypsy. But here on the island, the only Gypsies people had ever seen were those who showed up as part of some wandering circus, and those were just white folks dressed up and passing as exotic. My grandmother's mulatto looked like a real Gypsy. The only things that gave him away were his flat nose, the brilliantine that tamed the curls of his hair, and his lips that were per-haps a bit too full.

Needless to say, the concert was a disaster. All those second-rate mu-sicians once again failed to faithfully bring the contradanzas and op-erettas to life. They sweated, trying to feel the music, but it was obvious their hearts were elsewhere. And such seems to be the fate of those born on this island, to put their hearts where they don't belong.

Abuela set hers on the mulatto. He played the clarinet feverishly, and between his fingers the contradanzas sounded like something else altogether. He had a strange, new tone, which the conductor tried to subdue. When, annoyed, the mulatto lowered the intensity of his playing, he let his eyes roam over the faces in the crowd, as if looking for something he hadn't lost. What he never lost ("Well, girl, never is an exaggeration. Never in the course of a few nights," Abuela corrected herself when she saw the surprise on my face) were Maru's eyes. The good girl my grandmother had once been couldn't stop staring at that statuesque, darkskinned man, no matter how hard she tried not to. From afar, the mulatto read her like a music sheet. Heat began to climb up Abuela's legs through her pomplín petticoats and a light sweat began to scent her Dutch lace underwear. His eyes glued to her blushing face, the mulatto made music leap out of the raging valves of the clarinet. The conductor gestured wildly with his hands to no avail, trying once more to get the mulatto to tone down the intensity of his playing, the nimbleness of the arpeggios woven between the elegant fingers he inherited from no one knows who, perhaps a Negro basket weaver or a black stonemason and mosaic maker, all of it lost in the deepest recesses of his genes.

My grandmother Maru was smoking the whole time she was telling me this. She always smoked those long, dark cigarettes, and had from the time she turned fifteen. Her aunt's bad influence. ("Aunt Adela's damn vulgar streak," my grandmother used to joke every time she lit a smoke and held it between her wrinkled fingers.) But since she was raised to be a lady, she knew she had to sneak out to the patios, bathrooms, or remote corners of the places where they took her to socialize with members of her own class.

After the concert, she became agitated and then uncomfortable when her emotions opened her pores. ("Señoritas never sweat, even on

135

a tropical island in times of drought," was another of my grand-mother's pronouncements.) Maru excused herself and, faking a cool composure, slipped away to Casa de España's gardens. Once she was at a safe distance, she lit one of her cigarettes, which she had hidden inside her corset. She smoked cautiously and scattered the smoke with her fan so the smell of tobacco wouldn't linger in her hair.

The mulatto found the spot. Who knows if he was led by his sense of smell, or if he was simply looking for a quiet corner to rest after his per-formance. "He said his name was Víctor Samuel. He was a fox." My grandmother Maru talked to Samuel for what seemed like an eternity. Oddly enough nobody came looking for her. She doesn't even recall the topic of conversation. All she knows is that after a while she found Samuel's tongue tangled up with hers while his fingers played a deli-cate, tremulous arpeggio on her back.

There were frequent undercover dates. "By then," Abuela confessed to me, "I was already engaged to marry Ramiro, your grandfather." In a matter of months her fiancé would return from France, a newly gradu-ated surgeon. Full of guilty thoughts, she told her mulatto about the wedding plans. "So?" Samuel asked when he was done listening to my grandmother, resting on his bare side on the king-sized bed in the Hotel Central, where they spent their afternoons frolicking. "I've heard med-ical doctors have plenty of work and make a fortune."

The affair with the clarinet player lasted well into my grandmother's second wedding anniversary. After that, the mulatto disappeared from sight. They told her he had left the Philharmonic and started playing in bar bands and that he had opened a very successful business. Once, when they were older, they ran into each other somewhere and became friends. "*Poor Ramiro,*" *Abuela Maru would sigh mockingly, "what a cuckold. Serves him right, for all the infidelities I put up with. Oh, well, you know what they say: You won't see it if you don't look." And that's where her story ended.*

* * *

I would've never thought that Maru Villalona, such an elegant lady, her hair done at the salon, her dresses imported from Milan, would keep a lover until he left her for a bar band. But while my grandmother looked at me as if she had just given me the magic potion for all my problems, I rubbed my eyes, sore from constant crying, and wondered: "What the hell has that story got to do with the lover Efraín pampers?" Just as I was about to ask her that question, my grandmother filled the living room with a dense cloud of brown smoke and gestured for me not to interrupt her.

"It's been twenty years since your mother came crying to this apartment because of a similar problem she had with that father of yours. I gave her the same advice I'm giving you today, may God forgive me. In this life we have to be practical, my child. What's more, if you get a divorce, what on earth are you going to live on? Whatever the court orders your husband to pay? Or off that degree you got in college? What about the trips to Europe, the beauty salon, and the masseuse? No, my love. You have to lie to the rock on your finger the same way it has lied to you. And in the meantime, live it up. Nowadays, what with the women's revolution, a little fling won't even cost you your reputation."

I looked at my grandmother with an unhinged expression. I resisted; for seven months I resisted, but in the end I followed her advice. It was

137

easier than going headfirst into an unfamiliar new life. Damn Abuela Maru and damn the wrinkled mouth those words came out of. I hope she burns for all eternity in the seventh circle of hell, which is where she will undoubtedly go. This shit life is all her fault. If I had only gotten divorced back then, I would be safe now.

Convalescence

Two Wednesdays went by before I realized it was over between M. and myself. I don't know if I was trying to avoid the truth, but I started a ritual of waiting for her return. Every day I took my story notes, along with the papers M. had left at the motel, to work with me and then back home to the apartment. At first, I resisted looking through them, but I didn't hold out long. One fine day the temptation was too much and I started reading. After that I fell into the strange habit of putting her papers with mine, letting the two manuscripts sit in one pile and create a single text.

Every afternoon before going to work, I shuffled the pages, seeking unforeseen sequences that were different every time. Then I placed them on the night table in the bedroom Daphne and

I shared. I left them there, waiting for fate to take its course. An inner voice warned me it was just a matter of time before Daphne leafed through them. Daphne is a respectful woman who plays by the rules. But at some point her curiosity had to prevail. More than a few afternoons she had found me absorbed in reading those papers, shuffling pages, far away from her. She had to read them. I would've done the same. And for sure, I was counting on it. Those papers would give me away all by themselves. Then I would have no choice but to face the obligation to confess.

As far as confession goes I have to admit I'm out of practice. I'm no Saint Augustine in search of redemption and I'm not torn between philandering and guilt. I don't know what happened to the purifying Catholicism my mother raised me with, or to the hours of catechism at school, the childhood confessions delivered to solemn priests who tried to instill the fear of God in my heart and the weight of sin on my conscience. Frankly, I think they did a lousy job. If I find a logical or psychological explanation for my actions, I absolve myself and that's that. I'm cleansed of all impurities.

Even so, after M.'s departure I felt a terrible need to confess. To let Daphne see there was something definitely wrong between us. To be able to feel something else take the place of the confusing and muddled pleasure I had gotten used to with M. Maybe my need arose from the desire to drive away the suspicion that my life was returning to its simple, unbearable routines: working, waiting for one love to end, waiting for the writing to emerge blot by blot. And this time, to top it all off, I was working at a motel.

140

To me, that was a treacherous turn of events. Suppose what always happened, what happened at the newspaper, came to pass again? I mean, at first the job awakened the ink devil I carry around inside, only to lull it back to sleep later with routine and disenchantment. The naïve dream of making a contribution by broadening the critical minds of my country was again disappearing before my eyes like a ghost, trapped between the corrections made by the head of editorial, who had been my old teacher, guide, model, and mentor. How he rearranged my news stories ("Five white men murdered in South Africa") to create what he called a bigger impact. The first paragraph had to answer the five key questions: Who, What, Where, When, and How? Second paragraph, develop details and sum up reactions from the participants. Third paragraph, statements from international and local authorities. And finally, toward the bottom, in the paragraph nobody read: "Seventy-five black men also died in the skirmish. A number of Zulu women appear to have been raped. Eleven children between the ages of eight and twelve were also found among the dead."

Every week it was the same. With the war in Kosovo, the corruption scandal at the AIDS Institute, the struggle of the people in Vieques against the United States Navy. And in the centerfolds, death upon violent death, because that's what people like to read: who killed whom in a jealous rage, where did it happen, how (in every lurid detail), how did the mother of the deceased react, what about the neighbors, the police. The headline on the front page was better saved for human interest stories: the separation of Siamese twins, the missing child kidnapped by a woman driven mad with the desire to be a mother, the death of a nun chosen for canonization. But the real news ended up in the trash can or in the pages and paragraphs nobody ever reads, hidden under the veil of objectivity. Everything else was sales and advertisements, horoscopes and weather reports.

I didn't want to think about how I collected those news stories, promising them their due one day, perhaps in a book where humanity and reality mixed, where the dead assumed their tragic and painful nature once again, freed from the statistical environment forced upon them. I promised to return them to the page, one that would give them the ability to provoke indignation, reflection, and compassion from the reader. But there were so many that they turned into shit inside me. They fought for their turn. They wouldn't let me write.

No, I couldn't let that happen again. Now I worked at a motel. Here the devil was on the loose among physical bodies. Bodies that came one after the other, just like the corpses inside the pages of the newspaper. But here time was something else, circular and suspended. There was nothing to mass-produce. Nothing to edit or to tweak, nothing more to assemble than the piles of clean linen that took the place of the dirty sheets, which covered up stories not intended for general consumption. I could stop here, and watch my devil act out. Transcribe his mischief. I couldn't let our flame die out because who would I become if I lost my fiery devil? This couldn't be my place, this could only be a way station, as it is for Tadeo, for M., for Chino, for the countless nighttime lovers, for the entire city. The Motel Tulán was a small labyrinth in which I could momentarily lose myself, where I could do what my body asked and then run away.

A way station. That's what it had been to M. Her papers said so.

It was Franky who brought me to this motel for the first time. I met him at Miñi Miranda's house one afternoon when she asked me to pick her up so we could go to the gym together. When I got there, crazy Miñi wasn't ready yet. I don't know, she had the maid tell me something about telephone calls to an interior decorator who was helping her pick out new carpeting for the guest room. Miñi is such a liar. She was probably making me wait just for appearance's sake. . . .

So when there was a knock on the door and since the housekeeper was nowhere to be found, I had to answer it. And there was Franky. A little bit of cinnamon candy. He had clear, honey-colored eyes and skin bronzed by the sun. He was slender and wiry, with what we call an athletic body. He was my height more or less, so if I stood up on the tips of my toes, I could see the roots of his jet black hair, which fell down to his shoulders carelessly. Franky immediately identified himself as the children's tutor. I don't know if he noticed when I opened the door, but there I was, checking him out shamelessly.

I asked him inside and offered him something to drink to chase away the staggering April heat. Since Miñi kept delaying, we had a few minutes to talk. Franky told me he was studying psychology at the university. He was just starting his master's. His BA was in chemistry, and precalculus had ended up being good for something, since he was getting through school by tutoring math. I don't know how old he was. Twenty-something. I asked him why he had decided to change fields and he replied, "I don't know, maybe an allergy to ties and a settled life." He laughed. Lord of the seven winds, what a smile! He could pull down the walls of a city with that smile. And I, like the walls of Puerta de Tierra, could feel myself crumbling under its dazzling sparkle.

Miñi descended, pulling a shoe strap over her heel and straightening the wide shirt she used to cover her love handles and the loud colors of her gym clothes. "Gotcha. Don't you come here and try to steal my tutor." I smiled. I had foreseen the issue and gave Franky a card with my phone number, with the excuse that the girls were falling behind in science at school. If Efraín had a lover, why not me? I said good-bye to Franky, making him promise he would call, if only to recommend another tutor who could do the job. As soon as I got in my SUV, I gave in to the temptation of asking Miñi:

"Girl, where did you find that fine piece of work?"

"Who, Franky?" she answered, playing dumb. "Sweetheart, that's Felipe Arzuaga's boy. He's my husband's partner. If you only knew the headaches he causes his father. Now he's got it into his head he doesn't want to be a doctor."

"Really?"

"That's right, girl, he wants to be a psychologist, as if you could eat that with fries. I told Felipe to send him to college abroad. In the university here they brainwash kids and they end up believing that money is the devil's work. That's why I push my babies so hard. As soon as they graduate senior year, they're off to college in Boston."

I drove the SUV without paying much attention to Miñi's diatribe. She'd already given me all the information I wanted. The kid was no hoodlum. All that was left to see was how daring he could be.

Franky was much more daring than I imagined. He called me within a week to recommend himself as the girls' tutor. There was proximity, laughing, secrecy. Franky confessed women his age bored him. They had lived so little, knew so little about life. That was my cue to strike. Two weeks later, as I said good-bye to him by the gate (at the time, Efraín never came home before ten at night) I slipped him a kiss very close to his mouth, a kiss which he took very well. He was no fool either, my dear tutor.

But we had to cover our tracks thoroughly. Franky told the girls his midterms were coming up and he wouldn't be able to carry out his tutorial duties. He ceded his position to a pale, surly girl about to graduate in biology who needed money to attend a research internship in New Jersey. Then he called me and invited me out for a cup of coffee and (by God, I don't remember how it degenerated into this) within three-quarters of an hour we were paying for a deluxe cabaña at the Motel Tulán. Correction: "we" is too many. I was the one who paid the bill.

Every time we ended up in the Tulán, we arrived at around one in the afternoon. I don't know why but I began to grow fond of this motel. The rooms didn't have that humid smell, or the reek from faulty air-conditioning. The place gave the impression you could take a shower in its bath without fear of catching mysterious, somewhat difficult to explain infections in hard-to-reach areas. And the carpets weren't those shaggy things blackened by sweaty feet in plastic shoes. They had the discreet charm of the clean and safe carpeting in a doctor's office. There were no love machines in the rooms, or vibrating beds, although they did have mirrors on the walls and ceilings. Those endless hours of abdominals and lifting weights finally paid off. As did the hours enjoying the neo-hippie tastiness of my tutor's suntanned butt.

Two months later Franky disappeared, pursuing a doctor's daughter who planned to study ecotourism in Costa Rica. His absence was a *relief because it let me relax my state of vigilance. I didn't go back to the Tulán for a while after Franky, although it definitely had become my favorite motel. I only had one other lover after Franky, an attorney who compensated for his lack of youth with plenty of money for four-star hotels. But I never again felt the frenzy I experienced among those walls that smelled of talcum powder and cheap insecticide. Let's just say I developed a nostalgia for the place. Memories of better times, perhaps. . . .*

M.'s words captivated me just as her body had. Obscure and secretive but at the same time, free of self-consciousness, of judgment's unending labyrinth. Like an addict I found myself reading them day after day, unable to get out of their embrace, my eyes glued to the page's skin as if it were M.'s own. I was jealous of her. I always wanted to write in such a naked manner, without worrying about who would notice my dirt and my odors, concentrating only on getting them down on the page, hoping I could liberate myself from them. As it did for M., the motel gave me a place to see those sores magnified. But just the same, I had to put them behind me, I had to let go of the magnifying glass that enlarged my own sores so I could detach myself and turn them into writing material. It was a step M. wasn't interested in taking. It's the step that transforms confession into literature. M. avoided it by throwing the papers away. That paramount decision buried her paramount act of freedom. I envied her act of renunciation. But I didn't want to emulate her. Or maybe I did, maybe I was hoping my desire to be published was parallel to the act of throwing my manuscript into the trash, not caring who read or approved of it, and thereby freeing myself from the crushing self-consciousness that wouldn't let me write.

For that I had to escape the motel, as M. had done and as Daphne suggested, find myself another darkened desk and get back to my old life. But something told me it was not yet time. Maybe I was waiting to finish my story, or for M. to return. I don't really know. But why did I want to confess to Daphne and jeopardize everything? Instead of removing the stain of my betrayal on my own, why was I conspiring in what would require a confession? I certainly wasn't in love with M. Impossible. It had to be something else. M.'s body, her papers, the adulterous couples moaning, the odd encounters between drug dealers and union lawyers, and Tadeo's voice all confused me. I was pleasurably lost in the Tulán's maze. And I didn't want to go home.

On top of that, M.'s scribbling was having an effect on me. On me, the aspiring writer. On me, who had read so much. Once upon a time, my father gave me some advice. "A writer, eh? Well, you've got to read our great ones. You owe it to them. René Marqués, José Luis González, Emilio Díaz Valcárcel, Enrique Laguerre. They're the best we have." I sat down diligently in the study with the big old books. I took them to the beach. Took them all over the city. They didn't impress me at all. "The foreigners, perhaps," I told myself, a bit ashamed of catching myself thinking what everyone else thought: that the island's narrowness had to be overcome, that in this poor, pressure cooker of a country everything is still to be done and what is done already is screwed up. That's why, if it's foreign, it's better by definition. I then read everyone, and still do, from Shakespeare to Tabucchi, from

Thomas Mann to Saramago. And look who ends up having an impact on me.

It's curious. A writer needs to be marked by other writers, just like an empty page. And then to betray the hand that covered that page with ink. Only then can they gain access to confession, sorry, I meant, to writing. No, I meant both things, because to a certain degree, writing is a confession and an act of treason, the terrible treason of a rebellious reader not satisfied with being the subservient receiver of his Father's wise words, His Life-Giving Word; a reader who wants to give permission for his words to be said too. That's why he betrays, I mean, writes, with the weak spirit of the guilty and the ambitious audacity of the traitor. One and the other, pulling in opposite directions. Otherwise, writing's treason can't transcend its nature as a stiff, rhetorical invention. It doesn't arrive at what the Greeks called *moira*: it doesn't take its destined shape. All my life I've searched for the thing I could dream of betraying. And now, these papers which were never meant to be transformed into the "Word" were showing me how. Through her scribbles, M. invited a truer treason than found in any actual book. There it was, the living page, beating like I'd never seen it before, not even in the collected correspondence or autobiographies of famous writers. Because those expressions were written down after the "Word," they uncover the inner workings, the earlier evolutions of a writer's mind. This was definitely something else.

Maybe I'm mistaken, maybe I've made all of this up after the fact, surrendering to a desire to find some meaning in my actions. At this stage, none of that matters. Whatever the reasons, the important thing is Daphne read my papers at last, M.'s papers, and handed down her sentence.

* * *

"Do you have a moment?" Daphne said one morning. Her face wasn't bent out of shape. She even looked happy, although she wasn't smiling. It was the serenity of someone who confronts another person confidently, ready to say what's on her mind. I threw myself like a sack onto the edge of the bed. "It's been a while since we've been together."

"It's just that this job—"

"No, it's not that. You haven't been here, present, since before this job. Neither have I. It's nobody's fault."

"We're together now."

"Not even. I already left."

"What are you saying, Daphne?"

"That I don't want to be with you anymore."

The blood in my veins froze for an instant. For a moment, I doubted. Was this what I really wanted? For the relationship to end this way? The papers had served their purpose and now my intentions were blowing up in my face.

"Did I do something to cause this?"

"Of course you did. You became oblivious to the fact that I lived by your side."

"That's it?"

"That's plenty."

"Can I do something to make up for it?"

"Sure, but why?"

"Daphne, I . . ." And I left the words hanging out of my mouth. Suddenly my head filled up with a vast list of all the things I was losing. I made an inventory: the apartment, the flexible hours with a woman who in the mornings went to work and in the evenings waited for me. I thought about her body in my arms, when I arrived before dawn to find her still asleep and would slowly curl up against her back. I thought about her hair against my cheeks, her curly and rebellious cobalt blue hair, the silky fuzz on her cheeks, and her supple, round breasts, like two ripe fruits perched on her chest. My stomach recalled the soft pressure of her large, fleshy thighs, the cushion between her legs, and her small pubis, so much like a doll's. Looking at her dark skin, abandoned after years of systematic neglect, I relived the heat of her body, scented like freshly cut grass. I didn't know what to say. It wasn't like I was losing her now. I had been losing her for a long time. But only now, all at once, did I feel nostalgic.

"You know I wanted more out of life than to wait while you wrote," Daphne went on. "I wanted us to do things, projects, a house, maybe a kid, I don't know, but I was definitely looking for something else besides waiting around."

"I understand. You lost faith in me."

"Faith?"

"Faith in my project, in my novels."

"Excuse me for being so blunt, but what do I care about your novels? I don't sleep with them, I don't talk to them in the mornings either."

"But I do."

"And with me too. You used to sleep with me too. You didn't

have to replace one thing with the other. You didn't need to put off life or look for it outside in order to be able to write. Life is here, this is it. You are your words."

"I don't understand what you're coming to."

"I'm not coming to anything. I'm coming away."

I couldn't help smiling at her choice of words. Daphne stared at me sullenly.

"This is not a game of words, Julián."

"I know."

"And another thing. Those papers . . ."

"What?"

"The journal . . ."

"You read the journal?"

"Spare me the drama. You wanted me to read it. If not, you wouldn't have left it in plain view."

"Daphne, let me explain. It's over. It was over a long time ago, before it began."

"That doesn't matter, my love. I'm not leaving you because of that woman. I'm leaving you because of me."

I didn't say a word. There was nothing to say, really nothing. From the bed, I watched Daphne taking the keys out of her purse. She grabbed an overnight bag that was already packed, near the door. With her back to me, all ready to go, she spoke for the last time.

"I'm going to my parents' for a couple of weeks while I find another place. The papers are none of my business but I think you should give them back to your friend. Or at least return them to wherever she left them."

Pieces of M.

Amelia gave me a piece of advice: "Girl, you need to see my therapist."
She rummaged around in her purse while I kept complaining about the
way my head hurt. I told her my skull weighed several hundred pounds
and that I was scared to move my neck too much, for fear it would snap.
It felt like I was carrying a heavy sack on my shoulders all the time. And
I couldn't stop thinking. It was as if high-octane gas powered my mind.
My head was filling up with words all the time, while I slept, ate, took a
bath, went to the supermarket, waited for the girls to come home from
school. The eldest had a driver's license now and Efraín got her a car so
she could be independent. "You listen to me. Call my therapist and make
an appointment. You'll see how much better you feel," and she handed
me a small card with the edges worn from so much handling. "It's the
last one I have left." She smiled and changed the subject. "Did you

hear? Mario Andújar gave his wife a really hot Lexus for their wedding anniversary. If every husband was like that . . ." It was the sign to zip it. And I really wanted to talk to someone, instead of spending so much time having conversations with myself.

After I dropped Amelia at home, I spent some time walking around the house with the card in my hand. "Isabel Vigo. Psychologist." I remembered the time as a teenager when my mother took me to see a psychologist because I was out of control. I would only argue with her, wouldn't follow orders or advice. It was around the time Father got sick. My mother and I went to seven sessions. I kicked and screamed, and then went silent. Mother finally gave up and became convinced therapy was only making the situation worse. When Father came out of the depression that had left him bedridden, everything returned to normal. I went back to being the happy-go-lucky girl, the airhead, getting grades that were just good enough, going out to parties with friends. My mother took a deep breath. The therapist was never mentioned again.

The girls came home from school. We served dinner. Efraín was late, as usual, but he was in a good mood. We even talked a little about his work and made plans for the upcoming summer vacation. We might go to Cancún. There was no sex, but that night we slept in each other's arms.

Be that as it may, the next morning I woke up with my head full of words again. Terrified, I ran in search of the small card I had left on the dresser. "Dr. Vigo's office," answered a friendly voice, "How can I help you?" I explained to her that she came highly recommended by Amelia Mendizabal and that it was urgent. That everything in my life was okay, that everything was like it always was. There were even signs that it was getting better, and yet I couldn't stop feeling that my head would explode. I talked and talked without rest, choking on my own breath. My tongue wouldn't stop, and neither would the words.

"Very well, Mrs. Cáceres. Why don't you come by the office the day after tomorrow, at ten thirty in the morning? I think I can squeeze you in. And take it easy. Everything will be alright."

I spent the days that followed fighting with my head. Every time my neck started aching more than usual, every time I felt like I was going to start talking to myself again, I sat down in the bedroom or the living room and began to breathe in, one, two, and then exhale, three, four, following a technique I saw on the morning news. That was the only way I could calm down. The day of the appointment finally came. I don't even know why I went. The three months of therapy were useless.

Dr. Vigo was chubby. Round face and rounded hands, not even the heels of her feet had corners. At the center of all that roundness, the eyes of a big ugly cow looked at me, trying to communicate her understanding, but the only thing I saw in them was boredom. The first session went two hours nonstop. She made me tell her about my childhood and I told her everything, from beginning to end. It surprised even me how much I talked. I didn't keep her at bay by throwing a tantrum.

"My childhood was what you call normal," I told Dr. Vigo. "That's how I see it, from the little I remember. I went to school. I played with dolls. My mother made sure nothing was missing, and she and Daddy both took me to the pile of classes they signed me up for: swimming, piano, ballet. 'So you discover your talents,' Father would say. 'So you develop discipline,' my mother added. I liked them all, didn't have a favorite. I was good in everything but school. What I liked best was being with people, staring at my friends' moms and guessing what they were thinking while I jumped through the air and dove into the pool;

seeing everybody's faces when I made a perfect dive. That was every-thing, seeing and being seen by other people. But I could also go with-out playing the piano for months or fail out of the next ballet recital or lose a meet. I didn't care about being the best, or about winning medals, or even about making my parents proud by trying hard. The experience of them seeing me, and me watching them look at me, was enough. I knew there would be another opportunity for me to be seen and another and another after that. My parents would take care of it."

I told Dr. Vigo that I didn't have a clear memory of my early child-hood. But I remember some things: playing with a stuffed octopus I got for my birthday, the strange disappearance of a milk bottle surrounded by toys, the print on the quilt where they laid me down to sleep in the nursery. I think that's my first memory, the quilt for napping. Since my mother left early for work, we had a nanny living in the house that took care of me until I was old enough to go to school. Doña Alicia. She combed her hair in tight buns, and she was the color of mahogany, her bun, her skin, and her eyes too. It was as if someone had painted her from head to toe with a single stroke. Never a smile, very strict. Like clockwork, after each lunch she made me take a nap. I was never one to sleep much during the day. Even at night I have trouble sleeping. . . . But no matter how much I kicked and screamed or complained to my mom, not even God could force Doña Alicia to leave me alone. I had to take a nap. I had to take the goddamn nap. Since I couldn't sleep, I looked at the quilt's pattern until I knew it by heart. A stripe of red cloth, a green one, an orange one, a burgundy one, and then the red again, all of them crisscrossed by the beige threads holding the weave together. It seems like I can see them clearly if I close my eyes right now. Time flew by, a lot of time, but it was weightless, and I was amused by my little stripes. Then Doña Alicia would come, and I would pretend to be asleep to see if she would lift the sleeping sentence, if maybe she wouldn't make me lie there the entire time. She was very lively, that woman, but only when she was on her own turf. We ran into her once on the street, when she was waiting for her ride at the bus stop. She was talking to people, she was even laughing and her bun was coming undone. She looked like someone else.

But the strongest memory I still have came later. I must have been six or seven years old when it started, when I began waking up early some mornings because I was afraid of finding myself in a pool of urine. I wet my bed well into my teens. I don't know why. My mother and Doña Alicia pestered me about it constantly. "You've got to control yourself. Get up when you need to pee." Mom gave me advice in the neutral tone that's used with purebred dogs when they're being trained. "You just need to stop whining like a spoiled girl," hissed Doña Alicia every time she had to change the sheets, and my face would burn with embarrassment. Papi was the only one who gave me any comfort. "Don't you worry," he said to me, "I was a big pisser until just the other day." Mom looked at him with reproach, with that stare of hers that accused him of being so disinterested.

She loved me. Of that much I'm sure. She was a bit withdrawn, demure, but she never failed me. She gave me everything I needed, and even what I didn't need. Although few and far between, there were times when she was affectionate. I could count on her for anything, even to help me with the problems I had. It was just that she didn't love my dad. She didn't. She loved me, but not him. Who could love my father the way he lived, lost in sadness? Or maybe it was that his loves were all mixed up in the house, running into each other in the hallways *without making contact, lost in the bedrooms and the baths, calling out to each other quietly, but not loud enough for the other loves to hear, as if they were afraid of actually finding each other. It was like living in a sitcom, my childhood. Everything was fine, everything was perfect, but at bottom of the existence the three of us were building inside that house, something was missing: screams, fights, a simple spontaneous caress.*

I would've given anything to hear them fight, throw plates at each other and shatter the silence. I felt humming inside those walls. To hear them moan between the sheets of that flawless bed, which didn't reek of urine, like mine, and which greeted every morning freshly made, as if nobody had slept in it. O.K., yes, that's what I wanted to talk about. I saw them in bed together just once.

It was Saturday or Sunday. I know because even though it was early, there was none of the hurrying and running around of school days. I woke up to go to the bathroom, relieved I hadn't wet my bed. The door of my parents' room was slightly ajar. When I went over to take a peek, I heard noises from inside. Then I saw them, both of them, naked, close together in bed.

My mother leaned back on her elbows. She was looking at my father with sweet, sad eyes, as if seeing him for the first time, as if he was a gentleman she had just met or of whom she had dreamed and now discovered next to her, in a bed that was new and unknown. My father, on his back, was looking at her too. He gently stretched his arm over and touched her cheek with the back of his hand. As I spied on them from my hiding place behind the door, I could feel the murmur we lived with, the hellish humming, being transformed into a current emerging from that soft touching of skin, a current that overflowed and transcended the flesh to include me, and the sleeping house, which was dusty and inelegant but at that moment beating calmly. That was love. Why hadn't either of them shown it to me before? Why did they go to the trouble of making me, of making and unmaking each other, but never take the time for an unraveling like that?

* * *

Dr.Vigo looked at the clock and said time was up; we should meet again the following week. I went home somehow relieved, and for a whole week didn't feel the need to scribble in journals or lock myself in the car or bathroom to talk to myself. Afterward there was another session, in which I told her about Efraín. Then the paper madness returned. I no longer talked to myself. But I couldn't stop scribbling. I spent entire sleepless nights holed up in the study, pen in hand. My tongue became heavy and stayed on the bottom of my mouth, moving only when necessary. "You want me to heat up dinner for you?" "How did it go at school today?" Nothing more. But at night, alone, shut inside the study, I wrote until dawn. The ink was like a torrent of blood. It would have killed me if I couldn't stop. I was going to bleed to death. Feeling frantic and unable to wait another week, I called Dr. Vigo, told her it was an emergency, and went back to her office. I told her everything about Efraín, his negligence, his lovers, his contempt.

"Efraín doesn't pay any attention to me!" I screamed and cried to the doctor. "Not in bed, not in the house, and not at public events. I'm like a trophy, like a tame mare. He's there, at my side, but he doesn't notice me."

159

While I cried, Dr. Vigo paused, wiped her glasses clean, and settled her Buddha-like roundness into a more comfortable position in her armchair.

"You know I also offer marriage counseling, but your husband would need to come for that."

"I don't want him to come."

"Why?"

"Because that's not what I came here to work out."

"Why did you come, then?"

"Because my head is about to explode. Plus, I can't stop writing nonsense. Before I used to say it, but now . . ."

"What does your head say to you?"

"Get out, get out."

"Why don't you act on it?"

"How could I abandon my girls, my family?"

"Perhaps it's not them that you have to leave."

"Leave Efraín?"

"Perhaps."

Leave Efraín. If only Dr. Vigo had known that I'm not as stupid or weak as I look, that I had already tried leaving Efraín several times, that I was just about to leave him once and for all. If only she had known I had already talked to my lawyers, looked at an apartment big enough for me and the girls, that I was on the brink of filing for divorce when I found those damn papers and had to cancel my plans. I dropped everything out of fear, a terror so tremendous it forced me to quit therapy, to spend hours struggling with myself, to shut myself inside this motel room just so I could breathe. The entire house turned against me, as if it had come alive, as if it had found out that I knew it was an accomplice to

Efraín's cheating: "You're full of shit if you think you're going to find a place for yourself in here. I won't let you live within these walls. You get out now and take your stench and your afflictions somewhere else." I wanted to go back to my journals, but the house wouldn't let me write. So I came here, where it all began.

The papers on Efraín's desk. My God, what am I going to do? We will lose everything. . . . No, I don't want to think about it now.

* * *

I haven't told anybody this, nor have I written it down anywhere, not even in old notebooks or papers I've torn to pieces. I saw him with her one day. I knew "she" existed, but I had never had the nerve to stop by the apartment building where Efraín kept her in all manner of luxury, to look her in the eye. Amelia verified it, stirring up the melodrama: "An affair, darling. And in the office. With a secretary who's nothing compared to you, that you can be sure of, but in any case . . ." I avoided the places where I suspected Efraín took her out to dinner (very expensive restaurants he took me to before). I didn't want to run into them, to have to see them together, perhaps engaged in that which I thought bound him to me, I don't know, an afterglow, an invisible fire that appeared when we were happy. A shared hunger. The sparks that disappeared when Efraín began to complain.

"You never want to go out anywhere."

"It's just that I want to stay home with you, Efraín. Come on, the girls are asleep."

"Why don't we go out dancing? There's a party tonight at the Graffams'. The Mendizabals will be there. You know, Amelia, your friend."

"Amelia is a bore."

"There's an important client that might show up."

"I'm not here to entertain for you. Go by yourself."

* * *

Efraín went and I stayed home, with the girls sleeping and the hunger alive and overwhelming, so overwhelming it wouldn't let me sleep. How did this happen? How was it that no matter how often I put my hands around his neck, Efraín went on his way without so much as noticing I was pulling him toward the bed? Just like the girl from long ago, I only wanted to be seen. For him to hold me with his eyes and his yearning while I somersaulted in midair and dove headfirst into the water, or onto the carpet of the house, between the bedsheets, into the ocean of hours that separated us until later, when day was over and we found each other again. But now Efraín's hunger was directed at other things. Or was it always like this? Had it been me who had not seen it? The only thing I noticed was that Efraín was not satisfied with me, he wanted more. More clients, more friends, more parties, more work, another car, and more vacations. More evidence that he was Efraín, the powerful. And she was his accomplice in this intrigue. Still, I never imagined how deep Efraín's hunger and his intrigue went. Or how he was using that other woman.

The papers convinced me to do it. One day, without even thinking, like a robot, I found myself in an airport office renting a car with tinted windows. I drove back downtown to the industrial zone and waited for the end of the day, following Efraín after he left work. I tailed him to a fancy apartment building overlooking the bay. I saw him park and go up in the elevator. I found the woman's name on the directory and waited. I stayed in the car for hours, experiencing a rather peculiar calm.

Any Wednesday I'm Yours

My head was clear, my legs and my ears were humming; it was not an uncomfortable feeling but more like the prelude to peace. After nightfall, Efraín came down from the apartment on the eighth floor and drove away in his convertible. I walked in resolutely, as if possessed by some-one else. I pressed the intercom. She must have thought it was Efraín, who forgot something. I heard a careless "come up" out of the speaker, and a buzzer announcing that the lock on the door was open. I stepped into the elevator. I walked up to the apartment door and rang the bell.

A pale, thin woman opened the door. We looked the same age, al-though she was definitely younger, several years younger than me, maybe ten at the most. She had long, black hair, like mine. Her lips were thick and her breasts firm, bulging out of the tank top that tried to hold them. She had long, smooth legs, and her toenails were done in blue. Still, it was obvious from her face that she had lost that freshness life possesses when one barely knows anything about it. She knew who I was instantly. She tried to close the door but my arm got in the way, show-ing strength I had no idea was in me. As if I were someone else, I swear, as if all those years of swimming, of ballet, of gymnastics suddenly showed up in my arms. No god or earthly creature could have closed that door now. First they would have to break my arm with a machete. Even my mind couldn't have persuaded me otherwise, couldn't have made me question myself: "What are you doing? Why are you stooping before your husband's mistress? What's gnawing at your insides? Get out of the way." Not even she could restrain me.

After a brief struggle, she let go of the door and hurried to the phone. She dialed, waited, and said: "Efraín, darling, guess who's pay-ing me a visit? Your wife." She then listened, as if for instructions. When she hung up she looked at me defiantly, like she was ready to answer any insult, return any blow I might give her. I continued to watch her in complete silence from the doorway. I even smiled at her. I think my smile confused her, because she began to put her hands over her face, looking for cover and gazing out the windows. Surely she was just waiting for Efraín to come rescue her from her predicament. "Poor thing," I remember thinking and then, "You're fucking insane. How could you feel sorry for this cheap woman?" So I decided not to mention anything about what I'd found on Efraín's desk. Let her go down on her own, the same way she had wanted me to.

"Efraín is on his way over," she defiantly challenged me. I kept quiet. "So say whatever you came here to say and the rest, well, you work it out with your husband. It's not my problem."

"Oh, really?"

She looked away, out the window again. I continued to watch her from the door. I looked at her for a long time, until I memorized her completely.

"You know something?" I asked her then. "It's you who should talk to Efraín. And I suggest you speak frankly to him. And say hi for me. I no longer have anything to say to him."

I cut her off and left. As I walked over to the elevator I heard a door slam and later a stifled cry. I didn't need to cry; I was cleansed. That day I slept like a baby. I went shopping, stopped at the gym, and moved Efraín's things to the guest room. I don't know if Efraín came home that night. I didn't bother to find out. He had done everything possible to get rid of me, and now I did the same. Now something was irrevocably broken.

Mulling It Over

"Daphne left me."

"When was this, big man?"

"Yesterday morning."

"Listen, bro, truth is when it rains it pours."

"She took her clothes, some boxes, the flower vases. She emptied the house. Miracle she didn't take the pots and pans too."

I had to tell someone. Daphne's absence was turning the apartment against me. I couldn't eat, I couldn't sleep. Everything reminded me she'd left. The coffeemaker, the empty coat hangers she'd hung her clothes on. M.'s papers on the night table put the vacant space (inside and outside my chest) in sharper focus than ever. Once again I had that exposed feeling. I needed somewhere, anywhere, to avoid the intense exposure.

Tadeo listened to my story with a thoughtful expression. He understood how I felt. He bit his lower lip. He sympathized with my loss and went with me down into a silence so deep that it made me stop for air, plunged with me while I tried to find true north on a deranged compass that wouldn't tell me what I should do with my life now. Wasn't this what I wanted? Hadn't I instigated it by leaving M.'s papers out in plain view? Why such a feeling of doom now?

"I didn't get the chance to meet her, but, brother, from what you tell me, seems like Daphne was a good woman."

"That, she was."

"So then, why did you let her get away? Go and find her."

"No, no, Tadeo, things were just not going well between us. Our schedules, my projects. Maybe it's better this way."

"You know what you're doing. . . ."

A prolonged silence spread out over the night. A slow night, Tuesday, and then the beginning of Wednesday. If only M. would come and take my mind off things with that voracious and distant hunger of hers, if only she'd do whatever she wanted with me.

Tadeo was down too. He definitely had something he wanted to say to me, but circumstances forced him to keep quiet and wait for the right moment. It was only a matter of time. Tadeo was never one to wait long to speak his mind.

Within a quarter of an hour a gray sedan came up the hill. My heart skipped a beat inside my chest. M.? No, it was the same guy who just a few weeks ago had gotten out of another car to do business with Efraín Soreno and company. Chino Pereira's partner. Tadeo stood up slowly from the chair where he kept his eye on the night like a nurse checking the measured, intravenous flow of a serum administered to a terminal patient. He walked to the car unsteadily and crouched by the driver's door. Some ten, fifteen minutes went by. Seemed like the conversation, although subdued, was on the heavier side. Finally, an envelope came out of the car's window. Tadeo grabbed it with both hands. The headlights came back on again and the car left as it had come, disappearing down the Motel Tulán's exit ramp.

"The cards have been dealt, old man. I'm leaving the day after tomorrow for Miami."

"Shit, Tadeo, are you sure that's what you want to do?"

"It's what I gotta do if I don't want to die of shame around here, if I want to return to Baní someday."

"What's keeping you from going back?"

"A promise I can't fulfill, a promise I made to my mother, Julián, that I would build her a decent home where she could sit down, get some fresh air, and take it easy. A decent life, one in which she wouldn't have to root around on the ground like a dog just to put food in her mouth. No, man, I'm tired of living like a dog. And sick of not being able to follow through on my promises."

"But it's not for lack of trying, it's because you haven't been able to."

"Doesn't matter. Hasn't it happened to you, big guy? Don't you ever lack the strength to look yourself in the mirror for fear you'll fly into a rage and spit at your own face? Doesn't it seem to you that the 'Easy does it, keep trying, you'll make it someday' lie just doesn't cut it anymore? Shit, Julián, it's time to grab the bull by the horns. This is my chance. It's not what I expected. It's not what I'd choose. But my mother isn't fifty years old anymore, and I couldn't live with myself if I allowed her to die like this."

I kept quiet. Not because I didn't have a thousand things to say, to point out risks, the danger of deportation, the years of jail time if they caught him. Not because I didn't want to prevent Tadeo from engaging in that desperate enterprise, but because I knew exactly what he was talking about. The feeling that you really should be someone else, that you aren't enough of a man to deal with the minimum any man should be able to deal with, such as providing for his women and proving himself before his peers; that desire to at least be content with what you see when the eyes on the other side of the mirror look back at you. I didn't have an answer for his argument. If some of us still had places to hide in, I knew others did not. Tadeo, for one, had few hiding places and fewer opportunities to grab the bull by the horns in life. My bull (to my credit and disgrace) was made of paper and words.

"And who's replacing you while you're away?"

"You remember that skinny guy, the one smoking all the time when Chino came to the motel to pack up his product? I think they call him Bimbi."

"Tadeo, you're going to leave me alone with that asshole? What if he cleans out the register when I'm not looking? Or even while I am looking? The guy's a delinquent."

"And we're not?"

"Sure, but we are decent delinquents, like most people in this country."

We laughed, in spite of the joke, because we had to. We had to clear the heavy air bearing down on us, the pathetic scene we two men made, our particular miseries making us brothers in arms. I, abandoned by my woman. Tadeo, putting his life on the line for his mother. A good time to laugh.

We took out a couple of smokes and lit up. In unison we exhaled and waited for the night to pass. Silence filled our mouths again as the night's noises reached a crescendo. Tiny tree frogs and crickets sang out in all their glory. From down below on Route 52 there arose the drone of traffic speeding down the highway, as if a river were spitting out surges of water making a pattern of mad waves that washed up on the shores of sleepy tarmac. The air was heavy, like a wind from the north. It would rain at dawn for sure.

"Looks like the Power Authority thing is heating up."

"They already announced the date of the strike?"

"You don't know? It's all over the papers."

"Tadeo, you know I don't read the papers."

"Is that right? I thought since you used to work on one, you were the type who read all four on the island. Or are there five? In Santo Domingo there's barely two of them. Who would've thought that on such a small island so much paper would be wasted on political gossip?"

"Five, there are five," I corrected him. "And it is precisely because I worked on one that I don't believe a word in any of them."

Once again the feeling of being exposed to the elements gripped my chest. At first I read all the local newspapers and the Sunday *New York Times*. I even devoured the EFE News Agency wires like breakfast. What happened to all that?

We needed to change the room temperature, or maybe we just needed a beer, a joke, a line of blow, anything to drive away the anxiety amplified by the night as it crept along at the motel. I didn't want to think about how day after day, month after month, of reading the news had turned me into a cynic.

"So what happened?" I asked Tadeo, shaking off the ghost of my disenchantment.

"Well, seven transformers in the center of the island blew last night and the government accuses Power Authority people of sabotage."

"Perhaps that's what Soreno and his henchmen were working out when they met here."

"Could be, big man, could be. But then, why would they also meet with Chino's man?"

"To buy explosives?"

"No, Julián, Chino's not into explosives. Drugs, yes, and guns, yes, but explosives? I don't think so."

"Maybe what Efraín wanted was to buy some guns, just in case they had to protect themselves and use unregistered arms."

"For sure, man, that could be it."

A car came up the drive. It was César, the Bantu prince of my first day (night) of work at the motel, arriving with his usual lover, the mellow and affectionate older man who promised to save him from whatever catastrophe his desires might unleash. The kid was smiling, more confident of his prey than before. And the older man, perhaps worn down by so much love, followed in his steps like a tame lamb en route to the altar of sacrifice. But there was no mistrust in his eyes. Nor fear. It was as if he had come to terms with his lot, whatever it was, as long as he could be enthralled under that boy's enchantments one more night.

We gave them cabaña 23, *La Dama Solitaria*'s old room. I felt like I was committing an act of treason, or maybe revenge against M., for having left me alone for three weeks now. If she came back she would have to wait. She would have to understand she had lost the benefits of being a regular, that once again she was a soul in trouble trying to get through the night. She would have to take whatever Tadeo's steady hands or mine dealt her. Our compassion would provide her with shelter, a room with walls as thin as cardboard so her impulses and spite would be laid bare, or, to spare her the humiliation, a solid room in which the bags under her eyes and her nakedness wouldn't be exposed to mockery or scrutiny. We would decide. And the Solitary Lady would have to acquiesce. That is, if she returned. But what about her papers? What if she came back for her papers?

"If you could see how vain Efraín Soreno looked in the news. Fine shirt, expensive watch. A player. He definitely has no qualms about seeing himself in the mirror every morning."

"Efraín," I repeated out loud. Where had I read that name recently? Or maybe I had just heard it on the radio. I pulled out my notebook.

"What do you say I steal his name when I board the plane? Perhaps it will bring me luck. And if I raise suspicions, they'll look for him. Can that be done, bro?"

"If you find out how, fill me in. I'll change my identity too," I answered distractedly. Wasn't Efraín the name of M.'s husband?

"Well, there he was on the front page, standing behind the

union boss. That *tigere* denied all charges of sabotage, and accused the government instead. They wanted, he said, to drag the Authority through the mud and turn the public against the union. You know, the same finger pointing as always."

"And the negotiations?"

"Stalled by the investigation. The Authority said it wouldn't send any technicians to repair the transformers until the government commits to a specific date to sit down at the table."

"Well, then the Authority wasn't behind it."

"You think the government was involved?"

"The government stands to gain much more from blown transformers."

"So our theory on Chino Pereira and Efraín Soreno just fell apart."

"To the contrary, my dear Watson. Perhaps Efraín is playing both sides."

"Julián, this is not a who-done-it. For all we know, the only thing we witnessed was a big coke buy for some huge bash."

"Or maybe Efraín Soreno has personal reasons to stall the negotiations. Wasn't there some talk about privatizing the Authority? Maybe Efraín wants in on that deal."

"With Chino Pereira's money. No way. Wait a minute. You're not leading me into that maze. That really gives me a headache."

"Come on, Tadeo, we're just killing time, that's all. Who the fuck is going to listen to us if we go public?"

* * *

We spent the rest of the night mulling over our theories. All of a sudden, the duo who had commiserated over their fates a few hours before changed into honest detectives trying to battle the corrupt and powerful. A fight between good and evil, in which the sides were (even if only once) clearly delineated, precise, contained. Tadeo and I, aided by the simple superiority of our acute minds, would uncover the charlatans. Neither their power nor their influence would be able to beat us. We were amused by our little adolescent game, necessary to drive away the gray adulthood that didn't turn us into men, but instead infantilized us even more and in a worse way.

Morning came. M. never showed up at the motel. Tadeo swept up the cigarette butts with a broom while I sat down to close the register. Morning surprised a few guests who stayed on, passing the night's hangover among us. In the broad light of dawn, their bodies and faces looked like shipwrecks that had washed up with the urban tide. I looked at Tadeo with great tenderness, something like the bond between two cops, or two soldiers at the bottom of a muddy trench who survive the bombs. Our faces, our bodies were still recognizable. We had made it through the night.

"So you are really going to Miami?"

"Just for a couple of days, no more. And don't worry about Bimbi. He won't dare to get on Chino's bad side."

"No, it's not that. I'm worried about you."

A brief, an ever-so-brief silence took over the moment. Tadeo's broom, its repetitive brushing on the cement around the office, was the only thing breaking the echo of our thoughts.

"Listen, brother, I've never asked, but do you believe in God?"

An interesting question. Do I believe in God? Do I believe there exists a higher conscience who assembles our actions in a coherent manner, consecutively, leading them to an orchestrated end, for better or for worse, or, at least, for the improvement or the worsening of the species, of our existence on earth? Or do I believe, on the other hand, that what we call life is but a succession of errors, trap after trap after trick, for beings that collide like little balls of energy inside the walls of an atom, simply keeping all the energy moving along with their hatred, their passions, their urgencies, until the reason for that energy racing around the face of the earth runs out of steam and then nothingness envelops everything, just like that? Don't I believe in God? Do I believe? Do I have to believe?

"Sometimes."

Tadeo stopped sweeping. He was looking at a spot over the hills and far away, over even the high-tension wires where the morning's first birds perched. He seemed to be having a conversation with the pitch black expressway crossing the island, where the cars sped toward the city. He sighed deeply, grabbed the broom, and, without looking me in the eye, spoke very quietly.

"Well, reserve one of those times in my name, and pray for me."

A Night with Bimbi

Rain. The streets were slippery. Down on Route 52 the waves of speeding cars—if you closed your eyes all the way—turned into a nocturnal beach. On the entrance ramp, walking right down the middle of the lane with the studied swagger of a teenage hit man, my new motel coworker appeared. Bimbi, no first or last name. Talking on his cell phone—"The *gatas*, bro, the chicks just won't leave me alone"—a brand-new Rolex flashed on his wrist. The choreography of his hands as he searched for a light accentuated his watch, making it sparkle beneath the lampposts. The Rolex made me think of Chino Pereira, who had one just like it.

"I'm telling you, never give your cell number to a *gata* because then they want to control you," was his welcoming advice.

I didn't say a word when he walked in. I missed Tadeo already.

Judging from Bimbi's look, the way he wore his seventeen years of age badly, with the shadow of a thin mustache that barely qualified him as a man, it probably was just his mother calling.

"Since I've been with Chino, damn, I get so many offers. Jackie invited me to a party in Sellés tonight in, ya know, the projects. But that's just my luck. It had to be today, shit, and I've been checking that *gata* out for a long time, *viste*?"

Later Bimbi embellished the story with a precise description of Jackie: tall, dark, braids down to her ass—"They're extensions, *viste*, but she wears them like she was born with 'em"—and a smile that could melt a block of ice. Jackie was super thin, like a tent pole, even though she already had a kid. Anyone who saw her wearing her school uniform, sucking on a noontime ice cream cone, would never suspect how streetwise she really was. "An incredible woman. Bet you can't guess her age." Fifteen, all of fifteen years old.

I looked Bimbi over again. Maybe everything he was telling me was true, maybe even with all that acne, measly facial hair, and a scraggly, malnourished physique weaned on fast food and candy store sweets, the kid qualified as a man. To be strict about it, in the eyes of a project girl easily impressed by cell phones and a Rolex, he was definitely a man; and in the juvenile hall he'd be lucky to end up in; and, if he wasn't lucky, in the inside pages of a sensationalist newspaper. Maybe even in *La Noticia*. There he would qualify as a man, that is to say, as a statistic. I imagined the report Daniel or I or someone else on the desk might copywrite to inform the public of his lifeless body. "The dead body of a 17-year-old man was found early this morning on Route 52 along kilometer 15. Known as José Pérez, alias 'Bimbi,' a resident of Los Lirios Housing Project. His body was found with four bullet wounds in his chest and another behind his left ear." And then reports from police officers, witness testimonies, possible motives for the crime, before moving in a flash to another item about another dead body, eighteen or twenty years old. Our daily bread. I began to feel sorry for the poor kid, began to sympathize with him. In the final analysis, he wasn't to blame just because he was passing for a man at such an early age.

"That's your chair, and this is mine. We put the room keys on these hooks. At the end of the hall is the pantry, where we store the bottles for the clientele. And those are the cabañas of the illustrious Motel Tulán, the first one over here and the last one next to the hill there."

It wasn't me who was reciting those instructions, it was nostalgia for Tadeo taking hold of me. In his absence, the affection I had for him seemed even more tangible, a profound camaraderie I had never felt before for another man. Perhaps it was that we had much more riding together than I usually had with people in my life; something more than my reputation, or some money I didn't really have to have, because my parents or my family could always get me out of a tight spot. Now I had something far more serious at stake, here, in this motel, with Tadeo as my ally. Since I met him my previous life didn't count anymore, nor did the risks I'd taken before. Now my life was that of a man living precariously, with far fewer safety nets. And that's why Tadeo covered my back and I covered his. There was nothing more to it. Without him around, I was exposed to the elements.

To top it all off, this mutant of a man, who probably couldn't even kill a fly, was sitting in Tadeo's chair. It was unsettling whenever he asked, with a lewd leer, "So when does the action start, partner?" as if the job was like a sneak preview of a new porno flick. I tried to explain to him the art of motel work the way Tadeo had done for me. Not to call attention to himself, to try to be invisible, use his peripheral vision; maybe it was better to take off the watch so as not to provoke unnecessary temptations. "I put it on today to show it off today, bro. No, no, no. Whoever fucks with my Rolex fucks with me, get it? I'll be all over them in no time. And just in case . . ." Bimbi lifted his seven-times-too-big shirt, his personal favorite. There it was shining in the semidarkness, the butt of a .45.

I said no more. I couldn't say any more because I didn't want to blow a fuse, hurry out to my car, and leave the motel at the mercy of a child whose delusions of manhood grated on my nerves. Instead I stepped outside to the corner to gaze down the entrance ramp, pretending to be on the lookout for the coming clientele. I lit a cigarette and began to smoke. I would take the first arrival, the second, and the third. I would take them all even if it meant a discrepancy closing the register because Bimbi had gone through it. I would keep him out of reach of our guests. I could only imagine the trouble up ahead if he came on to one of the female escorts by making eye contact, gave some gay man with his lover a strange look, or offered himself to a lesbian couple. Then the shit would surely hit the fan, since it wasn't likely he was the only armed person in the motel that night.

The night's first couple arrived.

"Bring me the key for cabaña eight," I yelled at Bimbi from my corner. He immediately disappeared into the office and hurried back with the key ring in hand. Smiling, he peered over my shoulder to get a good look at the couple.

"Let me know what happens, *macho*, when you get back."

"Keep a close watch on the register and call me right away if another guest arrives."

"Where should I put them?"

"Who?"

"The next guest, what room should I put them in?"

I waved my hand and went to take care of the last couple, who had already been waiting in their car for several minutes. If Tadeo could see me. People never had to wait when the two of us were here. We had become a precise and silent machine, leading the adulterers to the rooms where they could hide out, without making them linger, without their hearing even so much as a hint of our voices. Everything was ruined by the intruder, interrupted by lazy workmanship. I was thrown off a bit, and the key got stuck in the lock. The guests (a man with the face of a medical supplies salesman, and a woman who was most definitely a secretary, judging by her long red hair and the stains around her fake nails) had to ask me how much the room was because I almost went back without charging them.

"How was the woman? What she do when you opened the door for her?" Bimbi assaulted me with questions as soon as I sat back down. I brushed them aside.

"Don't fuck with me, little boy. This is just like any other job. Why would I check out the women who come here?"

"What, you've never hit on a woman who wasn't satisfied with her trick and sent them off but still wanted more?"

"Not one," I lied, remembering the touch of cold fingers on my hands and the vision of millions of tiny mysterious wrinkles that had made me act so crazy. Where could M. be? Would I never see her again?

Once again, Bimbi broke the silence.

"Tadeo left this afternoon."

"I know that. He didn't want me to take him to the airport."

"He couldn't let you. Chino sent somebody for him, luggage and all."

"I hope nothing happens to him."

"Are you in love with that Dominican or what? Nothing's going to happen to him."

"What would you know about it?"

"More, my friend, than you think. My cousin Culey was a mule, Pezuña was a mule. If anything I envy that guy Tadeo. You get tons of loot for the little trip."

"But if you get caught, you're going inside."

"If they catch you here, if they get you there, the trick is not to let them catch you. Everything else is just geography."

Another uncomfortable silence arose between us. An ambulance blared in the darkness far away.

"But Tadeo is an illegal alien."

"And Chino knows about it?"

"I suppose he must."

"Truth is, he needs someone they can't trace back to him, understand? I offered to go myself."

"And why didn't he pick you?"

"Because I'm underage, and from Los Lirios, so they would immediately think of him. He wants me to wait until things calm down."

"There's less chance he'd be associated with an illegal alien."

"It's crazy the way those people are getting a piece of the action everywhere. I think they've already established a mafia here, well connected and everything. Those Dominicans are dope."

"They're like everybody else. They want to eat."

"I'm already eating, but what they're giving me isn't enough."

"And that's why you do your thing and they do theirs."

"For sure. But what about you, what's growling in your stomach that makes you work a job like this? You don't look like you're dying of hunger."

"Depends on what kind of hunger you mean."

Bimbi's cell phone rang. It was Chino Pereira. I don't know what instructions he was giving Bimbi, but they were short, just enough to make arrangements with a few monosyllables. Yes, no, and then the silence of consent. I took advantage of the sudden calm to take a break from my partner. The empty night spread out in all directions and the company drained it even more. The buzz of generators and crickets overwhelmed the quiet suburbs. I touched my hand and realized it was damp. The humidity of a tropical night, the steaming broth that so many of us solitary, empty beings swim in.

A hand on my shoulder brought me back to Bimbi's annoying company. With a smirky smile, the little runt held out the cell phone for me. I looked at him with an expression on my face as empty as the night.

"Take it, man. Chino wants to talk to you."

Chino Pereira. For me. He wants to talk. On the other end, a voice made out of I don't know what—some sort of thickly chopped grain or hollowed-out cement—greeted me.

"How are you, my man? How are things going at the motel?"

My mind was somewhere else. I was thinking, for example, that my words needed to sound as precise as did that strange faraway voice inviting me into a conversation. Every word had to fall cleanly off my tongue, without stammers, doubt, embellishments, or exaggeration. So I lied.

"Everything's fine. Bimbi is a huge help." Why complain? To prove I couldn't handle the situation, or take charge of a tadpole who thinks he's a big macho?

"You remember the invitation I made a while back?"

To tell the truth, I didn't. To a party, a restaurant, or a bar? No, Chino was not one of those who busy themselves with the same fatuous and repetitive rites of the "leisure class." He, like a lot of other men, had to be the type who takes advantage of every opportunity to strike a deal. The rest of the time he spends with his family (which Chino didn't have) or his women. Perhaps a Sunday at the beach jet-skiing and knocking back beers with friends. Where did Chino Pereira invite me so long ago, such a little while ago, a dazzlingly short time ago, on the day several centuries ago when he bewitched me in between clouds of marijuana smoke?

"There's a *tambor* this Sunday. You said you had never gone to one, so you're going to this one. I'll pick you up around four in the afternoon. Leave the address with Bimbi." From me, another monosyllable. From him, the dead sound on his cell.

An evil tremor surged through my blood. I decided not to think, not even say a single word. To verbalize anything at a time like this is to lose control. And the last thing I needed at the moment was even more vulnerability, especially in the face of that alpha male, Chino Pereira, who even from afar could make the blood in my veins boil. I, who felt like a puppy waiting for a caress or a smack from its owner, couldn't let myself believe that this tremor was a mirror of my lack of control. No hesitation now, at least nothing visible.

At the other side of my silence, Bimbi was running his eyes over the day's papers. "Because, bro, what with all the *gatas* calling, it ain't until evening that I can find out what's happening around San Juan, USA, *ciudad de la melaza*." Bimbi was another loyal servant of the dead leaves, like so many others who believe what they read in those pages, who believe they are undoubtedly keeping abreast of the times by reading those scribbles, a pile of words bent out of shape and blown off course. Immersed in his task, Bimbi's face changed; he no longer looked like a pint-sized macho dressed as a hit man, but rather like a child watching cartoons. But maybe, I thought, for Bimbi the newspaper represented something else, a type of action movie–obituary schedule. Something like a *TV Guide* that every so often threw in the names of those, like himself, who had risked life and limb in the war of the streets, but who, by the magic of ink and paper, reemerged wrapped in soft focus, as famous as outlaws, through a kind of magic only children and those far from the life can invest with a sort of fuzzy luminescence. The newspaper, a television on paper, a way to kill time for those not yet killed by time, illuminated

Bimbi's face, giving off a strange light. Bimbi amused himself looking at the photo of "Today's Girl," the new ad for the latest supermodel calendar, a special offer for Pampers for his kid or nephew, the air-conditioning specials—"For the heat, bro, with my next paycheck I'll buy one for *la vieja*"—and the gossip about politicians and entertainers. In between the lines, there was the latest installment of the daily feature: accident casualties, carjackings, the war on drugs. Dreaming about the other outlaws, Bimbi looked to see if he recognized any of the day's dead or captured and vicariously shared their fifteen minutes of fame with them. Fifteen minutes, the time it took to draft that kind of news story.

Through Bimbi I learned that another generator in the Palo Seco power plant had blown up, and that this new act of "terrorism" was being blamed on union members. The threat of a strike became ever more real. Unionists announced their disagreement with certain representatives in the negotiations, doubting their honesty at the table. The brotherhood's spokesman argued that sabotage of electrical equipment was a government tactic, which used agitators on the inside to discredit the union's governing board. But rumors were still circulating that certain high-ranking union officials represented different interests than those of the collective agreement. There on the front page was, among others, Efraín Soreno, union lawyer and star suspect of labor relation treason. In his statements, obviously, he denied everything.

"Look at the state of this country. Two-bit attorney by day, all front. And by night, he sniffs line after line of coke at some dealer's house."

"Don't fuck around, Bimbi."

As his sole answer, Bimbi noisily crumpled up the paper, which crackled between his fingers like something dried up and dead. Pointing at the photo with his nail-bitten finger, he added:

"That one is our customer."

"And a client here," I answered.

"So he's a womanizer too. He who paints can also peel. Who does he bring here?"

"Others from the union."

"Must be to do all the stuff he gets from us. Maybe he likes to come down by blowing up a few generators."

"All he buys from you is coke?"

"From us, yeah. What else is a lawyer gonna buy from us? Heroin, crack? No, bro, white boys don't touch anything else. Their thing is coke. If they like to go to discos, then a hit of LSD. Nothing more. They end up hooked to the gills and head off to Betty Ford, supposedly for problems with alcohol. But check it out: we once had a rich client, also a lawyer, who decided to shoot shit up. They don't last long, and they don't really buy that much. Soreno is a big fish. He bites a lot, constantly."

"So only a client."

"Far as I know. He could also be one of the partners, nobody says he ain't. You know, man, I'm just rank and file. They only discuss certain things in front of me. But that's going to change faster than you could imagine. You'll see. When Bimbi starts to rise, he'll rise like foam."

I started to think about soap bubbles, and how easily they pop in midair. Bimbi took a cigarette out of his pack and started sucking on the filter nervously, like a starving infant attached to his mother's sore nipple. The smoke disappeared like a shapeless, murky bubble without substance. I decided to join Bimbi in his habit. I lit my own cigarette and we began to wait for the next guest while we read the arabesques pouring out of our lungs. I don't know about Bimbi, but nothing was revealed in mine.

I couldn't stop going over the new information about Efraín Soreno. Regular client, perhaps even in cahoots with Chino Pereira. Unsettling how we ended up tangled in the nets of power without even realizing it. Where did Chino's power end? How many more men were on his payroll, each one not suspecting the other? Bimbi, Tadeo, myself, Efraín Soreno and the union officials, maybe even M. Or maybe it was the other way around. Maybe it was Efraín Soreno who wielded the real power, who secretly and with the simplest act of his unconscious will had us all trapped in this web of misadventures. Me, Tadeo, playing with destiny somewhere up in the air, the same way other people with power had forced him to risk his life in the middle of the ocean. Maybe not even Chino Pereira could escape the pernicious influence of those who wield power, the ones who have no need to get blood on their hands, or even ink; who have no need to amuse themselves watching the paper sold at the city's crossroads by boys whose smog-contaminated lungs advertise each headline as the plain and simplest version of the truth. They don't have to: they have the power and they always find a way to pay or force others to get their hands dirty, with blood, ink, or with the terrible weight of lead and paper.

There were no other guests that night. The silence became oppressive, as if charged with foreshadowings and bad intentions.

Not even the secrecy that we offered for a reasonable price at the motel was enough to provide a shelter for those simmering under the suburban night. Far away, on the hills surrounding Route 52, several shots were fired. Bimbi and I weren't alarmed. It was like listening to a *coquí* or a cricket or anything else that goes bump in the night.

"Forty-four caliber," Bimbi whispered.

"What's that?"

"How much do you wanna bet those shots were from a forty-four caliber? Dare you. I haven't lost a bet like that yet. Not even Pezuña, who's in charge of Chino's arsenal, beats me at guessing the caliber. How much do you wanna bet?"

"You play this game frequently?"

"What a stupid fucking question. Where do you think I grew up, in a gated community? In Los Lirios, since I was eight years old, all the kids played it. That's how I bought my first lunch box. So how much you wanna bet?"

"Not me, Bimbi. I know when I'm in the presence of greatness."

"That's smart. Oh, before I forget, give me your address. It's for Chino, he personally asked me to get it. Seems he likes you."

This he said with a mixture of envy and malice. I looked him squarely in the eye. Not to intimidate him, but I think that's how Bimbi took it. In reality, I was looking for information, trying to get past his eyes, to see if this poor thing in pants knew something I didn't. If perhaps he had the answer that would somehow explain my reaction every time I was near Chino Pereira. Maybe the same thing happened to him. The heightened pulse, the mixture of attraction and fear. Or maybe he knew how and why

187

Chino Pereira managed to make me feel what I felt and could explain the dealer's motives. Why this sudden interest in me? What did Chino Pereira want with me, with this pale and gangly ex-editor, a white boy fallen on hard times? What was my role in his plotting and intrigue? Was I prey or bait? I was out of it after fielding so many questions, but to my surprise, my needy look had the opposite effect on Bimbi: he was intimidated. And Bimbi, the armed and nervous mini hit man, stuck his tail between his legs, and avoided my gaze. Mine, my gaze, not commanding or threatening at all, neither confident nor controlling, but longing, lost, and shipwrecked. The crossed wires were finally working in my favor.

Bimbi got up from Tadeo's chair to contemplate the night and stay out of my sight.

"Don't leave without giving me your address. He's picking you up at four." He exhaled the smoke into the night air and in a hushed voice, added, "Don't cross that dude. You don't have to be smart to figure that out."

Oró, Moyugba

What do you wear to a *tambor*, a drumming ritual, a religious ceremony? I definitely would not be dressed in white. I didn't want to look like a believer, but I also didn't want to look like I wasn't one. Meaning I wanted to camouflage myself, but not blend in: to be outside while staying in. Being Puerto Rican, that is, an islander, means something but only to a point: I deny my blackness, and I'm white without assuming the role. A half-breed, half of something, the double's double. Which is just to say that I'm used to wandering through a maze woven across oceans by hungry monarchs: European monarchs, African monarchs, gringo monarchs. It's hard living in a labyrinth built over the water, one that promises an escape route through Europe, another through Africa, another through New York and another through Asia.

Even harder yet when you no longer carry the torch of nostalgia. That's what my deal was. I wasn't carrying the torch. I never wanted to be Spanish, African, French, or Chinese. I never felt like reneging on the heat and going to live in New York. I mean, I never wanted to be a gringo, even though the vast majority of the Caribbean does. In that, we are no different from the rest of the planet. But really, the fact that I don't want to embrace the red, white, and blue and its badge of modernity, productivity, and progress does not mean that I want to be *Caribbean* Caribbean. Which is to say, an *authentic* Caribbean, you know, wearing the hat and praying to the gods of the earth, living off what I fish out of the sea. It's too late for that. The mix of peoples is too great, the labyrinth too large. I don't want to be authentic. Never did. That's why I now found myself with the dilemma of not knowing what to wear to a fucking *tambor.*

I nervously checked my scant possessions—the stretched and partial pairs of socks in the drawers, the three tattered rags hanging in my dilapidated closet—to see if I had a clean, presentable shirt to wear to the *tambor.* As I searched between the hangers, my head was filled with images from that old horror movie, *The Serpent and the Rainbow,* scenes from a Discovery Channel documentary on voodoo, parts of *The Devil's Advocate,* with Al Pacino and Keanu Reeves, and bits of the ancient Michael Jackson video *Thriller.* And inside my head, the possessed, the witches, and the zombies were the most authentic things my mind conjured up as I grappled with the words *tambor* and *santería.* Films and television took the place of reality with infinitely more strength than any memory, story, or personal experience I might have had. And

I—who had spent two and a half years at a newspaper trying to build a more accurate and tangible image of the Caribbean than the one I had from my years in school (private) and college (in the United States), from the urbanized enclosure of my childhood—was now finding out that anybody knew more about this island than me. Drug dealers knew more, and so did illegal aliens. I opened my laptop and went online. Somehow, I had to be brought up to speed.

Rule of Ocha, *santería,* an Afro-Caribbean religion born on the same shores where I was born, from the blood and tears of the descendants of the kingdom of Ilé Ife, ethnic Yoruba, with influence from the Igbo, Ashanti, Hausa, Fula, Ewe, Congo, and Carabalí, mixed their pantheons with those of the poor Aryans, Rosicrucians, Masons, spiritualists, devotees of the Magnetic Stone and the One Spirit. And so were brought to life *Sarabanda,* Mother of Water, Mayombe Wood, the Madam, the Four Spirits, the Seven Lightning Bolts, the Guardian Angels, and the many Orishas of the Rule of Ocha. At least that's what the *santería* web page I accessed said. But all that anthropological exposition didn't calm my nerves. Or my ignorance. Or my sense of disconnect, the crazy compass of my life. There were a thousand more entries with information about the religion. Books, and more reference pages. Right there, at everyone's fingertips. Something that I supposed was mine from birth I had to learn about through the Internet. I was tempted to continue reading, but it wasn't the time to repair my millenarian ignorance. They would come for me at four in the afternoon, and I didn't want to make Chino Pereira wait.

I finally found a light shirt to wear along with the Gap chinos buried at the bottom of the closet. I had to look for the iron (did Daphne take it?), plug it in, turn on the fan (to counter the heat and avoid sweat stains on the clothes), and wait. How long had it been since I'd dressed in decent threads, in job-in-an-office clothes, fit for a man of my supposed social status, with a college education, a plan in life, and a mission? "The habit does not make the monk, but it identifies him," my mother used to tell me every time she saw me walking out the door in rags, with bags under my eyes. And I remember how, as a child, I was very composed and elegant. Thanks to her, of course. She would make me wear my Sunday best even to take out the trash. She had dressed me in my best clothes the day she made me accompany her to a medium. Doña Haydée, retired beautician and suburban medium extraordinaire. The knots of feathers and plantains she had hanging from her ceiling made my skin crawl. Candles, plaster saints, coconuts, and an unidentifiable aroma. The rustle of a deck of cards being shuffled on a table, hands covered with bulging veins, and the news that my father had a pregnant lover is all I recall from the visit. My hands started to sweat. Where had that memory of Doña Haydée, the beautician medium who had deciphered my mother's dark present and sealed the gloomy fate of my parents' divorce, come from? Because it turned out to be the truth. My father did have a lover and I a bastard brother. And after a visit to the madam, I had a lame family, a mother's desperate love during the week, and a distant, disgraced father on Sundays. I don't know my half brother. I've met him, but I don't know him. Sometimes I see him around and we acknowledge each other from afar, like two distant neighbors in a surreal suburbia, whose streets and picket fences are made of blood, but not shared or communal blood. Going to a *tambor* was to expose myself to dangerous premonitions. But canceling on Chino Pereira would seal my fate even more dangerously. My hands were definitely sweating for a reason, with or without the heat of the iron.

Chino stopped by for me at five after four.

"Ready?" was all he said when he called my house on his cell.

I looked out the window and there he was, the window down on his white BMW (how many cars did he have, in what colors?), while he turned off his cell. We spoke very little on the way to the *tambor*. I thought we'd at least smoke a small joint, but it seems the sacredness of the festivity did not encourage such activities. Two or three calls came in through Chino's cell phone, which he attended to with his characteristic no-nonsense brevity. In the meantime, Busta Rhymes boomed out of the BMW's stereo.

The trip was short. In the blink of an eye, an access-controlled gate, complete with electronic keypad and closed guard station, stood between the car and the *tambor*. Chino's driver punched in the correct code and the gate began to retract like a serpent's tail, or better, like the magic door which let Ali Baba and his forty thieves enter the cave where the treasure was hidden. Only this time the riches were spiritual ones, and we swift outlaws weren't forty thieves but three, if you could count me, regardless of the stretch, in this category.

I must admit there were wonders on the other side of the gate. Through the car windows, you could see house after house worth a quarter, a half, or a million dollars, with postmodern facades

(1930s neocolonial with glass walls and aluminum beams) and grounds expertly landscaped, skillfully blending ornamentals from Southeast Asia with the bougainvillea and lemon trees native to this country. I didn't expect this kind of scenery. I didn't expect to find European cars with the Euclid's logo from the bar association (scales, blind hand) on their license plates. Nor did I expect these carefully manicured suburban streets to serve as the stage for the beating of *Batá* drums, hosted as I was by a ruthless drug dealer. I don't know, perhaps the image of Doña Haydée's house was still too entrenched in my imagination. Perhaps the reek of candles, honey, blood, and rum, of plantains and feathers tied together on a shabby garage door, still informed my extrasensory experiences and always would. Maybe it was the movies. Or could it be there was another explanation for this scene? Perhaps drug dealing and *santería* were secretly acquiring professional status without anyone realizing it.

The house where the *tambor* was being held was the wealthiest in the entire subdivision. It was surrounded by two acres of land adjacent to a little hill dense with foliage, the remains of once open countryside, perhaps brimming with West Indian oak, flamboyants, and *tabonuco* trees. And right there were not one but two cement structures, offering shelter to the residents of flesh and blood as well as of spirit. The garden was a delight of red ginger, ferns, canary bushes, and Maltese Cross, teeming with white cockatoos, peacocks (yes, peacocks in the middle of the Caribbean), pheasants, roosters, and hens, all with their respective broods. Toward the back of the yard, there were two huge cages. Still in awe of my surroundings and to give some room to Chino,

I moved closer to one of the cages. It was inhabited by a family of spider monkeys. The other cage was even more spectacular because inside, gamboling around as if it were the most natural thing in the world, were a pair of deer, horns and all, who from time to time drew close to a small pool, full of goldfish, for a drink.

I had to rub my eyes. Where the fuck was I? In what part of the Land of Oz? In what circus mansion? Who, in their right mind, thought of collecting exotic animals in a two-acre backyard inside a suburb crisscrossed by avenues, bakeries, record stores, and car alarm shops? Or was it that these animals formed part of another, unbreakable code that I couldn't decipher and that was much more than simply voodoo, much more than merely religion, a code nourished on episodes of *Lifestyles of the Rich and Famous*, magazines, and the mythology of theater (carnal and religious), all of which were infiltrating the secret syntax to create a blend of distinct things: cement, peacocks, altars, professionals, cockatoos, and cell phones, all under a tropical sun? Which world am I in, which earth is it where I stand? Why is it spinning under my feet and I above it, when by the sheer tension of opposites everything should blow up into a thousand pieces, into earth, shadow, smoke, dust, and nothing, and then begin all over again? Without the horrors that we human beings commit.

A hand rested on my shoulder, a strong hand with wide, firm fingers. My nose detected an aroma of woodsy perfume; the corner of my eyes, a shiny Rolex on the wrist.

"Julián, don't get far away from me. You're new to this environment and the *tambor* is about to begin."

I stumbled along behind Chino Pereira. Like the white deer, he walked comfortably through that dreamland backyard as if he had been raised there, as if the titi monkeys and white cockatoos that perched on high-tension cables had always been his pets, and this, his concrete jungle.

"If a saint speaks to you and I'm not around, send for me. I'll interpret what they say." I was staring at Chino, more puzzled than ever. A saint speaking to me? Chino Pereira my interpreter, my spirit guide? In what language would the gods of the Yoruba pantheon speak to Chino as they traveled from the remote African heavens to enter the heads of their followers on this island? What hidden messages did they have about me that only he could decipher, and, wise interpreter that he is, make known when he saw fit? The thought of an Orisha appearing before Chino to talk about me—to expose my torments before everyone—ended up spooking me. I found myself absolutely without point of reference. Lost. Exposed to whatever might happen, with the harshest witness right in front of me.

Chino's driver began taking goods from the trunk of the car, and I helped carry them. Two trays of hors d'oeuvres, a gigantic red and black piñata stuffed with toys and surprises, a bag of pears and green apples. They explained to me that the *tambor* was for Obatalá, lord of heads, sacred mountain, just warrior; white is his color, white his merciful beard; it was in his and his children's honor this *tambor* was being held. That's what Chino Pereira— serious as always—explained to me. He went on with his lecture. From his mouth (his mouth) I learned that Obatalá's children are cerebral beings, keepers of a wisdom that comes straight from

Olofi Olodumare, creator of all that breathes in the heavens and on earth. And that Obatalá is Olofi's secretary on earth. But he bears a heavy cross. They say that Obatalá is also the creator of human beings, their actions and oppositions. That one night while finishing the mold Obatalá drank so much palm wine he lost his head and his concentration, and from the drunken Orisha's careless mold there sprung the maimed, the crippled, the albinos, the blind, the one-armed, and the freaks. That's why Obatalá's children cannot drink liquor or consume drugs of any kind. That's why they have to stay as far away from drunks as possible. Because they lose their head easily. Their heads are always two steps away from madness and mistakes: like my head. So it seemed that Chino Pereira had invited me to the ideal *tambor*. Were I a believer, an Orisha like Obatalá would choose to ride me as his horse.

Inside the house, near the pool, a structure of wood and cement made a roof for the throne. It was a beautiful place. There's no other way to say it, even if I run the risk of sounding corny or simply clichéd. The throne room was pure beauty, something these eyes trained on harmony and platonic moderation had never seen before. It was as if a still life had exploded right in front of me. A still life somewhere between baroque and kitsch. Dozens of green apples and pears were scattered on the floor, surrounding four white cakes with sugar flowers decorating their edges like tiny islands. Bottles of cider and champagne completed the offerings. White grapes overflowed silver vases. Snowy tulles and satin fabrics, all white with silver borders, hung from the walls. More fruit was spilling onto the floor around the throne. There at the exact midpoint on top of an embroidered linen cloth was the mystery itself: Obatalá manifested in a china vase the size of a large urn. A handful of bead necklaces spilled down from the top. Necklaces with tiny coral beads adorned the vase in various spots. On the curtain behind the altar an insignia woven with silver threads took the shape of an incomprehensible arabesque, something like a coat of arms. Finally, hanging from the ceiling was a long animal tail, capped with a golden handle inlaid with beads of many colors, which gave an air of respect and sublime royalty to the whole arrangement. Obatalá, king of heads, lord of *orí*, white the color of his beard of mercy . . .

I didn't let my jaw drop because I still know how to fake it; in other words my mother taught me good manners that I still remember. Even so, the throne impressed me more than the pair of deer or the white cockatoos flying through the suburban sky. I don't know, it was as if everything was strangely familiar, as if I had just bitten into a piece of candy I'd never tried before, but beneath all the spices the distant flavor of something I knew, like a taste from my childhood, burst forth. I settled down little by little and, although I still felt out of place, the threat of dark premonitions no longer spooked me. I thought I had found something beautiful, something that in some strange way was conversing with me. Now that I think about it, I can't say exactly what came over me at that point. I let myself go with the emotion and the aesthetic sensibility that always kills me. I can't explain it very well. The only thing I know is that I calmed down and decided any dreadful premonitions were worth the trouble if they allowed me to witness the event.

Suddenly Chino threw himself to the ground, his head first, touching the floor. I was startled once again. Right in front of him, a short man, almost a dwarf, in high-heeled white boots, touched first one shoulder and then the other while uttering incomprehensible words in a loud voice, of which I caught only something like "*Didé*." Right away, Chino Pereira, the invincible, got up from the floor and crossed his arms over his chest, bowing first to one of the little man's shoulders and then to the other, before engulfing the little man inside his muscular embrace. After a brief, hesitant smile, Chino told me:

"This is my godfather, Ojuani Jekún." The little man stretched a ringed hand toward me and then continued with his ceremony of embraces. Music began to play outside. The *tambor* was getting under way.

It was an extremely long afternoon, filled to the brim with the dry sound of the drums bouncing off the remnant of the hill in Ojuani Jekún's compound. That tiny man was the hacienda's owner. The owner of the cockatoos, the *tití* monkeys, the pair of deer, and a fearful reputation that made him one of the island's most powerful *babalawos*, a skillful shaman when he needed to be and an infallible healer with thirty years as a recognized holy man, and another twenty or so in *Ifá*. Ojuani Jekún, black, small, powerful, had been the godfather to innumerable godsons whom he saved from sickness, jail time, and death. As payment for his services, he had received everything that now constitutes his lot. And today, his saint's day, he was giving infinite thanks to his father Obatalá, without whom he would still be an electronics salesman and numbers runner.

How can I describe the sound of those drums? The intricate variations in tone that flooded the air, shifting imperceptibly between songs? How can I describe the people who converged in that confusing place, full of all that was good and bad; kids, mothers, prepubescent girls, humble people, obviously from the ghetto, and professionals, maybe even neighbors of the powerful Ojuani Jekún, as well as drug dealers and professional musicians? And how can I count the times those drums resonated in my ears, or in my chest, when my eyes were closed, or with my eyes open and my hands pleading and upraised? And how the people prayed, their mouths repeating Yoruba chants and their bodies dancing in steps whose majesty has never been seen in films or documentaries. The atmosphere of a secular party, the jokes and fooling around that was not in the least bit holy, legs resting against the hoods of cars, cigarette butts on the floor, and bottles of rum lifted out of trunks, by people who came for the *tambor* with red eyes, their own party already under way. All of it was subsumed in the relentless presence of the sacred, which celebrated its arrival in that place. Children who tried to feed chips and Vienna sausages to the monkeys interrupted a matron who danced in honor of her mother Yemayá, asking for help in the face of approaching death. Everything together, everything mixed up, the body and spirit, the music and faith, sensuality and the distressed soul seeking solace. Everything was reflected in the feverish drums, solemn and joyous, never silent; by the chants in the language of dead slaves. The moving bodies and sweaty skins of dozens of their descendants, some white, some mulatto, some black, danced to the rhythm of music both earthly and sacred. The music was a heartbeat. In the ceremony of the drums, each beat counts; losing one beat of the music was like losing the pulse of life.

"They chant to Elegguá, the first and last, god of good fortune and pathways, and then to a string of deities: fresh water, seawater, wind, the inside of the earth, and fire. The *oró*, the first part of the *tambor*, is over," was how Chino explained it to me. "Now the newly crowned saints will be presented."

It was an endless line. There were thirteen or fourteen people recently born to their saint, all dressed in white, all walking escorted by men and women who were preceded by someone cleansing the path for them with water from a gourd. All of them had their heads shaved, covered with handkerchiefs, and, in their left hands, bracelets of colored beads which identified the angel who now ruled their heads, clearing the pathway for them and delivering them from evil. One by one they drew closer to the *tambor* with their eyes lowered, and once there they began their first dance before the congregation, their first full prayer with their bodies, offering not only their heads, but also their skin and their intestines as vehicles, horses for the saint to ride. The saint could ride them if he wanted, or use them as instruments of his eternal power, manifesting his primeval force through them: the forces of nature, fire, air, sea, wind, rain, all of them speaking through human tongues to the beings of this earth.

The ceremony we had come for started after that. I felt it immediately, that it had begun, because the air became charged with a different density. It wasn't the peace, the splendor, the faith of just moments before. It wasn't even the boisterous crowd surging and ebbing away at the *tambor*'s edges. It was something else, some other presence that came into the setting. The air started to get hot. Everyone was sweating.

The first drum beat, and then the second, and by the third someone far away began to convulse. A tightened face, eyes opening and closing uncontrollably. People formed a circle to keep the horse from escaping. An Orisha had chosen this person to show himself that night, right there, in Ojuani Jekún's garden of incongruous delights. A release of energy was unleashed in that person's body. A dark mulatto, very tall, one of the flock. The guy looked as strong as an oak but he was trembling like a leaf. Only the whites of his eyes were visible. The drummer got up from his seat and approached him. The singer shouted words of welcome in the ears of the possessed:

"Padre mío, eni o gbogbo so rojú, babá so rojú, babá so rojú."

"Come to this, your house," Chino repeated for my benefit.

Then, and only then, Obatalá came down to earth.

And then many Orishas came down. An incredible surge of energy that touched everyone.

"There go three Yemayás, one Ochún, one Changó," said one of the people with Chino.

"That's nothing, look who's coming."

Obatalá made another entrance into the ceremony. In all the confusion I hadn't realized some followers had carried the oak man, the one touched by Obatalá, to the back. Now they brought him back to the front decked out in full regalia. He was not the same. Now he was a god in the flesh, in all his magnificence, wearing a crown and a white satin suit with silver studs, his horsetail adorned with ribbons and collars, waving a cloth that removed the bad energy from those in need. The *tambor* did not stop, even for an instant. I exaggerate; the drummers would sometimes take a break and so there was a sudden silence. But the silence was so fleeting, it didn't quiet the booming of those three drums in my ears, in my chest, in some hidden part of my being, making my senses more alert than ever, more awake, without fear. No, I wasn't afraid. Curiosity filled up all the space left over from the *tambor*. And even though I didn't stray from Chino's side, it wasn't out of precaution, or to be under his influence. I stayed with him so I could ask him one thing after the other: what did that chant mean, which Orisha had just come down, what should I do when one of the trembling women jumped and crashed to the ground as they saluted the drummers? Because when that happened, people touched the floor reverently. And it was he, Chino Pereira, dealer by day and humble follower, who guided me through. His tongue opened the way for me more generously than before, as he deciphered the mysteries unfolding before my eyes.

"Who is your patron?"

"Patron?"

"Yes, your patron saint."

"You mean my guardian angel. Elegguá, god of the roads. And my mother is Oyá," Chino finished his explanation.

"And who is Oyá?"

"She who has charge of cemeteries."

Then what I feared happened. Obatalá walked straight into the corner where Chino and I were talking. The god covered me with his cloak and spun me around while he shook the cloth over me and then the horsetail adorned with beads. He passed his hands over his sweaty face, the sweaty face of his horse. I stared at those big hands, as hard as rocks. Wet with sweat, he ran his hands over my face.

After that Obatalá looked at Chino out of the corner of his eye. He didn't stand right in front of him. Nor did he speak to his face. As if he were speaking to some other presence, he growled:

"*Orí* will fall. *Gbogbo orí* will fall sooner than you think. *Meta orí* presage your fall. Stop veering people off their course. Don't continue, Omo Elegguá. *Ikú* walks behind you."

Obatalá repeated the same ritual with Chino he had done with me, plus he told him that another god, I don't know which, wanted a blood offering, a lamb. Where in hell was Chino going to get a lamb? That's what I would've asked, but Chino was not intimidated and he humbly promised to comply with Obatalá's request without delay. My face stung from the sweat of the saint, or of the saint's horse. That moisture—someone else's and unasked for—snapped me out of the trance. It seemed like the most disgusting thing that had ever happened to me, and my mind was once again crowded with scenes from horror movies and our visits to Doña Haydée's place. I couldn't even hear the drums anymore. By then all I wanted to do was to go home, to shower and wash the sweat off my face with lots of soap and a sponge. The man's perspiration was unforeseen and invasive. I didn't understand what that was all about, and I didn't want to know. Whatever the reason the saint had to sweat on me, no one had the right, whether secular or religious, to invade another person's cleanliness. Wasn't my own sweat enough? I had to be forced to mix it with someone else's?

A long-haired woman touched by Yemayá began to dance with a bucket of water in her hands. She walked halfway out in the backyard, emptied the bucket, and came back in, setting the bucket down on its face. That ritual marked the end of the *tambor*. My face was still stinging. I wanted to go but Chino told me we had to wait for the food. Plus, he had to consult with his godfather about the proper time to sacrifice the lamb to Ochosi.

"That's the saint that asked you for a sacrifice?"

"Yeah, that's him. You stay here with Gabo. I'll be right back. As soon as you finish eating, we'll go."

With the excuse of having to use the bathroom, I slipped away to wash my face. I couldn't deal with the itching, or with that damp sensation anymore. It was all I could think about. But en route to the bathroom I bumped into someone I knew, a friend of my father's. An attorney, like my father. The guy smiled at me, then looked serious, and then confused.

"Don Vicente?"

"Julián, how are you?"

We exchanged nervous greetings. We made small talk, superficialities, nothing that would give away our discomfort at running into each other at such an odd place, such an unlikely place for "our class of people." I couldn't stop asking myself what Don Vicente Hernández, attorney at law, my father's colleague, was doing at the *tambor*. Wasn't this for the initiated, for the poor inhabitants of the slums, still caught in the primitive web of superstition? How many more white collars would be here, asking for a favor from their guardian angel like all the others, promising lambs, hens, candles, raising their prayers to the African powers from far away? How many of those present also lived in this closed-off suburbia, members of the island's highest spheres, which Ojuani Jekún had slipped into thanks to favors from his godchildren? How many of his godchildren were doctors, businessmen, attorneys? And how many were drug dealers? Pretending to follow the conversation with Don Vicente, I took a look around. And I discovered more familiar faces. One faith, a thousand roads, a thousand skin tones, a thousand social classes, all present, all out of place. This *tambor* was turning into another maze.

"Well, Julián, give my regards to your father."

Then I realized that my father's friend was looking at me, equally puzzled. And Don Vicente, what must he have been thinking about my being there?

When I got back to Chino's sidekick, he was waiting for me with a full plate of food in his hand. I couldn't refuse. Goat and chicken fricassee, white rice, black beans, salad, cake. Inside somebody was handing out fruit, the fruits from the throne. Kids clamored around Chino, who broke open the piñata and shook it so that candy and toys were evenly dispersed to the loud swarm of children pulling at his pant legs. I sat down on the edge of a flower stand to eat and counted the minutes to my return home.

Back in the car, Chino became even more taciturn than before. I doubted whether I should break the silence around him. But now that my face was clean and my stomach full, my curiosity came back, along with the sheltering peace that had surrounded me while in the presence of Obatalá's throne. I worked up my nerve.

"Chino, tell me, what does *orí* mean?"

"Head."

The translation for *gbogbo orí* was "many heads."

"And *meta*?"

"Four."

"What about *ikú* or *irú*, however you say it?"

"*Ikú* is death." Chino was looking away as he answered.

* * *

"Many heads will fall. Four heads mark the fall of yours. Death walks behind you." That was how I deciphered the saint's message. I didn't feel like asking anything else.

Chino Pereira's cell phone rang. A few monosyllables. It was Pezuña. He called to let Chino know there was a problem with the operation: Tadeo had been stopped by Customs in Miami. They had him locked up. The shipment was lost. Chino told me all this as if he were relaying the latest ups and downs of the stock market. And I, with the echoes of the drums booming inside my chest, felt an incredible desire to cry.

The first head had fallen.

The Saint Disappears

"So now you know, bro. Don't worry, I don't feel bad. I had to pay my dues one day. Take care of yourself. And don't forget about me."

"Tadeo, we must be able to do something. Maybe Chino can."

"You're barking up the wrong tree, brother. Chino is going to stay far away from all of this."

"And what if you help the investigation?"

"So they kill me when I get out, or even worse, while I'm in here? No, Julián. I'd better grin and bear it."

"We have to do something. Chino told me he saw some chances."

"You do whatever your conscience tells you. I've got to get off the phone soon. We're running out of time."

"Tadeo—"

"Take my confession. Maybe it will help you with that book you're writing."

* * *

It was on the ocean that Tadeo became lost. The man steering the boat swore to everyone on board that he knew the way by heart, but he seemed incompetent. "I'm no sailor. I like to keep my feet on dry land, big fella, where what's underfoot doesn't move," Tadeo said to me. Those mountainous black waves rising from the bottom of the sea drove him mad.

Thunder crashed and the wind blew. It wasn't cold but a high wind was soaking them to the bone, drenching them in sea salt. There were eleven of them. Only one woman, which is odd, because these days most boat people are female, although they don't set out for Puerto Rico. Women go even farther, to Spain, the Netherlands, far away, where nobody can see them do whatever they have to do to survive and send a few bucks back to their families, who if they saw them doing what they do, would stop speaking to them. Distance makes any kind of money look clean.

They thought they would never get there. Not one buoy light could be seen, not even the Mona Island Lighthouse, which was the halfway mark. At times the light on the bow disappeared under a wave. The woman began to scream. At first, Tadeo thought it was out of fear but then he heard shoving, panting, and more screams. He looked down where the woman had settled hours before. And he saw a pile of bodies on top of her.

"There were four of them. Pedrito, who had left Baní with me,

210

grabbed one of her legs. Another one who claimed to be from Montecristi had her by the hands, and the poor thing had the fourth one on top of her, his pants halfway down. You could only see the guy's buttocks thrusting and pulling back, and you could hear her screaming for help, for the love of God. The rest of the boat was dead silent; the air was full of foreboding and disaster. I don't know, bro, it was as if any moment something far worse was going to happen. We felt condemned to death.

"The others looked out to sea, at the huge waves of that inferno of water rising and falling, the guy's buttocks rising and falling, and somebody passing a bottle. The eyes of the boat's captain were fixed on the waves, looking for anything, hoping maybe by some miracle he could make out a light in the distance. He stopped just to yell, 'Hey, *tigeres*, see you keep your voices down for shit's sake, you're making me nervous.' And the young woman went on screaming like a cow in a slaughterhouse.

"I couldn't take it anymore. Staggering and tripping I made it over to where the young woman was. The third one was already on top of her, and was biting down on her mouth. I began to push. I was gonna save her, I had to save her. Someone had to do something for her.

" 'Damn, man, what if it was your sister, or your mother?'

" 'I'd fuck her all the same,' Pedrito answered. 'I don't mind dying if I'm fucking a beautiful brown-skinned bitch when I go.'

"Then she looked at me. Her terrified eyes were filled with tears, and her face . . . I can't describe her face. It wasn't human. It was the face of someone who had been human, but wasn't any longer. Someone who would never be human again."

A fire began burning inside Tadeo's body, rage and desperation for all the work he'd done just to end up as a meal for a shark
at the bottom of the ocean. He had pawned his mother's furniture, her pots and pans, the little wedding band which was the
only reminder he had left of his old man, all so he could go in
search of a better life. And this was how God paid him, with this
coin made of black water full of monsters waiting for his flesh.
This hell of salt.

"I wasn't going to let God take my flesh just like that, tender,
soft, free of all sin. If something was going to be forcibly taken
from me it was my own kindness. Death would have to get its
hands on me as corrupt as they come."

The boat pitched harder and harder on the waves. With one
hard shove, Tadeo pushed Pedrito off the woman and, hard as a
rock, climbed on top of her. She didn't know what to do. Her
moist and warm flesh was like a grave in which Tadeo alone was
going to bury himself. He thrust inside of her two or three times,
and she looked at him with the most sorrowful eyes in the world.
He couldn't finish. His conscience awoke. He pulled her out from
under him and grabbed his head savagely over and over again
with both hands. The woman crawled behind Tadeo and sat there
sobbing. Tadeo pulled out a knife he had in his pocket, a switch-
blade, and stared at the other men in the boat, the scream for
blood sounding loud and clear.

" 'Whoever touches her will take this knife in his gut down to
the bottom of the sea,' I shouted defiantly. Nobody else bothered
her. I opened and closed the blade thinking it should be me who
gets it in the gut. I swear on my mother I did."

He didn't know how much time went by. The storm slowly died down. They were still lost, but exhaustion and shock made them nod off. The boat smelled of vomit, alcohol, blood, and spilled semen. Everyone, save the captain, fell asleep. Until a siren woke them up.

"It was a ship from the coast guard. They were arresting us, taking us back to Santo Domingo. It was all the same to me. I couldn't care less whether I was dead or alive. But all of a sudden I thought of my mother's face, when she saw me coming back after losing everything, everything of mine, of ours, for a caper that I dragged her into even after she tried to resist: 'Don't go, my little angel. Don't go in that boat, because if you come back to me with your belly swollen with seawater my heart will just stop beating.'"

The coast guard crew had their megaphones out, and they ordered the captain to pull the boat alongside theirs. The little waves the ship made put a smile on Tadeo's face. The roll of the sea would never again make him afraid.

They arrested everyone. Everyone but the young woman. When they were being led off the boat, Tadeo looked toward the bow because he wanted to help the girl. To apologize to her and ask for her forgiveness, and beg her to accuse each and every one of them. But she wasn't there. Nobody saw her disappear. Perhaps she felt safer at the bottom of the ocean, where the waves could give her a sharper and trustier blade than Tadeo's.

"Sometimes I even think we imagined her. But no, a shoe, a bag of clothes proved she was there. I haven't told anyone about this, *titán*. But locked in here, I'll explode if I don't get it off my chest. I'm telling you. That's why I'm not complaining about getting caught. Maybe it had to happen. I had to pay somehow. God gave me plenty of chances to take care of my debts and I couldn't do it. So this is how the bill arrives.

"Don't worry about me, really. I'll get out of this somehow. And who knows, maybe we'll even run into each other somewhere, at the cafeteria maybe. The waves have smoothed out at last. I feel cleansed of the guilt I was carrying, which was making me do things I couldn't justify. I don't know if it'd be worth it to try and be different now, to live another way. Maybe you can come and visit me. (After six in the slammer, don't forget.) To tell the truth, I'd really like it if you came. And I swear to that motherfucker God, that by then the house in Baní will have electricity in every room."

On the other end of the line, I swallowed hard and kept quiet.

Diary Entry

I know he's here in one of these rooms. After picking that man up, he came here. He couldn't go to another motel, he couldn't shake me loose. He doesn't know the car I'm driving. That's why I rented it. That's why I leave mine at home and escape in a cab to rent another car, so if any of his friends or go-betweens pass by the house they'll think I'm still in there, waiting.

But no. I'm here, in one of these rooms, doing what he does behind the walls close by. Just as he does. Betrayal. Living a lie similar to his. Plotting a way to get rid of him. But I'm not leaving his world without first getting some payback. First this carefully planned scheme, then the next.

For all the nights in which he left me alone, for all the lies and all the half-truths, for all the times he made me feel less than a woman, for the lie he forced me to live with to cover himself, so that he could go on being lord of the manor, the most high and mighty. For all those other times, this is my vengeance. Without mercy. . . .

Light and Asthma

"Strike." A single word in every headline. More inside, in the new pages. The Power Authority had decreed what everyone feared. Starting at noon Wednesday, the island would be without power.

The city was a chaotic mess. People were taking money out of the ATMs, running to the hardware store to buy generators, filling their tanks with gas, going shopping, double-checking their savings account. The masses lost their heads, running out of stores with more than they intended to buy: mascara, towels, canned goods, as if a hurricane were heading their way, as if those articles could, by some strange magic, provide comfort while the city went without power and therefore without life. People bought batteries to run the games they played to pass the time, the portable radios, mini televisions. They filled their shopping carts with dozens of packages of batteries in every size, afraid that the silence would swallow them up like a wild beast and then spit their bones into the open night. A national work stoppage was declared. Negotiations came to a halt. The island was left to its own devices.

To top it all off, labor attorney Efraín Soreno was nowhere to be found. On page two of the paper there was a quarter-page photo showing Efraín Soreno and his family. Police sources said his whereabouts for the last four days were unknown. He hadn't shown up for union meetings on Friday; no one knew where he was. His wife (second from right) had told authorities he hadn't come home Friday night. They had been having marriage problems for some time, so she didn't make much of it. The photo, in black and white, showed two girls, and a dark, long-haired woman with deep-set eyes surrounded by millions of tiny wrinkles. Definitely, without a doubt, it was M.

The photo shocked me like an electric charge. At last, confirmation. In her papers M. kept mentioning an Efraín, that Efraín, like an unreachable spirit. So, that Efraín was Soreno. And then the Motel Tulán was never a hideout but rather a place for plotting and intrigue. Perhaps they had both ended up there by chance, she looking for a moment of peace, and he using it as a base of operations. But then she caught him and began to plot her revenge. I had read it myself. In the last fragment of her papers there was a short note, full of rage, in which she vowed to make Soreno pay the bills. But then, what was the connection with Chino Pereira?

Why wasn't he showing any signs of life? He was also nowhere to be found, although no newspaper reported the fact.

I didn't sleep well at all. News of Tadeo's capture in Miami put me on edge. I moved about clumsily. Every time I tried to move around the apartment, I only managed to bump into walls and tables. My thighs and my arms were covered with bruises. The night we drove back from the *tambor* Chino told me to call him, to see what he could do to help Tadeo. I had also received a call from Tadeo. A call with a terrible revelation. Since then I had been trying to get in touch with Chino. I called him on his cell phone. It was the only number I had for him. But he never answered. A day went by after I called. I called again. A voice informed me his cell phone had been disconnected. He was nowhere to be found. Where could he be? Maybe harassing the partner in disgrace. Maybe dead next to the body of the labor lawyer. And in the meantime, Tadeo was dying of remorse in jail.

Three were missing: Efraín Soreno, Chino Pereira, Tadeo. And now the photo of the fourth one emerged in the halftone ink of the newspaper. The wife with the dry face, expressionless, holding on to the little girls' hands. And I had a hunch. Perhaps if I got in contact with M. I could get in touch with the lawyer, and through him, to the elusive drug dealer. Anything to save Tadeo. At least that's what I thought at the time, although in a secret part of my conscience I feared my intentions were different, that I was really just using Tadeo as an excuse to see M. again.

But this time I didn't let my imagination intimidate me. Chino had given me his word. He wouldn't abandon Tadeo to his fate.

And I would make him follow through. Although, what good was the word of a man like Chino Pereira? It could be as hard as mineral rock or as insubstantial as air. I didn't have the slightest clue.

I started to get dressed. I didn't feel like going to work. I didn't know whether the Tuláns had already heard about Tadeo, or if they had gotten a replacement to be my nighttime coworker. The uncertainty of new company made up my mind. Now was the time to quit. I had been so stubborn, so committed to staying at the motel, only to see everything dissolve and leave me with nothing to show for it but the bruises on my hands: a bruise from being abandoned, a bruise from a mysterious woman's body, the bruise from Tadeo's words still ringing in my ears, and the bruise from the wicked charge Chino Pereira unleashed in me. All these bruises still did not coalesce into the tapping on a keyboard. It was all empty, it was all a symphony of silences and scratches. No, I couldn't let things remain like this.

Then I received a phone call. The entire area around Route 52 had been without electricity since early that morning. And there was a problem with the emergency generator. The motel would be closed today. I was on call for tomorrow, when the technical difficulties would be resolved. The Power Authority was giving me the opportunity to get back in the thick of it that day, even if "it" meant the chaotic daily life of strikers. I wouldn't waste this opportunity. I changed from my inconsequential shirt of humble motel work to one from the old job. I ran down the stairs and set out for the newspaper.

Fortunately, Daniel was in his cubicle. I bumped into everything before finding my way to him.

"Julián, *muchacho*, what's up? And how are things? Better than around here, I hope."

"I wish."

"I still don't have any news about your old job. And now with the strike . . . all the reporters are covering the walkout. We're just here waiting to dot the *i*'s. The new boss is running around like he has three feet in every shoe."

"I came to ask you for a favor of a different kind."

"You came at a bad time."

"No, man, listen. I want to pick up Soreno's trail. I think I have information you might be interested in."

"Me? Why? I'm a lowly copy editor."

"Didn't you always want to be a reporter?"

"That was a long time ago."

"Well, I have an exclusive for you, in case you're still interested in getting off your ass and uncovering some truth."

Daniel looked me up and down suspiciously. Perhaps too much time had gone by and he had already thrown his dreams of becoming an investigative reporter into the trash. But when his eyes began to sparkle, I knew his dreams were still there deep down at the bottom. Or at least the illusion of recovering them was directing his gaze to the bottom of the trash. And the pile of garbage was me.

"What have you got? Weren't you working for a zoning agency?"

"You could say so. You have no idea what I found in there."

"What does it have to do with Soreno?"

"I'll tell you everything if you get me his residential address."

"He's not there."

"But his wife is."

"And what does she have to do with his disappearance?"

"Much more, I suspect, than people think."

Suddenly, the office lit up with the sound of fax machines, ringing phones, and the tapping of computer keyboards. The energy making all those devices work seemed to move sluggishly through the wires and outlets, as if what before had flowed effortlessly was now hard. I figured the paper had turned on its generator. Outside, you could hear cars honking on the highway and a deafening hum in the distance.

"Come with me."

"Where are we going?" I asked Daniel, but he replied by getting up, turning his computer off, and touching me on the shoulder to get me to move out of his way. I followed him quietly through the newspaper labyrinth until we reached the end of a hall filled with the smell of cigarettes, even though it was forbidden to smoke in the air-conditioned space. We ended up in a small office. There were no paintings on the walls, no plant life, or natural light. A hallucinatory tube cast a cold neon glow that distorted the contour of things and made them vibrate, as if they were also made of that strange energy. There was a shortwave radio, tuned to the police channel at full blast. At the end of the office, which felt more like a closet or a niche in a mausoleum, was a fat sponge of a man sitting in front of a phone and an overflowing ashtray, studying negatives with a magnifying glass. His name was Francisco Pedraza.

In my years at the copydesk I had heard talk about him. I think

I saw him two or three times, creeping slowly down the hall or getting into his car at the end of the day. We had never spoken. Few actually knew him. I didn't know Daniel was one of the privileged ones. But everyone at *La Noticia* knew his story.

Francisco Pedraza was the living image of a finished man. But strangely enough, he wasn't dead. He smoked constantly, in between cups of coffee, which was the only thing any human in *La Noticia* had seen him ingest in the years he'd been working there. And he had been there many years. Too many. From street photographer he'd moved up to chief of photography, and since then he hadn't gone out to take a single shot. Now he just sent his staffers to the scene, oversaw the cash "incentives" paid to the cops for information on the bloodiest accidents, and crawled from negative to negative like an inchworm, making sure the most shocking shots ended up in the paper. Since *La Noticia* set out to beat the yellow press competition, it kept publishing bloodier and bloodier photos. And the one responsible for the show was Pedraza. Nobody was better at picking the most repulsive shot. You could say Francisco Pedraza lived off roadkill trapped in acetate. Maybe that's why he lived like a cadaver.

They say he hadn't always been like this; that when he was younger Pedraza won international awards for his photography. As a photojournalist he was renowned on the island and abroad. But then he dedicated himself to covering crimes and dead bodies. The people at *La Noticia* say the move was simply a commercial one, but it was also due to the fact that as he reached the peak of his glory, Pedraza began to develop a strange affliction that started to eat at him inside, until he lost his way, his capacity to work with anything but death. He developed a case of full-blown apnea, one so acute that it was said he could die while he was sleeping because he simply might forget to breathe. Since then he has never been able to enjoy a full night's sleep. At the paper, they say that's why he smokes like a desperado, drinks coffee like there's no tomorrow, and always has the shortwave tuned to the police band. Even at home. I don't know whether he keeps it on to fight sleep with the noise or if maybe he does it to shock his own conscience with nightmares, making sure he'll never reach the deep sleep of the just.

"Since when are you breaking bread with Pedraza?" I asked Daniel in a hushed tone as we approached the desk.

"When you left, he became part of our coke circle, bro. Seems like coffee is no longer enough to keep him awake."

Pedraza got up from his seat and welcomed me by stretching out his soft, watery hand. I thought twice about shaking it. Over the sound of the radio I heard Daniel talking to him, agreeing on the next coke buy. They had to talk to Gutiérrez or if not him then with Palacios, but that was now kind of risky with the strike. Palacios worked for the Power Authority. So that made Gutiérrez the chosen one. I found the contact's name odd. It didn't sound like the one we used to use when I worked at the copydesk. No matter, in these times not even drug dealers keep their jobs long.

"I'll call him over the radio in his squad car," Daniel offered. To my surprise the new *La Noticia* supplier was a cop.

I was getting impatient. It seemed like neither Daniel nor Francisco Pedraza really cared at all about my presence in the office, and I wondered whether Daniel had forgotten the reason we were there, concentrated as he was in setting up the next coke delivery with his new partner in crime. The carefree conversation they were having over the ten-fours and the police announcing "Nine gun shots in Trastalleres" and asking for reinforcements, or reporting car thefts and accidents, was making me lose my footing. It all seemed like an imaginary show, a series called *Journalists in Action* that narrated the misadventures of a young, frustrated copy editor who tries to speak to his boss, who's already knee-deep in corruption, something like what my life could've been if I hadn't gotten fired from *La Noticia*. And Daniel, playing the role of his life, was the young journalist who sees an opportunity to redeem his soul. But he has to play his cards right, show he's not really interested, behave casually, not let on his real intentions, so that his boss, even though they share drugs, won't later give the leads to some other journalist with a bigger name. Hence all the aloof airs and all the small talk. Yes, that explained it. I recovered my composure and patience, and started seeing Daniel in a new light. I was even proud of his wit. Maybe that's why he still worked at the paper and I didn't.

"And Pedraza, by the way, do you know anything about Soreno's whereabouts?"

"Why are you interested in him?"

"You know I'm always sticking my nose in what's none of my business."

"Rehashing an old reporter's dreams. Believe me, Daniel, you don't want to be a journalist. Stay at your computer and learn about the monstrosities through the paper, like the rest of the world. Don't lose any sleep over going after the truth. It isn't worth it."

"So, what is?" I interrupted. I thought it was high time to intervene.

Francisco Pedraza looked at me from within the shadows, as if I hadn't been right there the whole time. For a moment I saw him focus his eyes, red from the smoke, searching for something back there, in the storeroom of his thoughts. He opened his mouth, like a fish out of water. And then he sighed loudly.

"I don't know. But it's better not to know. It helps you keep on living."

"Because it makes you stay in pursuit."

"Pursuit of what, the truth? The truth is what you have left when you're done drowning in nightmares."

"According to you."

"Yeah, according to me. Unfortunately, it's been a while since I have consulted higher authorities. Since I discovered those authorities also didn't have a clue."

"But back to Soreno . . . ," Daniel insisted, looking at me from the corner of his eye, as if sending me a warning.

"Look, Castrodad—that's your name, right? Lately my memory has been failing me."

"Call me Julián."

"Well, okay, Castrodad. Let me be bold and share something with you that's been on my mind. Truth does not exist; neither does reason, nor the logical order of the universe."

"I know that already." I was afraid this guy was going to un-roll the tired postmodern act on me.

"The only thing that exists is the experience of truth, and that experience is unique and nontransferable."

"Now we're fucked," Daniel whispered to me.

"What do you mean by nontransferable?" I replied, ignoring Daniel's whining. "What about literature, history, photography, this very newspaper?"

"Failed attempts from the start. All that crap is but a reason-able facsimile of what we'd like to pass for 'the facts,' or for what hides behind the facts."

"You're turning Platonic on me, Pedraza."

"No, not Platonic, my dear Daniel, because at least those mad Greeks were ingenuous enough to believe that by giving life to the copy, the Idea existed. The Platonic thinkers were able to exist because the world was still young. But now who can swallow that nonsense?"

"I disagree."

"That the Idea doesn't exist?"

"The Idea, like that, with a capital *I*, does not exist, thank God. We both agree on that. What I disagree with is that the experience of truth, the experience each of us live of the truth, cannot be communicated."

"Let me ask you something, Mr. Castrodad, does your life make sense to you? Don't you live it as if it were a lie, as if every-thing you lived was nothing but an obstacle to understanding that which lies beyond each fact, that which you don't notice but sense, and which builds a network of associations, an order underneath the one which makes you breathe, lie, seek other bodies, go to the bathroom, work?"

"Just about."

"Well, that search is the only experience that you have available of what could be called the truth."

"So then truth exists and can be communicated."

"As a pursuit."

"Yes, as a pursuit."

"The problem is that you end up losing yourself in the pursuit."

"And that's bad?"

"Sometimes it's a huge relief."

"Well, I hope you guys are done with the recommended dosage of office philosophy. Because I still return to the faithful rendition of truth and I would like to know, Pedraza, if you have any clues as to Soreno's whereabouts."

"Daniel . . ."

"Boss, I appreciate your concern for my mental and physical well-being, but I've been stuck in the copydesk dying of boredom for centuries. I didn't spend five years at the School of Communications and rack up two student loans I'm still paying off just to correct typos. My friend here says he's got some confidential info that could help me be the one who finds out what's up with the attorney right in the middle of a union strike. I don't know how or why he stumbled into this info, or what he gets by giving it up. I also don't care to ask. That's his experience of the truth. Mine is that if I don't make it out of the copydesk soon, I'm gonna start killing people."

The two of us laughed for a minute at Daniel's outrageousness while he seemed on the verge of pulling his hair out at any moment. The laughing made Pedraza abandon the philosophical fatalism of before. It wasn't that he was enlivened, that was impossible for him. But Daniel was making him forget about himself momentarily. For a minute I thought I knew why Pedraza was giving Daniel his time. Perhaps Daniel reminded him of the way he once was, when he was younger, or how he could've been, if he hadn't photographed so much blood, or lost his ability to get a good night's rest.

"And what is this clue your friend has, if I may ask?"

Daniel looked at me carefully. It was my turn to speak. So I told them everything.

"Everything" is an exaggeration, of course.

I had to choose, transform, and hide some facts. I didn't mention anything about Tadeo specifically. Nor of my job at the motel. In the version that suddenly came out of my mouth I ended up as a friend of Esteban Tulán Jr., for whom I administered the motel while he went on a badly needed vacation. I never had the affair with M., nor did I read her papers, but I did see her coming every Wednesday to the motel, meeting once with a mysterious lover, only once, and then disappearing from sight. I also didn't tell them how Tadeo ended up getting caught further and further in Chino Pereira's web, but it was him alright, without first or last names, transformed into a simple motel employee whom I had caught safekeeping drugs for Chino, who in turn would send one of his cronies every once in a while to pick up the stash at the motel. In my story I saw myself at the moral crossroads of deciding whether to tell the police, but I didn't out of loyalty to the owner who would return from his vacation any day. I would then inform him, and he could decide what was the convenient thing to do. I didn't want to assume a position of authority he hadn't delegated to me. I told them all this to get to the crux of the matter. And that I did narrate in all luxury of detail. It was the day, the night, I mean, in which I surprised those two cars parked at the bottom of the entrance hill, exchanging packages with lightning speed from window to window; the cars of both Soreno and Chino Pereira.

"That's what I got, my friends."

"Well, you got more than the police."

"You think so, Pedraza?"

"I'm sure of it," he said, pointing with a yellow, nicotine-stained finger to the shortwave radio. "What they know since about an hour ago is that Soreno is no longer in his car. They found an abandoned four-by-four out on a country road connecting to Route 52."

"The motel is on 52."

"The four-by-four is Soreno's."

"Bloodstains?"

"None. They're not ruling out a kidnapping. But nobody has contacted his wife or the union asking for ransom money, and that's not how they do kidnappings here."

"Could be he was supposed to meet someone out on that road. That he was running scared. Maybe whoever picked him up killed him as well."

"Could be. Who benefits if Soreno shows up dead?"

"The union."

"No, Daniel," Pedraza answered before inhaling a thick mouthful of smoke and washing it down with coffee. "Now, with the strike on, the union does not want one of its lawyers turning up dead, no matter what kind of trouble he's in or how much money he's embezzled. It's easier to make him a scapegoat and link him to the government."

"Pedraza, Daniel, maybe you didn't hear what I said," I interrupted anxiously. "It's obvious Chino Pereira is the one who took him."

"I doubt that very much, Castrodad," Pedraza replied calmly.

"What do you mean you doubt it?" I snapped back, somewhat upset. "Soreno was mixed up in some shady business. Maybe he used the union funds to maintain his coke habit, or maybe he was laundering money for Chino. Maybe he bought arms or explosives from Pereira, or just hired him to sabotage the Power Authority's transformers. Who else could be behind this?"

"Your interpretation of the facts is very good, Castrodad, but you're lacking in one particular."

"What's that, Pedraza?"

"Not too long ago some coke suppliers began to spring up inside the Authority. And the police already knew about it. Those inside the Authority took advantage of the strike to cease operations."

"Julián, I'll be honest with you," Daniel said, getting up from his chair. "When you came to my cubicle with Soreno's story I already had an idea about it. Through Pedraza and our connections I had noticed something was going on at the Authority. I thought the union was in on it because it seemed like too big a coincidence that a strike was declared just when a narcotics investigation was being waged on the agency's grounds. I didn't mention it to anybody but Pedraza, to see what he thought about me working the story on my own, so that they'd consider me for an investigative position. Now that you've come with Chino's story, everything falls into place. Soreno wasn't kidnapped or executed or anything. He's hiding out."

"But, Daniel, now is when he actually needs to hide the least. Now he's safer than ever."

"Castrodad has a point, Daniel."

"You think he was kidnapped?"

"No, Castrodad is also wrong about that. If Soreno owes money or if there was a falling-out between him and Chino, the dealer's not going to put a hit out on him when the entire country's eyes are fixed on the Authority and when the police are investigating the little business they've both got going."

"Well, then, where's Soreno?"

"He's with Chino," I insisted. I wasn't about to reveal that Chino was also nowhere to be found, that in fact I didn't care about Soreno in the slightest. He was just the bait I needed to get to Chino so that I could help Tadeo. And maybe also get to M. once again, to see her one more time.

Pedraza got up from his desk and moved slowly around the rectangular office. He emptied the ashtray, lit another cigarette, and looked at both of us like a teacher who can't solve a mathematical problem but who at least knows his students' theories are wrong, as if he had ruled out those theories centuries ago.

"There's someone here who wants everything to come out in the open, someone who wants the police to shut down the dealing, someone who wants to get rid of both of them, Chino and Soreno. The question is who?"

At that moment I hesitated over whether I should tell them what I'd discovered. But there wasn't another option. If I didn't, I would never get the attorney's address. And I had to see M., just had to. So I sat down, lit a cigarette, and, without a hurry in the world and with a careful heaviness in my chest, I told Pedraza and Daniel what I had read in M.'s papers.

The Coin

Today I tried to go to the district attorney again. I called ahead, made an appointment, bathed, got dressed, and took the car out of the garage with every intention of going into the office and waiting my turn. But all of a sudden I found myself in the DA's parking lot unable to leave the car. My face was burning. My hands were shaking. I burned rubber as I sped away, not knowing where I was going. I couldn't help but think, "This is not my life. My life is not like this, it can't be unfolding this way. This is some other woman's life." Once again I felt my mouth talking by itself, letting itself be overrun by tons of words independent of my will. In the heavy traffic I could hear myself saying: "Whatever happened to the silent understanding I had with Life? I wasn't going to ask for happiness; I would settle for a functional substitute. She, on the other hand, would leave me alone. And look what she's doing to me. Life is a fucking traitor." I was scared but not by that crisis of words again. So I waited for nightfall and returned to the Tulán.

And now I'm here, thinking like a crazy person. Maybe I've become one. Maybe that's what I was from the start, crazy, a crazy madwoman searching around for herself, and so much searching has her more lost than a cross-eyed crab. But it doesn't matter. What does it matter what other people think, or even what I think about myself?

Last night I found the papers. I was walking around the house like a madwoman, looking for a little notebook to write in, to see if maybe I could find some peace for my head. Dr. Vigo had prescribed tranquilizers. I had the prescription in my purse, with a lab referral, nothing really, a blood test, a normal procedure, or so said my madness. But my chest was about to explode in rage. I was now going to end up like my "friends," drugged out, happy, mixing highballs with Xanax at the tennis club. I wanted to think, before the pills and the highballs turned me into a mummy. I wanted to say good-bye to my torrential outburst of words. Explain to it that I didn't have a choice left. I needed to reclaim my head.

I went into Efraín's study to rummage in his drawers. That was his private space, forbidden to the rest of the family. But I imagined he'd have some notebooks in there. Plus, why respect his private spaces when he didn't respect me? I wanted to shake him up. I wanted him to know someone had invaded his sanctuary. So I messed up everything I could. I opened and closed drawers, moved files from their places. I found the damn notebooks I was looking for and took what I wanted. All of them. When I grabbed a bunch, I noticed a group of papers wedged under a plastic cover. I sat on his chair to read them. I wanted to get on his nerves, to offend him like he offended me. They were account statements from an account that wasn't even in his name, or in both of our names, or in the law firm's or the union's. It appeared under the name of an invented company, in which Efraín was listed as one so-called Pereira's partner. Others were under her name. The account balance was impressive. No wonder Efraín could afford the luxury of supporting two expensive homes, one for the missus and one for his lover.

* * *

I'm coming back from Abuela's house. I wanted to show her the papers. For her to help me ask Efraín where he got so much money. To have gotten it from the office would have been impossible. Since he's been working for the union he almost didn't have other clients. We called the bank. The joint account remained untouched. The bank's computer had no record of withdrawals from the stock portfolio. "Ay m'ija, this is not good," whispered Abuela. I felt my heart stop inside the center of my chest.

Abuela promised to take care of everything, to call her contacts to find out about that guy Pereira, supposedly my husband's partner. And she would let me know whenever she had something more concrete. In the meantime, I had to wait. My head wanted to burst. I had to occupy my mind with something. So I decided to have the lab tests done, buy the pills, and get high.

I waited my turn like everybody else. I replied dryly when they called my name in that professional, objective tone that is supposed to comfort you and calm your fear of the needle. The nurse read the referral for tests.

"Xanax?"

And she kept looking at me with an empty face, awaiting an answer. I didn't offer any. Let her think I'm another hysterical woman, depressed, a legal junkie, whatever she wants to think. I don't give a fuck about what she thinks. I don't give a fuck about what anybody thinks. I'm sick and tired of keeping an eye out, ready to address or correct everybody else's mistakes. I'm tired of paying attention to my mom's advice, my Abuela's, my friend's. I'm tired of trying to get revenge on Efraín or trying to persuade myself to forgive him. I'm tired of trying to become what my father is waiting for as he looks sadly out the window. I don't want to be me anymore. I'm sick of myself. Sick. I hope they discover something strange about my system in these tests. I hope I have AIDS. I hope this life strikes me once and for all and I can free myself from so many battles. It's high time I realized that I can't continue living in the fast lane. What's more, I don't want to, because it's exhausting. It's exhausting to be looking for so many answers. So fuck the world. I'm crazy.

And there, next to the counter at the lab, I felt as if I was standing in front of a wall. It was a see-through wall but as solid as the densest and hardest rock on the face of the earth. A wall made of a diamond nobody wants, a diamond that isn't worth millions and millions, as if suddenly the whim of men had decided that diamonds were now worth the same as dogshit and everyone had gone out in a hurry to pulverize them and mix them with water to make this huge wall, transparent and sharp, against which any scream can break. And I was standing before it. On the other side, a shadow called out to me, a shadow that was me, the other one, the one who wants to be left alone, who wants Efraín to pick up and leave with his business, his lover, and his fucking life and go to

238

the very gates of hell. Let him take the girls, the house, the dog, the cars, the gossip, the office, his tired eyes, his weariness, his desire to be victorious. Get him out. I contemplated the wall and through it that shadow calling me. And then I felt like getting a head start, running as fast as I could toward the sharpest edge of the wall and crashing into it. Leaving my flesh and my blood and my insides on the other side and, with the loneliest and happiest part of myself, penetrating the wall and going to meet the one calling out to me.

I saw it clearly in that lab's waiting room. I saw my desire to leave myself behind and my hunger, a vast hunger burning on my skin, and most of all on whatever's left between my legs. I fill myself with things to quench that hunger. I go to the gym, I get massages, take the dog out for walks, watch Efraín closely while he sleeps, and look for lovers. I visit Amelia and swear at everybody. I go to my mother's house to pick a fight because she didn't love me when I was a young girl, because all she did was work, because she left my father, her husband. I make appointments with the therapist, who keeps identifying my ailments: lack of self-esteem, codependency, sexual addiction. I leave her office thinking "I'm crazy, crazy" and feel more relieved. But then that outburst of words floods my mind and my lips begin to move on their own, in the car, in the house, on the road. Then I'm overwhelmed with fear. I have to come here, pull out my notebook, start writing, and get drunk so I can stay on my feet while I calm down; while this hunger for everything I can put inside me settles down. A hunger that threatens to overwhelm the empty space between my legs. But, at the same time, I want to be completely torn apart and rescued from where I'm stuck, frozen by fear. Someone, please lift the life that is crushing me, the life that's preventing me from turning into a shadow who goes far away. Would someone *come and go through me, push me to the bottom of my own being, push me until I come through the other side of life, free from myself.*

I didn't want to be paralyzed again between hope and fear. I wouldn't allow it. Hope and fear are two faces of the same coin. Those two same faces were the ones deciding the fate of those of us waiting there. Heads or tails. The coin flips in the air. Sitting to my right there was a good girl, with her boyfriend. College kids both of them, son and daughter of professionals, you could tell. They weren't over twenty. Overhearing their conversation I learned they were waiting on pregnancy results. If they were someone else's kids, with simple country people who lived far away as their parents, if they were recently graduated from vocational schools or working at fast-food restaurants, they wouldn't even have bothered with going to a lab. They would've patiently waited for her period or they would've bought her a case of warm yeasty beer or a bottle of aspirin, and forced her to flush it down the toilet, or else she could be walking around in oversized clothes to hide the belly from her dad, who, if he ever found out, would go searching for the father with gun in hand to make sure he recognized the kid and paid child support, because he wasn't going to raise nobody else's children. The coin flips in midair. To my left, a lady with her retarded son awaited the results of a breast biopsy. May God prevent it from becoming malignant, because what would she do with her son—who would take care of him when she was gone? Further down there was a Jamaican couple, or maybe they were from Curaçao, fighting with the nurse to have the results ready earlier. They had flown here to have the tests done because in the islands they didn't have the right equipment. The hotel was expensive. They couldn't wait another day. Heads or tails.

Then it was my turn. I sat down calmly in the chair and rolled up my sleeve. I endured the prick without blinking, looking at the transparent test tube filling up with blood, thick blood, as if it were made of slow-moving, wine-colored clay; it seemed to be aged and alive and full of mysteries and extinguished fires, but that's precisely what made it more powerful. The nurse filled one tube, then another. The muddy sea of blood continued to stain the edges of the tube and I amused myself watching the liquid flow out of me. I said to myself, "A good measure," I don't know why. The nurse pulled the needle out and took off the rubber tourniquet, putting some gauze on my arm. She made me bend my elbow in. "The results will be ready in two weeks," she said. "Please stop by the counter on your way out."

The coin is still flying through the air. I have to wait to see what side my luck will fall on. Wait for news from my Abuela, for the lab results so I can get my pills. Wait. In the meantime, how do I spend my time? Just now there was a knock on the door, someone delivering my order. When I opened the door, the young man almost tripped down the stairs. He's not bad looking. Tall and skinny, just how I like them, and he has a harmless face. A little lost, a little naïve. I'm such a fool. So crazy. That's exactly what I thought about Franky when I met him. But it doesn't matter. Right now, with all this waiting, what the fuck do I care?

A Band Apart

As soon as I woke up, I called Chino Pereira's cell phone a few times. I got what I expected: no answer. Little by little desperation was overtaking me. I was the only person Tadeo could count on and, in addition, the only one who could get a hold of the contacts Chino possessed to get him out of jail, bail him out, whatever it took. I couldn't leave him to his fate. I had to do something, anything, because of all I owed him. I waited half an hour and called again.

Temporarily disconnected. Once again. My hands were starting to sweat. All I could think of was going out to Paralelo 37, but it was risky asking around door to door to see if I could locate him. For sure no one would tell me what they knew, no one would give me anything helpful to my search. Plus, I would raise suspicions.

I didn't even try. I needed to solve the problem by other means. So I finished my coffee and went out into the streets to find M.'s house.

I was acting out of desperation, or by intuition. I really didn't know what I would find in that house, or what I'd do once I discovered Chino's whereabouts. My relationship with M. was not the type that would allow me to simply get out of the car, ring the doorbell, and exchange greetings at the door as if nothing had happened. And I wasn't the type to try, "M., how are you doing? Long time no see. I was in the neighborhood and decided to pay you a visit. . . ." We had shared our bodies several times, and some conversation, but that didn't give me the right. Ours was the type of relationship you find in the city, in motels. How ironic, to be able to probe our bodies but later on not even be able to greet each other on the street, to go to each other's house to ask for a favor that could save a friend's life.

"Las Palomas, Fifteenth Street, house G-fifty-three . . ." When I found the place I realized it was a gated community. There was an electric fence bluntly and irrevocably blocking the front of my car, with an armed guard observing me warily from the booth. He grilled me about my name, my address, my car's license plate number, my destination, my intentions. Suddenly I remembered that I had some heavy artillery in my inventory. I had never disposed of my press pass and this was the time to use it again. Surprisingly, a completely calm voice emerged from my mouth, one that answered all the guard's questions clearly: "Julián Castro-dad, Associated Press, BFX eight seven five. I'm going to the Soreno house, the lady's expecting me." And perhaps due to the frequency of such visits since the attorney had disappeared, the guard let me through without another word. A real miracle.

When I found the street and the house, I saw there wasn't a single car inside the garage. Nothing, no one. A golden retriever trotted carelessly through the backyard. I decided to wait a while until someone came home. I made myself comfortable as best as I could inside my piece of junk, stretching my legs and closing the window to block out most of the glare. I had nothing better to do. Waiting at home for something to happen would only end up fraying my nerves. I hated feeling that way, cornered and useless. I'd been feeling like that for too long. And although I feared that I wouldn't be able to help Tadeo's situation, or mine, I didn't have it in me to wait and let the chips fall where they may. I had to act. Act. Not think, reflect, ponder, nor outline, but act. So that my actions spit me out somewhere, even if it was the wrong place.

And yes, I felt fatally afraid that there was already nothing I could do to help Tadeo. I had warned him, pointed out he was an illegal, an illegal alien of Haitian descent, the worst possible kind of immigrant in these parts. If he were Cuban, there wouldn't be a problem. The exile community would go to any length to concoct a story of oppression at the hands of the communists and something would happen. But an illegal like him, poor, black, with his accented Spanish, not the Dominican cadence the entire world was already getting to know, but instead some other textures tangled on his tongue. Tadeo was a half-and-half, raised on both sides of the Río Masacre. Not even from the capital. And to top it all off, they had caught him with a shipment of drugs. My friend would probably rot in jail.

But Chino had given me his word. He had said, in his usual cool and dry voice, "Let's see what can be done." And I had to find him so he wouldn't keep his arms crossed. At the time, with everything that was happening, Tadeo would certainly occupy the lowest position on the drug dealer's list of priorities. Soreno was surely at the top, a mess that could've been caused by so many different things, such as betrayal, debt, business problems, and so on. I was tired of mulling over so many theories. I didn't want to uncover the mystery. Or, well, maybe I did, if it allowed me to find Pereira, or better yet, if following its lead would make me cross paths with M. once more. Because now there was a question that made me want to look for her even more. I had to know if M. was a murderer.

Four hours went by and nobody came home. I spent all morning watching that pile of manicured cement and the dog that kept trotting around the property. I smoked almost an entire pack of cigarettes. I had a few left, but had to save those for later. I would give most of them to the security guard to win him over. I would definitely be back, and I didn't want him to give me any trouble. Finally I decided to make the most of the afternoon and to head over to the newspaper. Perhaps Daniel had something interesting to tell me.

I went into the newsroom of *La Noticia* as if I still worked there, forgetting, for an instant, that I was just a visitor. I found Daniel talking on the phone in the last cubicle. He looked at me as if he'd been expecting me.

"Come on, let's go to Pedraza." I walked behind him with firm steps, as if I were taking in the vast hallway with my feet. Daniel carried some papers in his hand.

Inside his office, Pedraza was examining some negatives with a magnifying glass. It looked like he'd been there doing the same thing he had been doing the day before, when we talked, the whole time, as if that conversation had never taken place, as if time had done a somersault over itself and landed on the exact moment I had gone to see Daniel in search of M.'s address. There are people who inhabit different dimensions, different at least from the one I inhabited. At that moment I was sure Pedraza was one of those people.

Daniel closed the door behind us and then, triumphantly, set the papers he'd been carrying on Pedraza's desk. Pedraza took a black marker and began crossing out some of the lines of what Daniel had written.

"What's going on, chief?"

"We can't publish this just yet. Forensics hasn't corroborated it."

"All the same, if I may say so, the two bodies found are believed to be union lawyer Efraín Soreno and staff member Eugenio Palacios, who had both gone missing the night of September first. . . ."

"Soreno was found?" was all I could say. Inside my chest, my heart was a wild horse running fast.

Daniel and Pedraza looked at me in silence. They took a minute to study me carefully, trying to decide whether to share the information they had dug up through Daniel's inquiries and the police scanner.

"About half an hour ago the police found two charred bodies up on a mountain in the interior. An anonymous tip. Looks like Soreno is one. Forensics is still trying to identify the other," Pedraza said.

"That's Palacios, for sure it's Palacios."

"Don't jump to conclusions, Daniel."

"Shit, Pedraza, you know that when we called for delivery, Palacios's friend told us the situation was hot and that nobody had seen him since Friday morning, the same day Soreno disappeared."

"To tell you the truth, that guy talks way too much for a dealer."

"Did he ever . . . His tough guy airs probably got him in trouble and they took him out."

"A minor player. . . ."

"Yeah, a minor player who could have opened a can of worms. I just talked to that kid at the union, and guess what he said."

"Tell me, Mr. Know-it-all."

"The government's team decided to accept the employees' demands, but substantially cut the salary hike. And it seems the union is going to accept the counteroffer and lift the strike. Why, I ask, if all of this was orchestrated for better wages, does the union back off now? Well, because if not, the police will air their dirty laundry, making it known that a public agency's employees were involved in the dirty business of drug dealing. And then the union gets its comeuppance and prays for everything to just go away. The stench could rise as high as the legislature and bring about plans for privatization. A happy end for all."

"But then, why kill Soreno? His death would really stick out, draw too much attention."

"You, who always renounces the logical order of things, cannot see, my dear chief, that even the most corrupt minds make mistakes and are overcome by desperation? The corrupt trustees probably wanted Soreno to shut down the operation. And the man probably saw himself between the rock of his legal partners and the hard place of his illegal supplier. One of the two did him in."

"That's your version?"

"Yes, Pedraza, that's my version."

* * *

I kept quiet, almost not following the conversation. My mind was a maze. Daniel's governmental conspiracy theory seemed very likely. But, like Pedraza, I also had a hunch some other hand was stirring the cauldron from afar, and sought the same consequences my friend talked about. Whose hand was it? Couldn't be M.'s. She, no matter how mad she was or how much rage she felt, didn't have the steady sleight of hand nor the power to weave this web of murder and deceit. Or maybe she was taking advantage of the coincidence to cover up a vendetta that had nothing to do with the union lawyer's illegal dealings. Her plan was perfect. Who was going to suspect a jealous wife would end up killing her husband if the husband had for quite some time been digging his own grave with his involvement in shady deals that were getting out of hand? One shot and that's it, a disappearance, one charred body among so many. Nobody would point the finger at her. But then again, M. could lose it all as well. Every purchase would have to be seized and analyzed to determine if it was made with dirty drug-trafficking money. Her name would forever be associated with Soreno's in public opinion. "That's the drug dealer's wife," they would all say, like that Amelia she was always mentioning in her journals, and the high-society wives she used to visit: her father, his family name. I couldn't imagine that M. would be so embittered by hate, or so affected by rejection. But it was a possibility.

* * *

"Julián, did you find the widow?"

"She's not home, but sooner or later I'll find her."

"Better sooner than later," Daniel answered in an authoritative tone I had never heard him use before. He spoke with an unusual detachment, as if it were someone else speaking through his mouth. "This story is coming out as soon as forensics confirms the fact. Right, boss?"

Pedraza didn't say yes or no. He simply continued studying the negatives he had on his desk. I looked at the clock and said good-bye to both of them. It was almost time to go home, to try calling Chino's cell phone again and get ready for another night at the motel.

Blackout

I couldn't believe my eyes. A long line of cars stretched from the gate all the way down the hill to the highway while the occupants waited patiently to enter the Motel Tulán. Inside the office it was total chaos. The administrator's son, his wife, a cousin, and even Don Tulán himself were all working, and they still couldn't take care of all the customers lined up for the night. When I got there, they didn't even mention Tadeo. They just exhaled with relief and sent me to accommodate guests in the few rooms that were still available.

"Entire neighborhoods have been left without power, and people want to sleep with air-conditioning. We're lucky we fixed the generator." That was all the explanation I received. Never, in all the time I had been working at the motel, had I seen it full to capacity.

We filled all thirty-four cabañas. The huge tide of people had abated. As soon as we turned the NO VACANCY sign on, the cars turned around and headed out to the highway in the hope of finding another motel opening its doors to the city folk looking for a place with electricity where they could sleep. There were no couples taking advantage of the silence to escape, no terrible nocturnal cannibals looking for a hiding place. Whole families were getting out of the cars, single mothers with babies, like a group of war refugees, or hurricane victims looking for the reprieve of electricity. Once they had found shelter, calm returned as it does after a terrible storm.

No one came out of the cabañas. The Tulán family left me, along with the cousin, in charge for the rest of the night. Although it may have been the time to make conversation, my head was filled with too many things, and I also have to confess the ghostly member of the owner's family did not inspire conversation. As soon as the Tuláns left the office, the cousin sank down in Tadeo's chair. I couldn't help but wonder where Tadeo was now, on what cold jailhouse floor, in which detention camp. The simple thought tightened my chest and filled the night with nostalgia for Tadeo.

I had to get my thoughts in order. Soreno, or the body they were trying to pass as his, had been found in a hill thick with brushwood. Chino Pereira was missing. In M.'s papers I had some incriminating evidence I could maybe use to help my friend. At least to get him a good lawyer who could negotiate a reduced sentence if I gave some information to help solve this other case. What did I know? My head was buzzing. I couldn't tell the difference between the worthwhile material and my desperate conjectures. I couldn't even understand why I was so interested in Tadeo's predicament. He was a grown man, and he had taken the risk with open eyes. What else could I do? What if the actions spoke for themselves? If Tadeo had gone into that mess even after I had warned him, why couldn't I stay put in my little corner, waiting for the crisis to end so I could leave my hiding place? What was the strange anxiety that came over me, that made me go to the newspaper, talk to Daniel, confess my relationship with M., and ceaselessly call Chino Pereira's cell phone? It wasn't me who was sinking. Not me. It was a world that was sinking, a world I had entered by chance and by chance it offered me a way out. All that world surrounded by a sea of tarmac that made up the Motel Tulán. Now a simple rushing flash flood of that dark water was threatening to swallow it whole. What was I still doing there? Why didn't I make for the shore, if I had always known that this world was just a passing place, a temporary way station and never a home?

But where could I go? Toward the raw atmosphere of the night. Over there, lights twinkling in different places, the city beckoned me and whispered: "Lose yourself in here, inside me, wander and seek." But I didn't want to hear it. I didn't want to follow that voice. At the same time, the different voices rushing at me pell-mell kept me from hearing anything distinctly. I had to organize my thoughts. I pulled out my notebook and grabbed a pen. I found a corner in the office in which to hide from the conde-scending eyes of cousin Tulán and let myself go.

I began with a straightforward list of facts and unknowns.

I went over it. M. arrives at the motel. Why? I come to the motel. Why? Soreno goes into business with Chino. What kind of business? There's a drug front established inside the Power Authority. Who proposed it to whom? With whose money? With whose material? The police investigates. A strike is declared. Soreno is found dead. Who killed him? I find M.'s papers. Why me, why did she sleep with me? Her revenge ended there, paying him in the same bad currency for denying her the pleasure of being watched as she somersaulted through the air. For denying her the love, and leaving her alone with words crowding her mind. She at least betrayed him under a shared roof. But then, why make me an accomplice? What about Tadeo, and his mother, the effort to leave her alone and without resources, the rush to complete his return? All these passions seemed destructive enough to provoke one death, maybe two. But where was Chino Pereira?

The dark ink flowed from my fingers. Like a brook, like a bloodletting, as if black tar was seeping out of my fingernails. I couldn't stop, I had to write it all down. That was my only hope. The paper would tell me what the mind, the facts, and the people refused to explain.

I continued writing, but by then I was obeying another force that was taking me over like frenzy. The notes became something else between my hands. Once in a while I interrupted what I was doing to take care of a guest's order, French fries and soda, but then I'd return to my corner in the office and forget about everything, about the cousin, about the night, and about the reasons why I now found myself caught up in a vortex I could not understand. And tangled up in M., in my memories of the way her body smelled like a ripe papaya, a smell I still carried on my skin. I don't know if I was interested in saving Tadeo, saving M., leaving everything behind, or simply just surrendering once and for all to that contact between my hand, the ink and the paper—a way of losing myself because I could no longer deal with myself.

It wasn't about emptying myself, it wasn't about searching for something underneath anyone, but it was the slithering of a live body, one that was weightless, without a cause, and without depth, but precisely because of that, infinitely more abysmal. It was about slithering through the body of paper in that corner of the Motel Tulán's office. Forgetting about everything. I didn't even notice when the night was over, or when the cousin touched my shoulder and announced the morning shift had arrived. I wanted to continue slipping and sliding down the page. I looked for the key to the utility room, the only room that was vacant all night. The key was there, hanging from the same nail as always. When I stepped out of the office the sun blinded me like a sea of milk crashing against my eyes. Tripping my way over, I came to the small room, switched on the light, sat down, and continued working my way down the page.

There was no depth to the papers, nor in what I wrote: only the recital of facts, feelings, questions. If depth had been present, there would've been the promise of an end, a bottom. But the endless flatness of the paper seemed like another place for loss. To describe M. and how I met her. What I had seen at her home, her wandering dog, her papers. What had happened with Tadeo on the never-ending nights I waited for her provoked a similar sensation as the one I felt when she let me sink into her body. She sank me: a delicious defeat. And there was no end to my purpose, my discovery or debt. Only that soothing motion. To become someone else in the absence of the "I," the one who is always searching; to lose the motive of the search when contact is made and to not even be able to ask where I am because I remain so lost. So lost that the distance between the searched-for and the searcher has disappeared. So lost that the entire distance was the only thing that existed, you lost in her, becoming part of her, her body, the particles of the body of desire, with death itself announcing that the fallen heads will roll, never to rise up again. And I, by sheer willpower, one greater than mine, was calm enough to place my head at the foot of those papers so that they could eat it. By M.'s feet, by Tadeo's, so they could devour it, by Chino's feet and the charge he rushes through my veins. I offer my head as payment for being lost, deliciously unencumbered and outside of myself. Never before had I felt such calm in the face of such fatality.

I was hungry and so I supposed some time had gone by. I had to eat something. I went out to the bakery, leaving the dozens of papers without beginning or end in the spare room. Upon my return (I had ordered the breakfast to go so I could eat it at the motel) I looked over what I had written. I grabbed all the papers and made a single pile. I put M.'s papers inside, as if my scribbling could protect her. I took them out to the car and headed into the city. On the radio I learned that the union rank and file were meeting with their leaders. That now, enigmatically, one faction was ready to accept a reduced wage hike. But the strike was still in effect. The greater part of the metro area remained in the dark, including my neighborhood. It didn't make sense to go to my place, so, on a hunch, I took the quickest route into the Los Lirios housing project. And the hunch produced what I was hoping for.

Sitting there in the stands at the basketball court was Bimbi. Pezuña and a few others were hanging out with him. I don't know why, but that day the guard that was supposed to be at the project's access-control gate wasn't there, so I didn't have to explain the reason for my visit. I stepped on the gas and went into the project. I had never been in one before.

Dozens of four-story buildings stretched from one side to the other. In front of each building, a yard of scant grass served as a playground for an unsupervised bunch of kids. It was impossible to say why, but even though the buildings were painted and there wasn't any visible trash, the project seemed to exude a rotten odor, something different from what you breathe in any suburban subdivision. That sterilized air was definitively absent. And lots of people, more people than you'd suspect could fit in the space provided for in each of those buildings, were loitering around. In between the yelling and shouting, boom boxes blared from the apartments. Girls with hot pants or miniskirts way more revealing than you'd expect for their age were sitting on the curb sucking on lollipops. But over on the far end, the basketball court remained strangely empty. Only Bimbi and his friends were keeping watch.

I don't know where I got the courage. I don't even think it was courage. It was just willpower or frenzy that led me on. So I let myself be taken to the court. Bimbi recognized me from afar and came over, cutting me off before I got to the stands.

"Who sent you here?" was his greeting.

"Nobody. I'm looking for Chino."

"Well, join the club. Nobody has seen him or his shadow since the new shipment arrived."

"The one Tadeo was bringing in? Didn't Customs seize it?"

"Yeah, man, but by the good grace of nature, Sambuca came to the rescue and recovered it. No wonder he's the oldest dealer on the island. He's better connected than a telephone line. Although there's a cat in a box around here somewhere, because suddenly they put Chino out of business. Orders are coming directly from Sambuca now."

"And Chino?"

"Right now he's not seeing anybody. Maybe he's being punished."

"Maybe he's dead."

"You're crazy, big man. This is no Hollywood movie. Anyways, Sambuca wouldn't have his own nephew killed."

* * *

I wanted to think a little bit about what Bimbi was saying, that Chino Pereira was Sambuca's nephew. But I didn't have time to ponder the fact. I was taking care of other business. To get over the surprise, I lit a cigarette and offered him one. I exhaled deeply and swallowed hard. The pause made me take a breather.

"Well, if you see him tell him I'm looking for him. I'm worried about Tadeo's situation."

"Whatever, man. Your poor friend got stuck with the shit. Why did he let himself get caught?"

"But Chino said—"

"Chino says many things. Word up. At the moment of truth, only those who want to run the risk take the risk. If you get caught, careful with what you say and grin and bear it like a man. You finish your education in jail. That's how it was with Chino, who being who he is, had to pay some time. That's how it was with Pezuña too, *viste, primo*. That's how you measure a real man, brother. The big house is trial by fire. If you make it out on your own two feet, you're given the rank you deserve. If not, well, you weren't cut out for this shit. That's how it is."

I shook Bimbi's hand and headed home. There was no light back at the house. I took a short nap and was woken up by my own papers. I dreamed I was writing, without rest or truce, scribbling on page after page some strange arabesques I couldn't understand, although my own hand was making them. Somewhere in the dream, I was in prison, writing, and that prison was the motel, my house, the cafeteria, the newspaper, cabaña 23. It was my car from where I watched M.'s house. Other things happened, but I only remember myself writing.

I woke up in a sweat. The fan wasn't working; neither was the electricity. I decided to leave early for the motel and take advantage of the generator-powered fresh air. At least I could find a little light. Then maybe I would be able to finish bringing that dream into the reality of my papers. That fragile reality.

Vigil

M. came out of her house and walked straight to my parked car. She was wearing jeans. Too bad she wasn't wearing a slip. The bags under her eyes were even more pronounced, creating a dark aureole around the little wrinkles that crowned her eyelashes.

I pretended not to notice her walking over. It was the second morning that I had staked out her house. The first time I had been fooled. Since I hadn't seen any cars parked outside I assumed nobody was home. But when I saw that on the second morning the dog was not complaining for the lack of attention, that his dishes next to the garage door had fresh water and food, I knew somebody was in there or would come home soon. About half an hour after parking across the street, I saw the drapes move slightly and a shadow shifting through the house. I had been discovered.

Judging by the secretive nature of the sighting, I supposed whoever it was didn't want to see me, or that maybe the shadow was
also waiting, expecting. It was a matter of time. Either the
shadow would call security and I would be forced to leave in a
few minutes, or it would decide to establish contact. Two hours
went by before anything happened. Then the shadow, M., walked
over to my car.

She touched my shoulder. I raised my eyes from the papers I
had picked up while waiting for her to make up her mind. When
I came across her gaze a small smile escaped from my lips. A
small smile of joy that simultaneously apologized for my intrusion.
I expected to face a cold wall, furious eyes, an insult I deserved for
daring to be there, forcing my presence on her after the pain of so
many losses and misfortunes. But I only found an empty silence,
like a wind with eyes watching me from the flip side of reality. A
tired and empty wind.

"I've come to return your papers," was all I could think to say.

On the other side of the window, M.'s face, wrapped in silence,
recovered a little of that sparkle in the eye. She seemed to be
awaking from a long sleep, as if she was under the influence of
tranquilizers, drugs, or in some altered state that made her respond with scant emotion to everything that happened. But her
eyes lit up. I don't know if with rage or caution, alertness or relief,
but I knew myself spared of any more silences.

"You want a cup of coffee?" she asked me. I don't remember
what I said. But she opened the car door and took me by the arm.
I allowed myself to be led into the house. Even if Chino's hit men
were waiting for me inside that house, or the police, or Tadeo's

ghost, I would've still gone in. Even if M. had been holding a shiny knife in her hand, I would've followed her just the same. At the time, I would've followed M. to the end of the world, to the bottom of myself, to wherever she wanted to go.

She opened the door to her house, led me to the couch, and put a steaming cup of coffee in my hands. She took her sandals off and cuddled up in a chair in front of me. She waited for me to speak. I told her how her papers had ended up in my possession, how a maid at the motel had confused them with a lie and picked up her notes from the trash thinking they were mine. I told her how I'd started to read them and then suddenly stopped. How I never saw her again at the Tulán and since I missed her I decided to console myself with the next best thing. I should've thrown them away, or returned them to where she had left them, followed Daphne's advice, who, before leaving me, suggested I do so. But I couldn't do it. Each week I read a little more, a page, a paragraph, a sentence, fearing I would finish reading it and then she, M., would completely disappear from my life. Until I got to the end. The end in which she wrote about what she found in her husband's study.

Then M. spoke. She told me the whole story, where she had taken the balance statements from the account her husband had kept secret, receipts for a new boat and his lover's apartment, everything paid for in cash. She had taken them to her grandmother, who suggested asking a friend for help, one Víctor Cámara, her old lover, the former clarinet player who was now a successful businessman. And he took care of it. He took her to one of his partners, an old employee of his, who was now a federal district attorney. They gave the documents to him in exchange for protection, and brokered a deal in which the joint account, and the house, would not be seized as part of the investigation. And she wouldn't need to testify. The DA assured her that the documents were enough. She thought it was all over. She asked Don Víctor to tell Soreno that everything was arranged so he could plan his escape and save himself, unless he decided to turn himself in. Don Víctor promised he would do so. And now the police were telling her they had found Efraín's body up in the mountains.

M. spoke and I just stared at her feet, those long, thin toes without nail polish, so innocently clean and transparent. I thought: "How can I trust what she's saying?" But I didn't care. I didn't care to know the subtlety of her words, those words coming out syllable by syllable, her frenzied mouth speaking without secrets.

She continued to speak while I pretended to listen.

"Someone called Pereira," she said. But my attention could not leave her ankles. Strong, lean ankles, crisscrossed by little branches of reddened veins. I couldn't help asking myself: "How serious is what she's telling me?" But it didn't matter. The only thing that mattered was the texture of those ankles that I had once upon a time rubbed with some part of my body, without even realizing it. That time I had lost the chance to delve into the mystery of those ankles and get underneath them. And underneath them were those veins, her pale white skin, white like mercy, like a mountaintop, like the inside curvature of a bitten pear or an apple. And I felt like crying my eyes out, like resting my head by the feet of those ankles. "The police came this morning," she said.

"Charred bodies, two of them. One was a man named Palacios, who worked at the Power Authority and was also missing." They explained to her that Efraín was involved in illegal dealings, drugs, she said, and a shipment that had also disappeared from Customs. Palacios was the connection to one man named Pereira. The police were looking for him. They said not to worry, she told me, that they would keep an eye out. She assumed my car belonged to an undercover cop the first day she saw it parked in front of her house. But then she looked at the driver carefully. She thought she recognized me. She decided to come out.

She sipped her coffee. A hand that should've been mine stretched out to her ankles. It was mine, that hand, with fingers hungry for the touch of her skin. It was definitely my hand. That hunger burning on the tip of my fingers is a feeling I will never forget. M. got up. I don't know if to avoid my touch, or to distract herself from her own words.

"Two," she said while she walked to the other side of the living room. And then she continued: "The other body couldn't be Efraín's, it can't be. He would never wear a Rolex, it was never his style."

My head shook savagely, as if the ancient amphibian splashing around in the bottom of my blood suddenly sensed danger. A silent voice said, "Tadeo." But I no longer feared for his life. I knew he was on his way to a prison, that sadness and desolation but not death awaited him. "Tadeo," the voice repeated and then I thought: "Chino is dead." But I didn't care. I didn't want to care, at least for the time being.

"Do you want more coffee?" she asked me and I snapped out

of my trance. Something that was alive throbbed in my hands, a half-drunk, warm cup of coffee.

"What are you going to do now?" I asked her.

"I don't know. Sell the house, enroll the girls in another school," she said. "Make a life for myself." And then silence and a shrugging of shoulders. I moved close to her but this time my head did not want to ask anything else. This time I put my arms around her and comforted her as best I could while she sobbed. I breathed in the damp smell from her hair, a smell of algae, like seawater after a rainstorm. I stood there quietly, without asking any questions, at the edge, while she sobbed and repeated the phrases: "I didn't want it to end this way. I wanted him to leave, but not like this."

But one more question was necessary.

"What should I do with your papers?"

"Throw them out," she said while she stared into the deepest part of my eyes. And there they were, the wrinkles and the deep, dark gaze that my eyes could never hold in their entirety. What swam around inside that stare, by the sharp corners of her eyes, was a mixture of relief, pain, hope, doubt, and I don't know how many other things. Down there, in that unfathomable bottom. Why hadn't I noticed it before? Down there in the deep there swam the same thing that splashed around the bottom of my own eyes.

I don't know what else we talked about. All I know is that suddenly I found myself following her up the stairs, putting her to bed, tucking her in, and then going downstairs, closing the door, and walking out quietly to my car. When I got on the highway, the tarmac was shiny with the first dew of the night. I took an exit I thought was a shortcut, and ended up on Route 52. Far away I could see the Motel Tulán's pyramid blinking in the suburban night. Its yellow waterfall of lights first, then the green neon like an eye, and finally the red letters advertising vacancy in front of the entrance hill. I sped on past it, on my way home. Inside of me I knew I would never go back.

I parked on the shoulder of the expressway. I took M.'s papers and tore them into little pieces again and again. I started the car and drove to my exit. A dark green sea, bustling with the sound of insects and amphibians, stretched out on both sides of the highway. I started to throw what was left of M.'s papers out the window, watching how the wind blew them over into the ravine next to the asphalt. But on the passenger's side another stack of papers remained untouched. There was a frozen river of ink, flowing clumsily over its mistakes. Honest mistakes, mine, more mine than anything else on the face of the earth had ever been mine. I turned on the radio and my fingers began drumming on the steering wheel. I was neither happy nor sad. Those dancing fingers weren't celebrating anything. They simply moved over the surface, in anticipation of the keyboard that waited for them to continue dancing. The asphalt stretched beyond my old car toward a row of blinking lights. Breathing in and out, the city waited for me.

The Promise

Art is artifice
More like a typewriter
Than a smile or a flying fish
But just the same
Love is artifice
A passionate construction wrapped around a touch more than
    five feet of skin blood and bones
Everything conspires against the poem
And yet
Everything loved felt and thought is a great metaphor
               —Nemir Matos-Cintrón

These days I keep busy, waking up early, going to the newspaper, and writing later at night. I'm back at *La Noticia.* They called me because they needed a new staff writer. I accepted the offer immediately, although I negotiated a different shift. Later I found out I was doing Daniel's old job. He had been "let go" by the director, who claimed he was too tense and exhibited personality problems that prevented him from effectively fulfilling his duties.

Right before starting to work for *La Noticia* again, the day before to be exact, the press offered its version of what had happened in the murder case of labor attorney Efraín Soreno. According to government sources, the attorney had been killed by a gang working out of the Los Lirios housing project. Soreno had illegally appropriated union funds, which he used to purchase real estate and boats, and to invest in the drug trade. The narcotics were distributed through the housing project. The gang members decided to cut in on Soreno's profits, but there were fights, and the murder followed. The charred body found next to Soreno had been identified as that of line inspector Eugenio Palacios, resident of Los Lirios and the man responsible for putting Soreno in contact with the project's drug-trafficking gang. There was no mention of Chino Pereira anywhere, or of the drug-selling operation inside the Power Authority.

In the following pages the labor leaders denied they had anything to do with Soreno's shady dealings. The more vocal members argued Soreno had used the instability caused by the strike to promote his own agenda. Consequently, the public should understand that the union was just another victim of a corrupt lawyer, they said, one who had stolen a substantial part of the union's funds to invest in drug trafficking, a crime particularly deadly to the moral fiber of our society. They also added that now, right in the middle of negotiations with the government, the union was facing a demoralizing situation that could very well

compromise its credibility with its members and the general public. That in light of the facts, they had to reexamine and reevaluate
their leadership, and even decide whether it was necessary to
hold special elections to change it. However, regardless of these
hardships, the union was committed to upholding workers'
rights. What was important was that everything was out in the
open and that the incident had not turned the government
against the negotiations, since the union was understanding and
receptive, and also interested in battling drug trafficking on all
fronts. The union spokespersons reaffirmed that the syndicate
would comply with the pertinent authorities to guarantee that
none of Soreno's partners in crime still hiding inside the Power
Authority ranks would elude prosecution, even if it meant
changes to the leadership. As a result of that commitment, the negotiations between the government and the workers had acquired
a new air of cooperation and good faith. The union predicted the
labor dispute would be resolved sooner than expected.

I also learned that Tadeo was in jail. He was sentenced to six
years, but he would be eligible for parole in a year and a half for
good behavior. He was lucky. Every once in a while we talk on
the phone and as soon as my employment situation becomes sta-
ble, which is to say that as soon as I manage to get a short vacation, I'll take a plane and pay him a visit.

The other night I ran into Daphne on the street. I was leaving
the paper and stopped at a fast-food joint to get something to go,
something I could eat at home while watching television. She was
with her new boyfriend, a recently divorced pharmacist she knew
from work. We talked a little. She told me she was doing fine

and, that being the case, it was probably better for me to stay at the apartment. If everything went according to plan, she and her new love would move in together in a few months.

I know nothing of M. I paid her a visit once after that night, just to see how she was holding up. I had let a week go by, a week in which I had surrendered to the hunger my fingers felt for the keyboard. I spent entire days and nights writing. Time passed. I wanted to see M. but I found an empty house and a sign advertising its sale. It was my turn to let her go, I thought, and drove straight out to the guard station and the gate.

I don't mind working again at *La Noticia*. I don't expect more of my writing than what I get, which is a bunch of stories that are half true and half false and which I have to check for grammar and spelling to make them seem to be "the truth." I'm honing my craft and at night I stay in my apartment in the middle of the city and work on my own story. Along with the day's headlines, it shares the strange beat of fiction, but perhaps because of errors in the text and the furious sincerity of those errors and pursuits, I hope it will be worth more than what the world tries to pass on as "true." It's another truth altogether that seeps through living ink, something very different from the struggle for power. I lend my fingers to let it flow. Parallel lines. I'm not completely sure of what I just wrote: that this other truth—mine—is so innocent. But that doesn't matter either. I gave in to uncertainty. It's the only way to go forward.

I still have a million revisions to make to the manuscript. Change a few names, go over the tone of certain passages. When I reread it, I ask myself whether it was worth it. But what motivates me to stay here, alone in this apartment but not empty, is the hope of finding another pair of eyes out there. Perhaps my story will allow someone to see their reflection in its muddy waters on some evening when they are lost and looking for shelter in the city at night. I can't guarantee them the reflection will be of much help, or that these papers will offer even a fragile roof over their head. But here between these pages is where the promise lives and breathes.

M

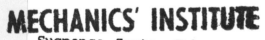